FLIGHT

Look for other books
by Chuck Black

The Kingdom Series
Kingdom's Dawn
Kingdom's Hope
Kingdom's Edge
Kingdom's Call
Kingdom's Quest
Kingdom's Reign

The Knights of Arrethtrae
Sir Kendrick and the Castle of Bel Lione
Sir Bentley and Holbrook Court
Sir Dalton and the Shadow Heart
Lady Carliss and the Waters of Moorue
Sir Quinlan and the Swords of Valor
Sir Rowan and the Camerian Conquest

The Starlore Legacy
Nova
Flight
Lore
Oath
Merchant
Reclamation
Creed
Journey
Crucible
Covenant
Revolution
Maelstrom

www.ChuckBlack.com

FLIGHT

EPISODE TWO

CHUCK BLACK

Contents

PROLOGUE

Relevant

Elias lifted his hand to knock on the bedroom door, but before he could tap the smooth dark gray surface, it slid away from him in four directions.

"I'm ready!" Brae was sitting on her bed, her back against the wall. Beside her was a tray of carefully prepared snacks, and on the nightstand was Elias's favorite drink. He couldn't help the smile that spread across his face as Brae looked up with a gleam in her eyes.

He sat down on the bed.

"I can see that. Eager for more story are we?"

Brae nodded. "You've never told it like this before."

"I'm not so sure about that, Brae. It's the same story."

Brae's eyes went to the window and the stars that waited there. "I suppose so. But I think I've forgotten much of it. I guess I've never listened like this before," she explained turning back to look at her father.

"Hmm." Elias reached for a cracker topped with spicy cream cheese.

"What?" Brae asked.

"You're not a little girl anymore." His eyes narrowed. "You're beginning to understand."

Brae knew what he meant, and she wanted more. An awakening inside her thirsted for more. The words her father spoke seemed so relevant in her life now.

Elias held the cracker, suspended in midair. "This story will change you, Brae…if you let it."

"How?"

"Understanding the truth of Ell Yon's power and great love for the people changes anyone who is willing to listen."

Brae seemed lost in thought for a moment as Elias bit into the cracker.

"Did Daeson find the oracle?" she plunged ahead.

Elias swallowed then reached for his drink.

"Let's find out, shall we?"

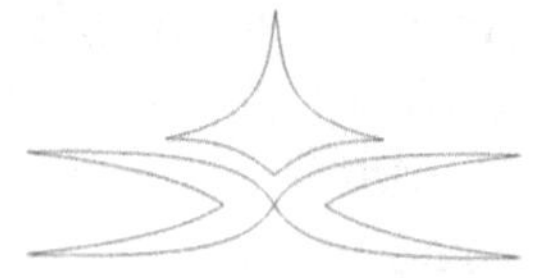

CHAPTER

1

The Oracle

Oracle – a man, woman, or child chosen by Sovereign Ell Yon to deliver messages to the people of Rayl and at times given the ability to demonstrate the power of the Sovereign to protect His people.

The coordinates for the Lamara Skies popped up on the nav computer screen.

"Thanks, Rivet."

Daeson smirked. Why was he thanking a machine? Something about the bot was forcing a personal connection, one he vowed he would never allow with a non-sentient.

Daeson's thoughts turned to Raviel and her parting actions. She had spoken no words, but she didn't have to. His heart quickened as he thought of the embrace she had given him. He tried not to read too much into what had happened but how could he not hope? His heart ached for a real relationship with her, but her belief in the mystical Ell Yon forbade her for reasons he couldn't understand. It frustrated him...no, it angered him. Yet something deep in the corner of his mind nagged him—like a child realizing for the first time that the world is not what it seems. And now with the entire race of Rayleans enduring the horrific persecution of the Jyptonian military, he was forced to admit his part in all of this. His life had completely unraveled and thousands had died.

The oracle…it had all started with her. Daeson was tempted to blame her for everything, but he knew that was ridiculous. No matter what happened now, he needed to see her one more time. He had questions that deserved answers!

The shores of a massive continent flashed beneath Daeson's Starcraft in an instant. Now skimming the thick, forested lands of the western continent, Daeson had to climb to skirt the mountainous ridge that bordered the shoreline just a few miles inland.

The Jyptonian city of Nimbiya was nestled in the mountain range far to the north, but the southern region of the western continent was largely uninhabited—the Lamara Skies. On the other side of the mountain range, Daeson slowed his Starcraft and dropped his elevation to a few hundred feet. He navigated carefully as he neared the region, feeling the tumultuous shifts and eddies of the odd gravitational fields even at the periphery of the floating islands. Navigating a Starcraft within the region would be foolish. Others had tried and not made it out. Even experienced pilots dared fly only at elevations high enough to negate the contrary gravitation fields.

"Remarkable," Daeson said out loud, forgetting that there was no one other than Rivet to respond.

Daeson took a moment to gaze at the spectacle all around them. The anti-graviton fields stretched as far as the eye could see. Some of the islands below were small and ever shifting in their position, at times colliding with other islands with gentle yet ominous results. As far as Daeson could tell, the ground beneath the islands was a no-man's land... treacherous to navigate.

"This is impossible. Where do we even begin?" Daeson asked.

"I would recommend starting with the coordinates that were just transmitted to our navigational computer," Rivet replied.

Daeson looked down at his display.

"That's oddly convenient."

"Be careful, Master Daeson. It could be a trap," Rivet warned.

Daeson followed the coordinates, scanning for any ships or weapons but detecting none. The coordinates led him to just short of the edge of the anti-graviton field, where he safely landed the Starcraft. On the ground, Daeson looked for some sign or message from the oracle.

"Do you see anything, Rivet?" Daeson asked.

The bot performed a three-hundred-sixty-degree scan. He stopped and pointed. "One human approaching from that direction."

Daeson unholstered his Talon and prepared to charge it.

"I do not detect any weapons," Rivet added.

Daeson kept his Talon at the ready just the same.

From behind a small grove of trees opposite the direction of the anti-graviton field and its corresponding no-man's land, a young woman with a shoulder pack approached.

Although not Oracle Sabella, the woman came directly to Daeson and spoke. "Put out your hand."

Daeson hesitated before offering his left hand, while keeping a tight grip on the Talon in his right.

She took a DNA sample, scanned it, and then tapped on a small display on her forearm. After a moment, she seemed satisfied and looked up at Daeson.

"I am Thenoras. I will take you to the oracle."

She swung the pack off her shoulder, reached inside and handed Daeson four propulsion boosters.

"Put these on," she commanded. "Have you ever used them before?"

"Not like this. I've only used propulsion boots," Daeson replied.

"You'd better learn fast," Thenoras said as she strapped a propulsion booster to each of her ankles and wrists.

Daeson wasted no time in matching her. When they were ready, Thenoras turned and looked at Rivet. "The bot stays here."

Daeson nodded. "Rivet, activate the Starcraft's adaptive camouflage and wait for me here."

"Yes, my liege," Rivet replied.

Daeson followed Thenoras as she walked toward the edge of no-man's land and looked up. Above them were massive islands floating at different elevations. Daeson couldn't imagine what she was expecting him to do.

She turned and looked at him with a twinkle in her eye. "Stay close and do not deviate from my course. There is only one path that will get you there safely."

Daeson felt flutters in his stomach. His last encounter with an anti-graviton field nearly ended in disaster, and that had only been one isolated field. Maneuvering here would be a thousand times more treacherous. He hoped this wouldn't turn into another terrifying few minutes.

"Wait," Daeson called out. "Why such secrecy?"

"The Jyptonian Elite want the Plexus, but others more powerful want the oracle. They know that she is the Raylean's only true connection to the Sovereign."

"Why doesn't she reside with the Plexus?"

"The Plexus and the oracle often don't see eye to eye. She is usually not welcome where they are." Thenoras refocused her attention above them. "Come."

She then leapt into the field and ignited all four of her propulsion boosters. Within seconds she was flying upward at tremendous velocity. Daeson shook his head and blasted upward after her. He watched as Thenoras twisted, turned, and adjusted her flight path with perfection.

Daeson struggled with every deviation; he knew he would have to burn precious fuel to make corrections. Getting the hang of four independent boosters strapped to his ankles and wrists while trying to navigate anti-graviton fields and avoid the crushing effect of moving land masses took every fiber of determination he could muster.

Daeson had to remind himself that just because he was "falling" upward, the threat of hitting a landmass from below was not diminished. It would have the same effect on his body as if he were falling in normal gravity hundreds of feet without a chute. Death was waiting whether he was "up" or "down." He found it helpful at times to shift his perspective of up to down and vice versa just to orient himself and engage his propulsion boosters properly.

For the next several minutes, they darted and dodged floating mountains, at times turning off the boosters completely and flying in the seams between normal gravity and the anti-graviton fields. At other times, all four boosters were needed to divert from a shifting island. One false move could send him into an unrecoverable trajectory.

Each moment seemed a life and death experience, but slowly Daeson began to master the art of the harrowing propulsion flight. He watched Thenoras and tried to mimic her actions, for her skill in this type of flying was truly remarkable. At times it looked as if she had wings. For Daeson, it was thrilling and frightening all at the same time. It brought back memories of his thrill-seeking days with Linden and Xandra...days that were now gone forever.

Finally, when Daeson knew his boosters had to have been nearly expired, he saw Thenoras slow and carefully position herself near one of the larger floating islands. She "slid" down a gravity seam toward the mass and finished with one final cushioning boost from her ankle boosters to land gently on the ground. Daeson followed, imitating her final move, and landed with almost as much finesse. Thenoras looked over at him with a pleased expression. "You survived...there must be something to you. Sabella is there." She pointed toward a cottage nestled in a grove of trees just a few hundred paces away. "She's been waiting for you."

Daeson nodded. He took a moment to gaze out across the mystical beauty of the Lamara Skies. This was a place made of dreams...surreal...majestic. He made his way toward the cottage where the oracle waited. Many questions were left to ask and many answers to find, but the one question Daeson needed to settle in his mind above all had to do with the oracle herself. Was she the real deal or just some self-promoted mystic that loved the adoration of people looking for false hope in a false power?

He carefully opened the door and peered in. Like a statue waiting to be looked upon, the young white-haired oracle sat at a black glass-topped table. Stoic, emotionless, sober. Daeson glanced about the room, confirming that the two of them were its sole occupants. He made his way to the table, feigning confidence and resolve but somehow already feeling the effect of the oracle's presence. He steeled himself as he sat down to face the one who had initiated calamity in his life.

Daeson looked across the table into the same penetrating eyes he recognized from that fateful night back in Drudgetown. It seemed so long ago and yet not so. He braced himself, remembering the inexplicable ability of this woman to make her words seem so dramatic...so personal. She had a way of peeling away his defenses until he felt exposed and vulnerable.

Not this time, he thought. *I will control this!* "I have questions," he stated.

"And why do you think I have the answers?" Sabella's stark white hair was in a dramatic contrast to her youthful face. But her eyes...her eyes seemed to hold the wisdom of a thousand years. She unsettled Daeson.

"Because you told me this would happen. You knew, and you must know more."

"I know exactly what I am supposed to know. Nothing more...nothing less." The oracle gazed deep into Daeson's eyes. "Never before have I given such a great message to one who knows so little about its meaning." She shook her head. "And even less about the one he serves."

"I serve no one!" Daeson rebuked.

The oracle smiled, as if watching a little boy throw a pointless tantrum.

"All of humanity serves someone, whether they know it or not. There are two powerful and immortal forces at work, Sovereign Ell Yon and his enemy, Lord Dracus."

The oracle reached into a pocket and withdrew a gold coin. On one side was the image of a lion and on the other a dragon. She placed it on the table and gave it a spin.

"Every person is like this coin...spinning and trying to figure out upon which side to land. It will not spin forever. It will fall on one side or the other—there is no other option for the coin, just as there is no other option for each of us."

The coin slowed and began to wobble, then rhythmically oscillated to one side. But before Daeson could see which side the coin landed on, the oracle covered it with her hand.

"Unlike a spinning coin, we have the capacity to choose the side upon which we land. By not choosing or, as some are inclined to do, choosing themselves, they unwittingly choose to serve the dragon."

The oracle's icy stare sent chills down Daeson's spine.

"You, Daeson Starlore, must choose..." The oracle then removed her hand to reveal the image of the dragon as she completed her statement, "...or the darkness will choose for you."

No matter how hard Daeson tried to keep from being lured into the absurdity of this mystic woman's words, he failed. "If what you say is true and we all serve one of these two mythical Immortals, why should one be any better than the other? What is the difference between Ell Yon and this Lord Dracus?"

The oracle looked perplexed.

"Supreme Ell Yon always surprises."

"What does that mean?" Daeson mocked.

The oracle slowly turned her head to look out the window.

"He has chosen you and yet you know nothing of him. There are countless Rayleans that would give everything to have such favor and to serve him with all they have. Yet..." She shook her head before continuing, "...he chooses you. He always surprises."

She looked back at Daeson.

"Lord Dracus has great love for himself, and he serves no one but himself. Sovereign Ell Yon has great love for his people and offers us freedom and abundant joy. Dracus promises the same, but in the end he only and always delivers bondage and despair. It is an absolute eventuality."

The oracle leaned forward. "Surely you have felt both the darkness and the light...and the author of each."

Daeson had no idea who this Dracus of which the oracle spoke was, but he did remember an encounter that shook him...Zaris Treville, the chancellor of the Galactic Alliance. Darkness was there. Daeson thought his adverse reaction to the chancellor was a result of his respect for such great power in this man, but deep down something else had caused him to want to flee. He could almost smell the evil on him.

If the oracle was telling the truth about this immortal named Dracus, Daeson did not want to meet him. But Ell Yon...who was he really, and what of him? Daeson tried again to dismiss the oracle's words as foolishness, but it didn't work. He allowed himself to truly consider her words, at least for the next few minutes.

"Sovereign Ell Yon is powerful, with resources and technology beyond anything we could dream of, but that is not what draws people to him. That is not why the Rayleans follow him."

"What is?" Daeson asked.

"I think you know. You've been close enough to know."

Daeson thought back to his dream of what he thought might be the mythical Immortal. Unlike most dreams, Daeson could remember every detail and the very real emotions that dream evoked. What he remembered most was in his eyes, those deep, penetrating, powerful eyes.

The oracle smiled as if she knew his thoughts.

He's good. The thought came, but Daeson resisted it, and he didn't know why. Perhaps it was because he still didn't believe in any of this.

The oracle broke his thought stream with more.

"This is a war for freedom, Daeson Starlore."

Daeson raised an eyebrow.

"You speak of the war the Jyptonians are fighting against us?"

"No. That is just a symptom of the Great War."

Daeson was confused yet again.

"What Great War?"

"The Great War for the entire galaxy. It's all around us. It is the war for power and control, and our freedom or enslavement will be the outcome."

"If it's all around us, then why can't we see it?"

Sabella looked as if her patience was wearing thin.

"The domain of the Immortals lies in a dimension outside our own...a fifth dimension. They have the technology to exist in both our four dimensions of space and time and also in their dimension in between...the dimension of the Ruah."

At that, Daeson scoffed. It was too much. The whole of the Raylean's beliefs rested on the absurd notion that the Immortals were invisible because they existed in another dimension? How convenient.

"I believe in only that which I can see. Everything else is a fabrication of the weak-minded. It serves to offer false hope to a hopeless people. My hope lies in my own abilities and in the opportunities I make for myself."

"If you truly believe that, then you of all people are the most enslaved, for you do not see the cage that you live in."

"Ha! Show me one soldier of this invisible war, and I'll believe. Until then it's all just mythical fanfare."

"Remember this, Starlore, when you lose sight of the enemy, he has every opportunity to destroy you. You will lose the fight before you even realize you are in one. And this Great War of which I speak will not remain hidden forever. It is coming here, and we are not ready for it!"

Daeson rubbed a tired hand down his face, trying desperately to make sense of what had happened in his life and to determine if this woman was mad. He looked at her and struggled. Her speech was so bizarre, yet something inside him knew there was truth in it. But he hated to believe it. He didn't want to become ideologically radical...on the fringe of society.

Deep down he knew that he couldn't take just a little here and a little there. To believe any of it meant he must believe all of it, and it scared him. For one fraction of a moment, he considered the possibility that her words might all be true. His heart raced as he took a brief glimpse into an existence that was infinitely bigger and more intense than anything his puny life could possibly absorb. He shook his head, rejecting the idea once more. He wanted to be done with the oracle, but there were yet two more questions he had to ask. He prepared himself for more cryptic responses.

"What of Deitum Prime, the agent that is bringing humanity closer to immortality?"

"The truth about Deitum Prime is that it doesn't offer the hope of immortality...it stole it away from us!"

Daeson couldn't help the stilted laugh. Here it was again—just as Raviel had claimed. If nothing else, the Rayleans were consistent in their delusion.

"You are mad, woman. Every quadrant of the galaxy knows that humanity has never been immortal. That is the whole point of Deitum Prime."

The oracle was undaunted by Daeson's rebuttal.

"Humanity was once immortal and shared in the splendor of Sovereign Ell Yon's favor. But it all ended the day his first officer led a rebellion against him. The rebellion spilled into the Aurora Galaxy in a way that changed mankind's existence forever. The absolute hatred of Lord Dracus for Ell Yon fueled his passion to create Deitum Prime and rob Ell Yon of his greatest love—his people—by bringing death to them."

"But the advantages that Deitum Prime bring to the human body are undeniable," Daeson countered.

"Is that truly what you believe?" The oracle eyed Daeson through narrow eyes. "Even now after you have been reclaimed...purged?"

Daeson's gaze dropped to his hands. He knew exactly what the oracle was talking about. Raviel had said it was so...the Omegeon radiation. He remembered the frail gray body he was still recovering from. And though his strength was not yet what it once had been, something was different. Something about him seemed whole. His thoughts were clear, and his body was growing stronger day by day. The only word he could think of to describe it was *renewed*. "Purged?" he sheepishly queried.

A nearly imperceptible smile briefly lighted across her lips. "You've been near to Ell Yon, purged from the outside in, yet not completely. You wouldn't have survived had Ell Yon completely purged you. No one would."

Daeson slowly closed and opened his hand. Even now he felt strangely free. "Why not?"

"Deep inside you Deitum Prime has infused itself into the fibers of your organs, and specifically your heart. The immersion is so complete that its removal causes death. You felt it, didn't you? During the purging?"

Daeson looked up at the oracle, remembering the days of lethargy as he lingered near the edge of death.

"Ell Yon is developing an antidote that will one day purge a person of Deitum Prime from the inside out." The oracle seemed lost to the future as if dreaming of the day.

Daeson struggled, torn between a lifelong indoctrinated paradigm of lauding Deitum Prime as mankind's salvation and this strange new doctrine about a mythical Immortal. It was much to process. "Your version of history certainly is different than that of every other race in the galaxy."

"That's because every other race has been lied to and is already enslaved by Lord Dracus."

Daeson sat silently for a time as his thoughts returned to the plight of the Rayleans. Regardless of how peculiar the words of the oracle were, the reality of the devastation was impossible to ignore.

"Do you know what is happening to your people?" Daeson asked.

"Yes."

"Then you know there's no hope. Soon anyone with any notion of fighting back will be dead."

Sabella lifted her hands off the table and crossed her fingers near her lips.

"What will you do?"

"Me? Do? I can't *do* anything. We are talking about the military forces of the entire Jyptonian world government!"

"You assume too much. In one respect you are exactly right. *You* can do nothing for the Rayleans. What you can do is listen. There is a place that is calling you."

The oracle slid the gold coin across the table to Daeson. "It is now your time to choose, Starlore. You are spinning no more. From this day forward this decision will define the rest of your life. Choose...wisely."

Daeson looked down at the coin. By what must have been a slight of hand, the image was now of the lion. He knew exactly what place the oracle was talking about. What he didn't know is how she knew: Galeo was calling.

Daeson picked up the coin and looked at it. That's when he felt the first tremor. It was radically different than the gentle motion of the massive island. This was more like a shock wave. He looked at Sabella and saw the concern in her eyes too. Just then Thenoras burst into the cottage. Gone was her demeanor of calm composure.

"They come for you!"

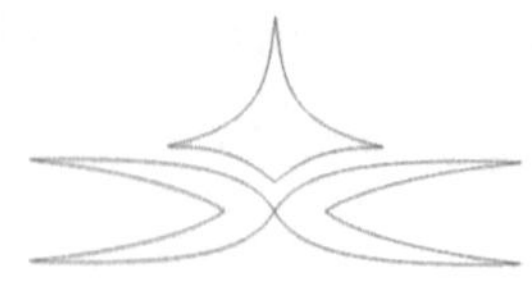

CHAPTER

2

A Glimpse Beyond

Galactic Alliance – A loose federation of planets unified in the cause to disseminate Deitum Prime to all regions of the galaxy. Chancellor Zari Treville provides leadership and acts as liaison between alliance members in conflict. Financial and technological support are privileges afforded members in good standing with the Galactic Alliance charter.

Sabella turned to look at Daeson.

"My time has come...they've found me. You must go!"

Daeson wasn't sure who *they* were, but if the oracle was concerned... "Come with me. I can help you both."

Sabella shook her head.

"I will only jeopardize the mission before you. Go!"

Thenoras threw a fresh set of propulsion boosters at Daeson, then grabbed Sabella's arm, encouraging her to come quickly.

"Sabella," Daeson called.

The white-haired oracle paused to look at Daeson one last time.

"Thank you."

Sabella offered the slightest hint of a smile, as if some weighty burden had been lifted. "The hope of a thousand generations be upon you. Goodbye, Daeson Starlore."

And then she was gone. Daeson stood confounded once more by her parting words, further rattled. The next shockwave shattered his contemplation as dust and debris fell from the rafters of the cottage. Daeson quickly donned the propulsion boosters and ran.

Outside, the peaceful, serene beauty of the Lamara Skies was gone. Large destroyers were not far away, methodically bombarding the islands with concussion bombs and energy blasts. Daeson didn't recognize the design of the ships, but he knew they weren't Jyptonian. Was this part of the Galactic Alliance force?

The mayhem was frightful. Rocks, boulders, trees, and water were being tossed a hundred directions, amplified by varying gravitational forces and resulting in a chaotic mixture of raining death. He sprinted toward the edge from which he had come and then saw an exotic vessel lift off through the roof of a nearby barn. He paused to watch. Its trajectory was straight up at first in an effort to bypass the effects of the anti-graviton fields, then it veered in the direction opposite of Daeson's destination—surely a diversion.

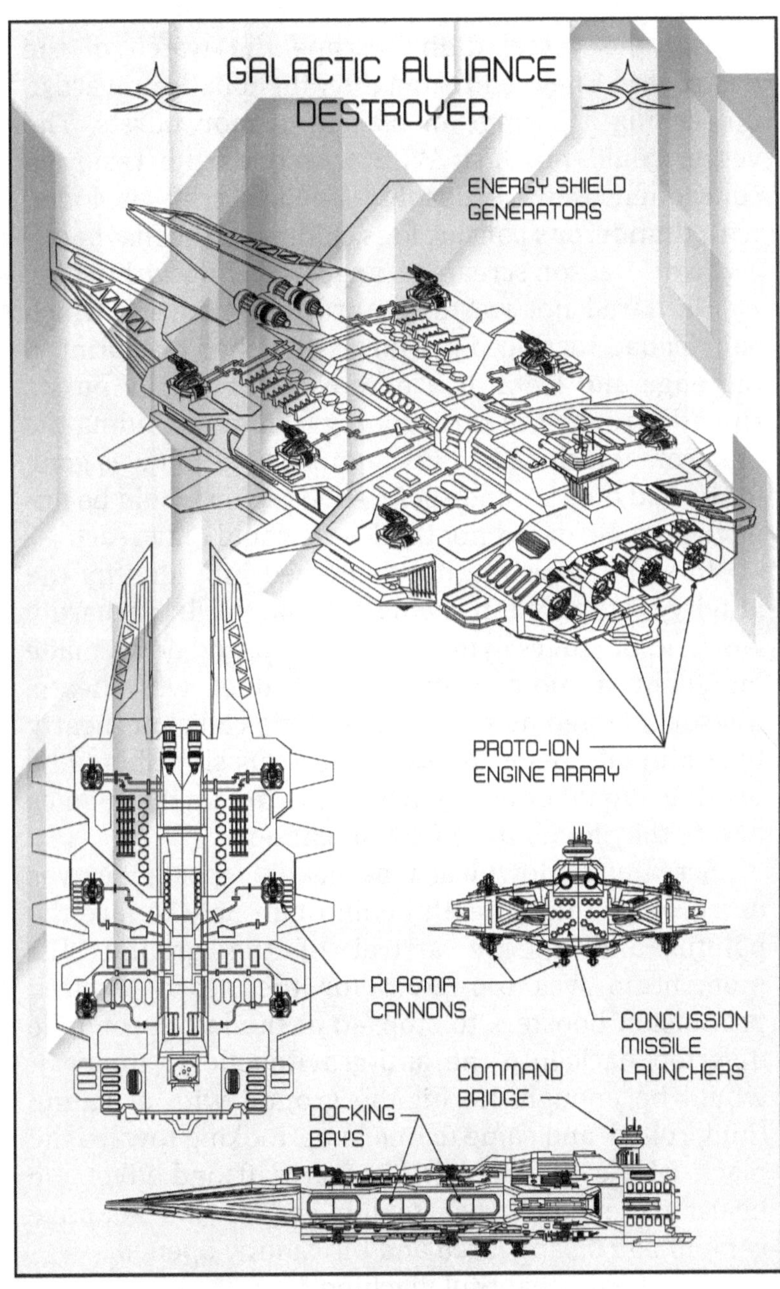

GALACTIC ALLIANCE
DESTROYER
ENERGY SHIELD
GENERATORS
PROTO-ION
ENGINE ARRAY
PLASMA
CANNONS
CONCUSSION
MISSILE
LAUNCHERS
COMMAND
BRIDGE
DOCKING
BAYS

But the vessel didn't escape the watch of the destroyers. They redirected their flight paths toward it, unleashing a barrage of plasma cannon bursts. The vessel could not last. Within seconds the resulting consequences were deadly. Sabella's craft exploded with thunderous concussions, adding to the mayhem.

"No!" Daeson screamed, anger swelling within him.

He dared not waste the precious time for which Sabella had sacrificed her life. He finished his sprint to the edge and leapt as a new wave of energy bursts ripped through the surrounding islands, including the one from which he had just jumped. Caution was gone for he had only seconds before the region would be un-navigable. He dared not think—he could only react.

In some ways the debris helped him identify the gravity/anti-graviton seams, but the peril was hardly worth it. Boulders flying right, left, up, and down made his flight a moment-by-moment duel with death. Daeson adapted quickly, but multiple collisions nearly took him out. Below he saw where his ship should be waiting. Would he even have time to fire up the engines before they found him? He thought not.

Screaming downward at deadly speed, he was outrunning a fiery death behind him only to face the painful and speedy arrival of the ground. His momentum was too great for the nearly expired propulsion boosters to stop, so at the last second, he diverted back into the anti-graviton field, hoping it would be enough. He hit the ground with a painful thud, rolled, and came to one knee, looking toward the place where he had left his Starcraft and Rivet. He heard its engines roar to life just as the adaptive camouflage disappeared and his canopy opened.

"Rivet, you beautiful machine!"

Sprinting to his Starcraft, he made the cockpit just as the engines gained full power. By now the sky was falling. Only small rocks and vegetation peppered the Starcraft as of yet, but massive boulders were close behind. One entire section of fragmented island was falling right toward them. Daeson flipped on the energy shield, lowered the canopy, and blasted off with full thrusters without a moment to spare.

His Starcraft screamed between falling sections of island as Daeson desperately searched for a way out. He accelerated to dive just beneath an enormous falling land mass then banked hard right to avoid another. Staying low, he hoped his Starcraft's signature would be lost in the surrounding chaos. Flying dangerously fast and low, he swerved a dozen times more before seeming to be clear of the collapsing world above him.

"Rivet, are they pursuing?"

"I do not detect any pursuit," the bot replied in his reassuring monotone.

Daeson's mind immediately turned back to Sabella and Thenoras. Why had they sacrificed themselves like that? If he had known what they were doing, he would have demanded different action. But in all probability, they would have all been dead had he done so. He clenched his teeth in anger and frustration. He didn't deserve to live any more than they did!

"Why...why did she do it?" Daeson muttered. He wished Raviel was with him to sort it all out.

"I do not have enough information to answer that question, my liege."

Daeson huffed. "Not a question for you, Rivet."

"But perhaps the oracle believed you are part of a greater purpose that you do not yet see."

Daeson scoffed at the counsel of the machine then hesitated...considering. He shook his head. *No*, he thought. *Not me. She died for nothing.*

Using the Starcraft's scanners and with a little help from Rivet, Daeson navigated undetected away from the broken Lamara Skies. They, like much of the world, were now in chaos. Daeson felt as if not only the Lamara Skies but also the whole of his world was collapsing too.

"What destination would you like entered into the navigational computer?" Rivet asked.

Daeson didn't answer. He knew that for some inexplicable reason, Galeo, the largest moon of Mesos, was calling him. But he was afraid. The image of the glowing night lantern was etched in his mind and filled his dreams. He needed Raviel, but he couldn't go to her—not yet. This was a journey he had to make without her. Though he could touch the hand of his love, there was an impassable gulf between them—so close, yet impossibly distant.

He had never felt so aimless and alone in all his life, as if he were wandering in a vast wilderness without a compass—thirsty, hungry, lost. He couldn't fathom anything turning his miserable existence into something worthwhile. He had the treacherous thought that Jypton with all of its inhabitants, Jyptonians and Rayleans alike, would be better off without him.

You are called!

Daeson shivered.

"What did you say, Rivet?" Daeson asked.

"What destination would you like entered into the navigational computer?" Rivet repeated.

"No...just now. What did you say?"

"I said nothing, my liege."

Daeson shook his head. Was he going mad? Was everything that was happening too much? He felt weak in every way. *There is nothing left of who I once was.*

Daeson numbly typed in the coordinates for the slipstream conduit that would take him back to the Omega Nebula and the moon that beckoned him. Before long he was exiting the conduit, and this time the flight to Mesos was uneventful. Jypton seemed incapable of dealing with anything outside of its own atmosphere now.

Daeson orbited Galeo a couple of times, looking for the right place to land his Starcraft. Though it was a large moon, gravity would be less, about two-thirds that of Mesos. As he entered the atmosphere and navigated across the terrain, it was obvious that the moon had indeed been colonized by the ancient people of Mesos. Daeson saw multiple city structures and manmade travel-ways connecting them. He chose one of the largest landmasses near Galeo's equator and set down at the edge of a small derelict city near a large lake.

Opening the canopy and jumping to the ground, he landed softly as he adjusted to the new gravity. Rivet quickly joined him. Taking a moment to look around, Daeson thought of Jypton and the desperate need of the people there. He should be going back, but there had to be a reason he was here—a reason he had been called to this remote moon in the far reaches of uninhabitable space. Or maybe there wasn't a reason and he really was going crazy.

"Well, I'm here. Now what?" Daeson asked no one in particular.

Rivet slowly turned his head to look at Daeson. The bot seemed distant, unaware; then the bot froze as if all of his circuits had shut down at once.

"Rivet?" Daeson frowned, but there was no response. "Rivet!" Daeson walked around the bot, but it was indeed lifeless.

"Great!" Daeson said. "And Raviel's not here to fix you."

"You will not need the android here."

Daeson spun about to see a woman standing behind him dressed in sleek battle armor, similar to what he had worn during his Talon training at the academy, but much more sophisticated. Perfectly form-fitting dark gray body armor covered her from neck to feet. A utility belt rested about her waist, adorned with various attachments of exquisite design he had never seen before. About her wrists and ankles were broad golden cufflets or bracers that appeared to be more armor or weapon than jewelry. Shoulder- length sand-colored hair framed her face. She was a warrior that possessed a beauty only possible for an Immortal— veteran eyes that seemed as if they had witnessed a hundred battles. On this ancient and abandoned moon, she looked out of place.

Daeson thought about reaching for his Talon, but although this woman was clearly well acquainted with combat, he did not feel threatened.

"Who are you?"

The woman's eyes narrowed. "My name is of no importance. I am a warrior of the Malakians. Follow me."

She turned and began to walk away, glancing over her shoulder. "And keep up."

With that, she began running toward one of the travel-ways he had seen earlier. Daeson hesitated. As peculiar as this encounter was, surely this was why he had come.

He sprinted after her and was soon belabored to sustain the pace she had set for them. They dodged fallen columns of ancient origins and navigated through a derelict city. Daeson was breathing hard, and his legs began to fail him. On and on she ran, seemingly unfazed by the physical exertion. At times, she glanced back at him, clearly unimpressed with his endurance.

Since his bout with the Omegeon purging weeks earlier, Daeson felt he had nearly recovered his full strength and then some, but this peculiar warrior was pushing him beyond his physical abilities. He was forced to stop multiple times and fill his lungs, but she did not.

He could only imagine how much worse he would have felt if this were happening under the full gravity of Jypton or Mesos. He managed to stay ten to twenty paces behind her, but only by pushing himself to his limits. Finally, she stopped amidst the ruins of an ancient courtyard. He slowed to allow himself a few extra seconds of rest, knowing she would probably sprint away once he caught up with her. She stood with her hands on her hips, breathing with hardly any strain.

Daeson did his best to stand straight on shaky legs and recover his lungs, but the effort was painful. "Where are you taking me?"

She looked at him with a gleam in her eye, then looked away and knelt on one knee.

As Daeson turned to see what had prompted this reverent response from such a warrior, his gaze fell upon the noble and familiar countenance of a mighty man. He glanced back toward where his guide had been kneeling, but she was gone. He dared look once more upon the face of the one from his vision months earlier. Once again, he was in the presence of extreme power and influence.

The man's eyes pierced Daeson's soul. Something about him exposed Daeson, revealing every flaw at once. Noble perfection—if such a thing were possible—stood before him in a man. Without a word being spoken, Daeson felt undone...unworthy. He tried to rally himself and regain his confidence, but he failed miserably. A man like this surely ruled worlds!

Daeson realized that he was in the presence of true royalty...royalty of a fashion mere mortals could not imagine. He felt something he had never experienced before, especially as a member of the royal family of Jypton—a need to kneel. Daeson could hardly hold the man's gaze. He lowered his head and knelt.

"Daeson Starlore." The ground beneath Daeson nearly rumbled at the sound of this majestic voice.

"Are you...?" Daeson began.

"I am...Ell Yon, the Sovereign of the Rayleans and of your heritage."

Daeson swallowed hard.

"Rise up."

Daeson mustered the courage to stand and look once more into the eternal eyes of this Immortal. He was face-to-face with the one he had considered a mythical fairy tale. If this man was truly the Immortal of which Raviel spoke, he was all she had said and much more.

"You are Raylean, Daeson Starlore. Quit fighting the truth."

Daeson lowered his head.

"Do you know why the Rayleans have been subjugated and persecuted for over twelve hundred years?"

Daeson considered the question but stayed silent.

"They're not simply the convenient solution to the labor needs of the Jyptonian Empire. They are the focus of the hatred of my enemy, Lord Dracus. They are the last and only hope this galaxy has of overcoming the complete domination of the evil of Dracus and his regime, of which the Galactic Alliance is a part. And I am the Raylean's protector."

Ell Yon's gaze left Daeson and turned upward toward the stars.

"It is time for the oppression of my people on Jypton to come to an end. They suffer hard under the rule of Lockridge. Through you I will set them free. They will be a people once more."

Daeson struggled to interpret his own thoughts and emotions before speaking. "The Rayleans call you their Sovereign. How is this so?"

"Because I have been with them from the beginning, and I will be with them to the end."

"But why? Why are you concerned with so small a people?" Daeson dared ask.

Ell Yon's eyes narrowed. "The fate of the entire galaxy hangs on this so small a people. The entire forces of Dracus's evil empire will be unleashed on them. Do not judge by what you see, but by what you know to be true yet do not see. The Rayleans are the future hope of many." Sovereign Ell Yon then looked deep into the soul of Daeson. "And I have chosen you to lead them in their darkest hour."

Daeson trembled. Everything inside of him rejected Ell Yon's command. *Why of all people should I be chosen? And beyond this, even with the great power this man seems to wield, the future of the Rayleans is pointless, isn't it?*

"But why should Jypton listen to me? What power do I have? What power do you have over such a great people? Their military might is unparalleled in the galaxy!"

Ell Yon's eyes became fierce, and Daeson's heart failed him.

"Watch!" Ell Yon placed his hands together in front of Daeson and slowly pulled them apart, revealing a translucent image of the planet of Jypton from deep space. Daeson was mesmerized. His eyes skimmed from hand to hand, and the image grew larger as Ell Yon spread his hands to the width of Daeson's shoulders. Daeson could detect no transmission devices, no optics, no technology, yet his home world hung perfectly in place before him. It felt magical.

Slowly the image zoomed inward, and Daeson found himself on a visual journey across the planet. Scenes began to unfold in rapid sequence like a video collage of events: thousands of sentries making raids on Rayleans across the planet, resistance fighters, fires, executions, battles, an assassination, and then the images fell still on the face of a little girl weeping over the dead form of her mother. When the image faded, the face of Ell Yon was in its place, a tear trailing down his noble cheek. But the eye that spilled the tear was not soft. It was still fierce, holding the fire of an ancient forge that demanded justice for the weak. How could Daeson refuse such a call from such a man?

Daeson looked into Ell Yon's powerful eyes and at once he fully understood what Raviel had been telling him all along about this Immortal. There was a perfect good about him that didn't exist anywhere else in the galaxy. And with that perfect good was perfect power and perfect knowledge. Daeson felt it all and somehow knew it to be absolute. It was as if Ell Yon had been watching him his whole life and was preparing him for this very day. But he was not ready…he could never be ready for such a mission.

"My Lord, what you're asking of me is impossible. I am just one man, and the Rayleans are not trained or equipped for war. How can they stand against the entire global forces of the Jyptonians and the Galactic Alliance? Linden Lockridge and Zari Treville are powerful…no one can stand against such might!"

Daeson had never been so conflicted in all his life. He had but a glimpse of Ell Yon's power, wisdom, and goodness and had been overwhelmed and pressed down by his mere presence, yet what was being asked of him was beyond human ability. Ell Yon was asking for everything, and he had nothing to give.

Ell Yon peered deep into Daeson's eyes with a gaze that shattered reason. "Don't you yet know who I am? The forces of evil in this galaxy will not stop nor be quenched by abdication. I will not abandon my people. Nor will I abandon you."

"But how, Sovereign? The power of Jypton is great, and I'm certain that I can convince no one, not even the Rayleans. Will you send a fleet of battleships beside me? Will you send an army of soldiers?"

"You will go alone."

Daeson closed his eyes and hung his head. The preposterous command collided with all reason and logic.

"Put forth your hands." Daeson once more felt the gentle rumble of Ell Yon's deep voice resonate into his core.

Daeson looked up at the noble brow of his Lord and reached out his hands. Ell Yon slid his cloak off of his arms to reveal an exquisitely beautiful vambrace on each of his forearms. Daeson was reminded of the cufflets of his warrior guide, which had a similar appearance, but these that Ell Yon wore were far more elaborate. The pearl white surfaces were inlaid with thin ribbons of jeweled technology that Daeson could not comprehend. They seemed to adapt and conform to Ell Yon's movements yet appeared as solid as armor. Ell Yon lifted one of the vambraces from his left arm, and it yielded its perfect fit to Ell Yon's control.

"This is the Protector. Through it I will lead you and my people. It will be light in your darkest days and hope where there is none. Its power is without limit. By this I will be with you."

Ell Yon lowered his chin and hesitated, pouring the fire of his gaze into Daeson's heart. Then the Sovereign's eyes softened, and Daeson understood why…it was love. Pure, relentless, undeserved love. Ell Yon placed the Protector over Daeson's forearm and pressed the seamless marvel downward. The sensation was unlike anything Daeson had ever experienced. The solid form yielded to his flesh, embracing him. Searing chills flowed from this elegant instrument of power, penetrating every fiber of his being. It formed a seamless shape about his arm in a flowing yet solid form, restricting nothing and protecting everything. Daeson gazed in wonder at the Protector. He looked up at Ell Yon, ignorant of the significance of the offer and the abilities it afforded.

"Here…it begins," Ell Yon whispered.

Something deeply painful filled the eyes of the Sovereign. Daeson didn't understand.

"You are the first of a new order…the order of the Navi. Dracus and the Scourge have created enemies of my realm that are fueled by the strength of Deitum Prime. They are crafty, devious, and strong. As a Navi, you will be trained to outfight them and outwit them.

The Protector is life. When wielded by one whom I've made worthy, it protects in a thousand ways and will destroy the forces of Dracus and the Scourge, no matter how powerful they may seem. One day it will be the instrument of complete victory for my people."

The Protector seemed to penetrate Daeson's thoughts, and it frightened him. It was a power that could not be stopped. Yet this fear was different than any other. It was a fear that revered the power behind it. He turned his arm over, looking for the seam that held it in place, but there was none. No hinge, no crack, no beginning, and no end. This technological marvel seemed to hold the very essence of the Sovereign standing before him. Daeson sensed the neuro-link of the Protector and knew immediately that Ell Yon was there…with him. Though the Protector was light upon his arm, he felt a heaviness he couldn't describe, as if he now bore the weight of the galaxy on his soul. What was this profound and weighty burden Ell Yon had laid upon him? With questions yet unanswered, he looked into the eyes of Ell Yon.

In spite of this technological wonder, Daeson still couldn't imagine how the Protector could overcome the power of Jypton and the Galactic Alliance, let alone this new Immortal enemy Ell Yon called Dracus and his Scourge. His thoughts turned back to the mission Ell Yon was asking of him, and he cringed at the thought of it.

"Sovereign Ell Yon…" Daeson began but his words choked within him. He feared the mission he was being called to, yet he feared to protest further.

Ell Yon looked disappointed, knowing what Daeson was about to say. His eyes narrowed, and a moment of intense anger crossed his noble face.

Daeson swallowed hard.

"Come!" Ell Yon said as he turned away, his flowing vesture exclaiming the power of his gait as he walked.

Daeson followed. They walked through the ruins of an ancient compound that surely was once some majestic royal court. Marble columns and toppled spires of granite testified to a once ancient but glorious civilization. Sovereign Ell Yon led him to an arched gate that was inscribed with markings Daeson couldn't identify.

When Ell Yon stopped and turned, his eyes still held the fury of his disappointment. Daeson shuddered. Whatever Ell Yon was about to do, Daeson realized that it should not have been necessary. But his trust was weak. *How can I do this impossible thing Ell Yon is asking of me? Surely, I and all who dare follow me will die.*

Without a word, Ell Yon turned back to the arched gate and stepped across its threshold. As he did, his form dissolved away to nothingness. Daeson could clearly see through the gate to the rest of the ancient courtyard, now in ruins, but Ell Yon was not there. He stepped closer to the gate and mustered the courage to step across its threshold into a world that took his breath away. The imagery of the ancient abandoned court of Galeo was instantly replaced with that of a new world. The sensation was not unlike that of a slipstream jump, causing him to feel for just a moment as if he were in two places at the same time. Once fully through the gate, Daeson became enchanted by this new world.

Standing next to Ell Yon, he whispered, "What is this place?"

"You have stepped through a dimensional shift gate. The Immortals reside in the fifth dimension called the Ruah. We are still on Galeo, but this..." Ell Yon motioned toward a city of incredible beauty, "This is my domain."

Daeson turned in all directions, beholding a technologically miraculous sight. Shimmering towers of crystal and metal were surrounded by structures that defied mortal architectural design. Ships elegant yet powerful flew every which way with precision and purpose. The city was pulsing with life, yet Daeson somehow knew that every single action had some perfect intent to which it had been assigned. The stature of the people here made a mortal fully immersed in Deitum Prime seem insignificant. Like his earlier guide, these were sober warriors of great confidence and strength, the Immortal race of the Malakians. Daeson felt as if he were walking among the mythical gods of ancient legends.

"Is this real?" Daeson asked as he reached to touch the marbled waist-high wall just to his left. Its cool, smooth surface was no figment of his imagination. "This is your city, Sovereign?"

"No. This is one of our galactic headquarters. Come."

Sovereign Ell Yon led Daeson a few hundred paces across a beautiful courtyard of magnificent stone, marble, water, and trees. Along the way, every warrior they passed bowed to one knee before Ell Yon. Knowing he was unworthy, Daeson honored their reverent respect by walking behind Ell Yon. They entered a building that appeared to be the heart of the city. Upon the arrival of Ell Yon, hundreds fell to one knee—silent, still, reverent. Only the noble nod of their king released them from their adoring devotion. The respect from these giants of immortality completely transcended the facade of devotion displayed in the royal courts of Jypton.

Inside, Daeson was again astonished by what he saw. The vast hall was a command center that pulsed with activity unlike anything he'd ever seen. Massive three-dimensional graphic displays surrounded them, as hundreds of men and women dressed in unique clothing that was both military and regal conversed and relayed orders for combatants in a war that appeared to span the galaxy. Images of star ships engaged in deadly battles, ground forces repelling a terrible onslaught of unidentified energy weapons, and numerous warriors on individual missions composed the tapestry of glimpses he was able to interpret.

At the center of the activity stood one of supreme authority—calm, sure, wise, and in all respects equal to Sovereign Ell Yon. He was a man of unequaled stature, a commander of warriors. Two mighty warriors stood next to him, one on the commander's left and one on his right. The Commander glanced toward Ell Yon, and the two seemed to know each other's thoughts without speaking a word.

Daeson felt so small in this place and next to these Immortals. He watched as the woman warrior who had guided him earlier approached the Commander and his vice commanders. The exchange was short and ended with a sharp salute. Ell Yon's gaze lingered on the leader in a manner that Daeson had seen before, much like a father watching a son work some task of ultimate importance.

Ell Yon glanced toward Daeson.

"We are in a battle to free the galaxy from the clutches of the Scourge. The Raylean people are the key to conquering Dracus and his forces of tyranny. By my power they will be free. Do not be afraid, for I am with you."

Daeson looked up into the eyes of Immortal Ell Yon and was humbled beyond words. So mighty a leader, so powerful a king, yet he had called upon Daeson for this task. Daeson didn't know how or why, but he did believe him and in him. Daeson knelt on one knee. "Forgive me, Sovereign. I am weak and unworthy, but I am willing."

Ell Yon hesitated. "Then rise up and go."

Daeson stood and looked into Ell Yon's eyes, his heart warmed in the glow of his approval.

The female warrior then came to him and pointed to the exit. Daeson bowed before Sovereign Ell Yon before turning to follow her. Outside she led him back to the dimensional shift gate and waited for Daeson to step through. Daeson looked once more at the world of Immortals, trying to remember every detail, for he knew that on the other side, time would begin to erase the reality of this world.

"The leader I saw you talking to...who is he?" Daeson asked.

"He is the Commander of the Malakians, Prince of the Aurora Galaxy. I would die for him," the warrior said with reverence.

"And you fight for freedom?" Daeson asked her.

The warrior hesitated as if restrained by some secret code. Her eyes narrowed.

"We all do," she said as she lifted her hand toward the gate.

Daeson nodded, then stepped across the threshold back into the world of mortal men, where the battle against an overwhelming tyrant waited...waited for a leader who had been called.

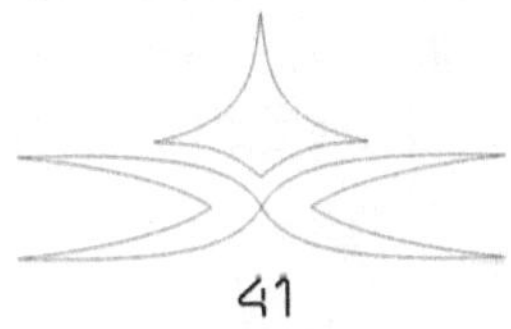

CHAPTER

3

Visions

"I will make a covenant with Rayl and will give to them and multiply them. I will dwell in the midst of them and protect them." – Eziam, Oracle of Ell Yon

Daeson stood looking out across the remnants of Galeo's ancient ruined city for a long time, processing everything he'd just seen and all of the events in his life that had led up to this point in time. Within minutes, he began wondering if what he'd just seen had been a dream or hallucination. How could it be real? Another dimension, Immortals, galactic battles, genetically induced mind control, secret conspiracies? He turned and looked back at the gateway. Perhaps one more glimpse would finally convince him. When he stepped back across the threshold, nothing changed. He simply stood one step away from where he had been.

What are you looking for? The whisper came.

Daeson lifted up his arm and saw the Protector in all of its technological splendor. He was ashamed. With all that had happened, he still questioned. The trust of

Raviel and her people humbled him. None of them had seen what he'd seen, yet they believed. He imagined his life from this point in time forward if he tried to ignore the call of the mighty Ell Yon.

He lifted his eyes to the hills, and something within him changed. In that moment—in the quiet of these ruins—Daeson embraced the truth once and for all. Whether he live or die, he could not turn away from the truth that Ell Yon had revealed to him.

"I will go, my Lord," Daeson repeated aloud.

He began his return journey to the Starcraft, hoping he could find the way without difficulty, for he had focused much more on not losing sight of the female warrior than on navigating the terrain of Galeo. The setting of the sun on Galeo was slow, but darkness was still a concern, so he quickened his pace. As he ran, new energy filled his legs with strength and his heart with courage. Something was rising up within him—the truth, as well as hope in a cause that brought ultimate purpose to his life.

Each stride he took drove the stake of determination deeper. His run turned to a sprint and his anticipation built until he could not restrain himself. He drew his Talon and extended the blade to full length. To his sprint he added the practice of his Talon training—jumping, turning, striking. And in the flurry of his journey, Daeson leapt from a rocky knoll and landed in a clearing before the form of a hooded warrior of supreme strength. The man's Talon was also drawn, wisps of blue energy arcing near the slivered edge of the blade's stasis field.

Daeson froze, his chest rising and falling to regain his breath as he considered the one before him. The formidable hooded figure appeared to have been waiting for Daeson. The waiting warrior slowly circled Daeson, who was trying to recover.

"Who are you, and what do you want?" Daeson asked between breaths.

The man responded by readying his Talon.

"I have no quarrel with you, sir," Daeson said, readying his own Talon.

"But I do with you," came the man's reply along with a powerful cut.

Daeson met his cut and retreated. Was this an enemy of Ell Yon attempting to stop his mission before it began?

"Why? What have I done to you?" Daeson asked, but his answer came in a volley of cuts and slices that were perfectly timed and powered by the skill of a master. Daeson did his best, but in order to stay alive, all he could do was defend and retreat. Within just a few strokes, his opponent had stripped Daeson's defense completely away.

Daeson knew the battle was over. Open and vulnerable, Daeson made a feeble attempt to recover, but the man's blade flew swiftly to its mark, stopping just a hair's breadth from Daeson's neck. Daeson could hear the arcing stasis field at full power as it encased the metallic construct of the blade that waited to tear into his flesh. The power and skill of this man were simply too great. *What is he waiting for?* Daeson wondered.

"You're not yet ready," the man stated coldly as he retracted his blade from Daeson's face. He removed the hood that had earlier obscured his face, but he didn't back away.

Daeson could barely breathe, and seeing the face of the one who had held his life in his hands just moments earlier added to his confusion. When he wiped the sweat from his eyes to see more clearly in the dimming light of the moonscape, Daeson faced none other than the Commander of all of Ell Yon's forces.

"You, sir…but why?"

"Because although your heart finally belongs, you have much to learn."

The Commander's eyes were fiery and fierce, and they frightened Daeson. The Commander grabbed Daeson's arm and lifted it until the pearled vambrace Ell Yon had called the Protector was clearly visible. Daeson saw that the Commander wore an identical Protector.

"The Protector is your life! Learn from me of its great power, and you will save many."

Daeson looked at the Protector and then directly into the eyes of this Immortal Commander. "Teach me, my Lord."

The Commander's eyes narrowed.

"You will live or die by what you learn here with me. Do not draw back."

"You have my word," Daeson replied with as much courage as he could muster.

"So let it be…your training as a Navi begins now."

This leader of worlds then released Daeson, and his training began.

That night Daeson slept on the ground near a thermal radiator provided by the Commander. As Daeson slept, his dreams lured him to another time and place. He was suspended in space as images of worlds and cities flashed before him. He saw people, briefly becoming them in the snapshots of lives they lived. Brilliant colors and scenes of dimensional shifts warped the space around him. The intensity of his visions escalated until his mind was frantically trying to make sense of any of it. He tried to look away, but the images were everywhere, taunting him because of his limited understanding. Technological wonders too complex to fathom, warriors, ships, battles, and millions of voices all pushed him to the brink of madness as they flashed faster and faster. He grabbed his head and cried out, "Stop!"

Daeson awoke and sat up with his hands about his head, just as in his dream. He was sweating and breathing hard, badly shaken from what he'd seen—no, experienced. He focused his eyes to see the Commander sitting before him in the soft glow of a crescent Mesos.

Daeson sat for moment in silence, trying to recover as the Commander waited. "The Protector is showing you beginnings." The strong, soothing voice of the Commander seemed to assuage his rattled emotions.

Daeson ran his left hand over the Protector, feeling its smooth, seamless outer covering. Even now it trembled with power...waiting. Was this the primary purpose of the Protector?

"Beginnings? How can there be more than one beginning?" Daeson asked.

"The beginning of life, of technology, of dimensions, of love..." The Commander paused before continuing, "And of evil."

Daeson shook his head. "But I didn't understand any of it. It was too much. How can I possibly understand these things?"

"Calm yourself and focus on one aspect of what you see. The Protector will guide you and teach you."

Daeson tried to calm himself, but the collage of images and emotions lingered. "It was different than a dream. It seemed so real. Was it real?"

"It was real for those who lived it," the Commander replied. "The Protector conveys not only the stories of what once was, but also the thoughts and emotions of those who lived them."

Daeson took a few more moments to recover himself then lay down again, unsure if he dared venture back to the realm of the Protector. Once calm, sleep came quickly, and so did the visions. As before, the experience threatened to overwhelm him, but this time he calmed himself and focused on one vivid scene that was forming in the midst of the vision. Slowly, the peripheral images dissolved away until Daeson was an invisible observer of a singular story.

To view these beginnings, he had entered the realm of the Ruah, in the abode of the Immortals called the Malakians.

Two young men stood side by side atop a ridge overlooking a magnificent city of shimmering gold and silver towers. Something distant and familiar about them nagged Daeson from the corner of his mind, but he could not place them. Elegant ships whisked across deep blue skies under the warmth of a yellow sun. A sense of perfection permeated everything in the scene.

"Kalem, have you ever wondered if there is more?" one young man asked the other.

Daeson focused further on the men and could sense their emotions as he concentrated on each one. This was far more than watching a screen as some disconnected bystander. Daeson seemed to be a part of the interplay between them.

"More? How can there be more?" Kalem asked. This man wore a smile as a natural and ever-present part of his countenance. Black hair framed a chiseled jaw and cheek line. His eyes glowed with friendship. "What do you mean, C'fir?"

C'fir pushed back a lock of blond hair and looked out beyond the horizon. "More to experience than what is here."

Kalem put a hand on C'fir's shoulder. "What are you talking about? Sovereign Ell Yon has provided everything we could ever need. Look!" Kalem exclaimed and spread his hands out across the scene before them. "We are on Tsiyyon…this *is* more!"

"Yes, this is everything we could ever need, but is it everything we could ever want?" C'fir asked.

Kalem eyed C'fir. "I have everything I need and want."

"Hmm. I wonder." C'fir raised an eyebrow as he looked over at Kalem and laughed. "It doesn't hurt to be curious, brother," C'fir chortled. "C'mon, the contests begin shortly, and our teams will be looking for us."

Daeson watched as the young men mounted exquisite machines that could only be described as extremely sophisticated aerobikes. Within seconds Kalem and C'fir were accelerating down into the majestic city that awaited their arrival.

Over the next few minutes, Daeson watched a collage of life events surround the young men and pass by as they matured into great men of intellect and noble stature. Others joined their circle of friendship, but Daeson could sense a bond of brotherhood between C'fir and Kalem that was unique. At first it was difficult for Daeson to mentally digest all that was being presented to him, but he carefully adapted and managed to retain as much as he possibly could.

He watched some men and women rise up and become leaders of Sovereign Ell Yon's people of the

Ruah. One named Galec excelled in the field of Quantumtech, authoring the creation of slipstream conduits throughout the galaxy that allowed fantastic voyages across vast regions of space. Within the Ruah, Galec organized and managed the building of entry and exit gateways that created the space-time shroud for such travel.

All slipstream conduits and their gateways were built in pairs, for each conduit was one-way travel. Because of the nature of their quantum existence, these same conduits existed in both dimensions and offered the space travel advantage to humanity when it was time for them to take to the stars. In the dimension of humanity, however, the physical gateways did not appear; thus, the slipstream conduits appeared to exist as anomalies in space.

Kalem's contribution was in the field of Geotech, where he designed both intricate and massive machines that harnessed the power of multiple energy sources, including Omeganite, to create focused energy beam cannons for resource recovery by boring into asteroids and lifeless planets.

C'fir's unique genius was in Biotech, where he created man-machine interfaces that were flawless and efficient. He quickly progressed to neuro-mapping, which enhanced their technology bio-interfaces further. Spin-off advantages from his research were yet to be revealed. Without the threat or distraction of war and conflict, the technology advancements of the Immortals within each of the tech fields in the dimension of the Ruah was beyond Daeson's ability to describe. In stupefied wonder, he rued the debilitating squabbling of humanity because of what it meant to the crippling their own advancement.

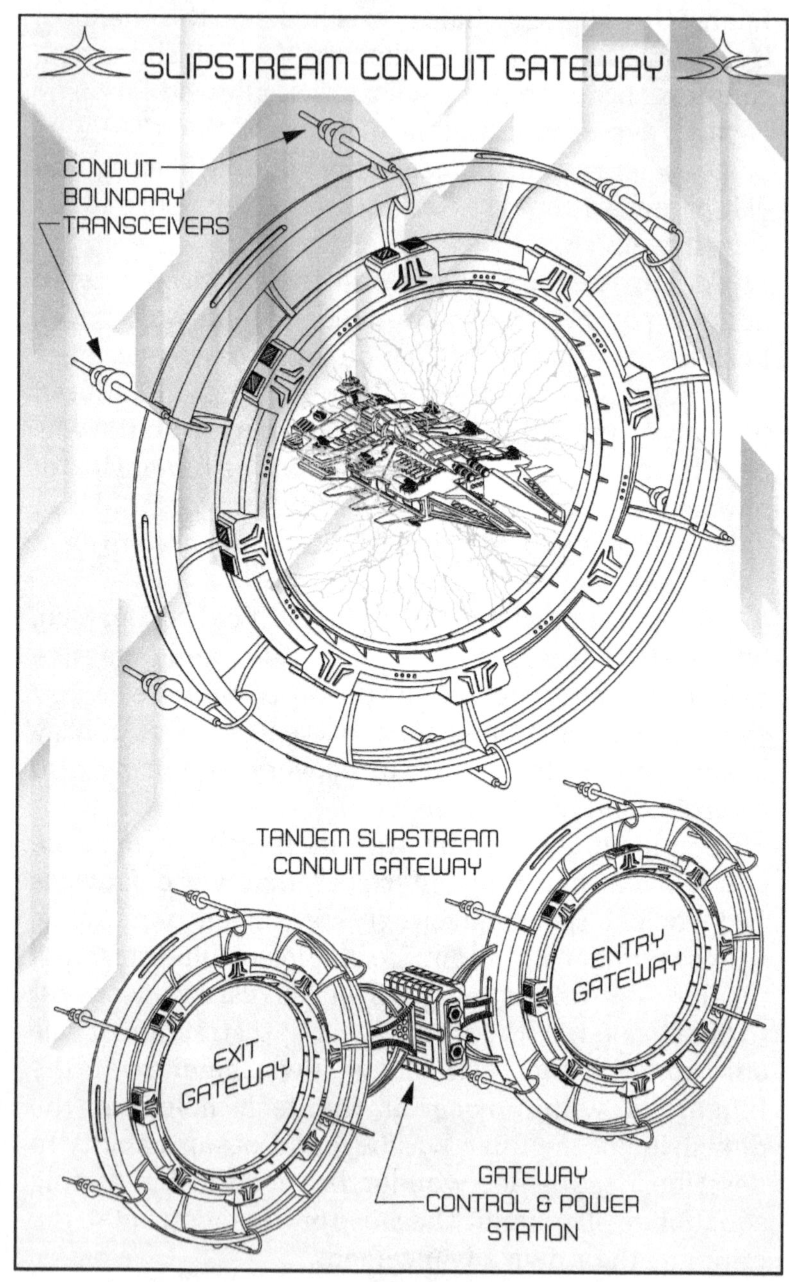
SLIPSTREAM CONDUIT GATEWAY
CONDUIT BOUNDARY TRANSCEIVERS
TANDEM SLIPSTREAM CONDUIT GATEWAY
ENTRY GATEWAY
EXIT GATEWAY
GATEWAY CONTROL & POWER STATION

C'fir, Kalem, Galec, and a few other select men and women who demonstrated incredible innovation and motivation were rewarded with consistent promotions and positions of leadership and responsibility. Although every Immortal demonstrated the utmost respect one for the other, contention was not absent. The most obvious tension seemed to exist between Kalem and Galec, two of C'fir's closest friends. But C'firs charm kept all at peace. His genius and innate ability to lead well won him the favor and special recognition of Ell Yon, as well as all of the Malakians that knew him. In time he was second only to Sovereign Ell Yon and his Son, the Commander. Daeson sensed no animosity toward C'fir from his closest friend, Kalem, but instead a great admiration and joy for his brother's success.

Slowly the scenes of the Immortals melted away, and Daeson returned to his own emotions for a moment. In the emptiness, he felt a deep ache as he remembered Linden. The brotherhood they had once shared was no more. He only hoped that this story of Kalem and C'fir would end differently than his own had.

Sunbeams broke through the leaves of nearby trees in shimmering brilliance as Daeson opened his eyes. Morning had come. Though he didn't feel rested, he wanted more of the story. But it would not be...at least not today, for Daeson's training would not wait. As Daeson began to train in the ways of the Navi, the Commander of the Malakian forces pushed Daeson beyond any limits he thought he had. In the midst of the training, Daeson thought of the academy and realized that his training there now seemed like child's play. From advanced Talon training to weapons combat, to Starcraft maneuvering and multi-ship engagements, Daeson was overwhelmed.

During one of his breaks, Daeson's mind turned to the visions of the previous night. "Commander, why is the Protector showing me visions?" he asked.

"In time, you will understand. Remember all the Protector reveals."

At the academy, Daeson had found such answers frustrating, but here, after catching a glimpse of the scope of what the Commander was beginning to reveal to him and teach him, Daeson was content. He trusted the Commander.

At the end of each long day of training, Daeson slept, and in the shadow of his dreams, the Protector gave him more of C'fir and Kalem's story.

One night as the visions began, Daeson was taken out across the stars of the Aurora Galaxy in close proximity to star systems and nebula of extraordinary beauty and splendor. Near one particularly large system of planets, multiple fleets of star ships had gathered, causing Daeson to stare in wonder. He turned his attention to a single fleet, struck by the details of the vessels. Their sleek design was unlike anything he had ever seen. He began to understand the functionality of the ship as the Protector gave him knowledge of the vessels, as well as information concerning the fleet admirals and the thousands of men and women they led.

Each admiral commanded a fleet of ships all equipped to accomplish specific exploration and mining tasks. Although many vessels appear equipped for war, it was not so. With whom would the Malakians fight? They had no enemies. Instead, all of the ships were furnished with Admiral Kalem's focused boring energy beam cannons, with power proportional to the size of the vessel. These systems utilized the beams to penetrate and split asteroids of all sizes in order to enable the mining of the precious resources within. The atmospheric-capable vessels were designed to accomplish the same on non-inhabited planets.

Most ships were also equipped with energy shields to deflect cosmic dust and debris when traveling through space, as well as to provide protection during mining operations should one of the asteroids send debris back toward them after being bombarded by a focused boring energy beam. Full loads of precious minerals were ferried back to the nearest processing outposts via space cargo ships.

Every fleet also had at least one advanced research ship to collect data and analyze the astronomical and cosmological findings in whatever region of space they were exploring. A typical exploration and mining fleet was composed of a star cruiser class flagship, five heavy mining vessels, eight-to-twelve frigate-class support vessels, six cargo ferrying vessels, an advanced research vessel, and twenty-to-thirty smaller six-man exploration shuttles, as well as another twenty-to-thirty one-man piloted crafts called extractors, which were equipped with small but powerful boring energy beam cannons. Extractors were also faster and more maneuverable than the exploration shuttles. A fleet of this size required over 8200 Malakians to operate all of the vessels at full potential.

The Protector guided Daeson to the largest fleet, where aboard the massive star cruiser flagship *Indominable*, he became a spectator at a gathering of the seven fleet admirals in counsel. He recognized most from his previous visions, including Galec and Kalem, and three others named Yelrod, Kyrsa, and Lucien. Yelrod had designed hyperlight communication for Sovereign Ell Yon's starships, whereas Kyrsa led the way in the field of Forcetech, inventing pion-charged propulsion engines. Her ship designs were elegant, and the power of the engines was simply stunning.

At the head of the counsel stood the confident figure of C'fir, festooned in accoutrements depicting rank that signified him as the First Admiral of Ell Yon's entire Aurora Galactic Fleet. Kalem stood by his side, Admiral of the *Advent* Fleet.

C'fir brought the counsel of admirals to attention and stepped forward to address them with a stolid countenance. The other admirals reciprocated.

"I have called you all here for our annual face-to-face briefing. I realize it takes significant planning to make this happen, but Sovereign Ell Yon deems it so."

C'fir glared at each of the admirals, then smiled. "And so, it is so—and it is good to see friends face-to-face once in a great while, is it not?"

The room's stoic atmosphere immediately dissolved away, and all of the admirals nodded in unison, returning his smile.

"Our exploration of the galaxy continues, my friends. Sovereign Ell Yon has granted us the authority and responsibility to expand our discoveries to all four quadrants. There is much yet to discover!"

"Here, here!" came the response from the other admirals.

"But there is now a new and intriguing aspect to our mission." C'fir paused, questioning with his eyes.

"Surely you speak of the subjacents...the humans...in their limited dimension on the planet Mesos," replied Admiral Kyrsa.

"Ah, yes. Have you been watching them?" C'fir asked.

"How can we not?" Lucien responded. "They are a curious people. Sovereign Ell Yon favors them greatly."

C'fir nodded quietly. "That he does. And they are on the verge of traveling the stars."

"But their affairs have nothing to do with Malakians," Kalem responded. "Sovereign Ell Yon has not commanded us in regards to them."

"Not yet, my friend," C'fir replied. "But his interaction with them is quite revealing."

Kalem's brow furrowed in confusion.

"Regardless," C'fir said, lifting his chin. "We have much to do... much to explore. Give me your reports, beginning with Admiral Lucien."

One by one the admirals provided a status report of their efforts to acquire resources, create slipstream conduit gateways, colonize habitable planets, and establish outposts and spaceports for building ships and establishing colonies. Each fleet research vessel shared their discoveries as needed, ever advancing the technological achievements of the Malakians.

Daeson thought of his earlier glimpse of the Commander's headquarters, where he had viewed hundreds of scenes throughout the galaxy of such things. His privileged view of the history of the galaxy in both dimensions was singular. No one had ever seen or heard such things before, and he was humbled to be granted access to the pages of history in a personal way.

When the briefings were through, the admirals enjoyed the rare opportunity to have relaxed conversations with one another, all except Admiral Kalem and Admiral Galec. Their avoidance of each other was obvious. After one quiet conversation with Admiral Lucien, Kalem looked rather troubled.

In his next vision, Daeson was taken once more to the far reaches of space aboard Admiral Kalem's flagship, the *Advent*. The fleet was in the process of mining one of several moons of a gas giant that orbited a red dwarf star. The red hue reflecting from the surface of every ship was slightly eerie.

On the bridge of the *Advent,* Admiral Kalem was reviewing a litany of reports with two of his officers. "Admiral, we are receiving a secure communication request."

Kalem turned from the display that hung in the air before him and his men. "From whom?"

"Admiral...Galec," the communications officer replied.

Kalem squinted. "Patch it through to my quarters," he ordered as he disappeared through the doorway that closed behind him. Inside his quarters, the display filled with the rigid face of Admiral Galec.

"Admiral Galec, what can I do for you?"

Galec's countenance was unusually grim. "I'm one slipstream jump away from your system. Meet me on the far side of the outer planet."

Kalem's eyes narrowed. "For what purpose? This is a secure communication transmission."

Galec scowled. "Let's be honest, Kalem. We aren't fond of each other. I wouldn't be paying you a personal visit if it weren't necessary. Come alone, and make your approach untraceable."

Galec's image instantly disappeared as the communication link was intentionally terminated. Kalem stood still for a long while, clearly stunned by the message. He shook his head. "This is not our way," he said quietly, as he turned to look out the large observation window. He stroked his cheek.

"Alone? What is this?"

Kalem returned to the bridge and spoke quietly to his first officer. The questioning look on the first officer's face quickly disappeared with the Admiral's next few firmly spoken words. The officer snapped a salute.

"I'll have an exploration shuttle fueled and ready by the time you reach the dock."

Kalem nodded and returned the salute. As he turned to leave, he looked back at his first officer. "Make it an extractor craft," Kalem ordered.

The officer hesitated, then nodded. "Yes, sir!"

A few minutes later, Admiral Kalem was launching from one of the *Advent's* bays aboard a fully fueled extractor craft. Daeson followed Kalem through multiple slipstream jumps, both within and outside their current planetary system, and eventually ended on the far side of the outer planet. In the shadow of the planet waited a frigate large enough to receive the extractor craft into one of its bays. Once the bay was pressurized, Kalem exited his craft and was greeted by Admiral Galec. The two men stood face-to-face in the dimly lit solitude of the hangar bay.

After a long moment of silence, Kalem spoke. "Why the secrecy, Galec? This is not our way."

"Our ways are about to change," Galec replied.

Kalem waited, and Galec seemed in no hurry to dispel the suspense, which annoyed Kalem greatly. Galec eyed Kalem suspiciously. Their lifelong tension seemed at its peak.

"Enough!" Kalem said. "Speak or I'm returning to my fleet."

"Are you aware of the rendezvous at Far Point?" Galec asked.

Kalem frowned. "What are you talking about? What rendezvous?"

Galec hesitated again.

Clearly exasperated, Kalem turned toward his extractor craft. "You've wasted my time. My fleet needs me." Kalem began walking back to his ship.

"Swear on the honor of Ell Yon, you know nothing of Far Point," Galec called out after him.

Kalem stopped and turned once more, disdain on his face. Galec walked toward him. "I swear," Kalem stated firmly.

Galec hesitated and then nodded. "Very well. I had to be sure...about you. It's good you don't know about Far Point. It means they don't trust you."

Kalem squinted, tilting his head. "Trust me? Who? And why not? All Malakians are to be trusted."

Galec shook his head. "Not any more. I've discovered a dark plot concocted to usurp the rule of Sovereign Ell Yon by someone close to us."

Kalem stepped backward away from Galec. Such words had never been spoken. He had never even had such a thought before. "What is this treachery you speak of? This isn't possible in the Ruah...against Ell Yon!"

Galec allowed Kalem a few seconds to ruminate on his words. "I know it seems impossible, but it's true.

There are plans to subvert Sovereign Ell Yon's rule and overthrow him," Galec continued.

Kalem shook his head. "Surely you're mistaken! Where did you hear such a preposterous thing?" Kalem asked.

"Two of my officers were invited to join this rebel group with hopes of taking over my fleet. I asked you to come here in person because we can't trust anyone...*you* can't trust anyone. Your own officers and many of your personnel could be involved. Although your absence is a danger to your fleet, your ignorance of the situation was an even greater risk. I had to speak to you in person...to see your eyes and decide if I could trust you. The fact that you aren't aware of the rendezvous tells me they consider you too great a risk to invite you."

Kalem's eyes grew fierce as he considered Galec's words. Although he clearly didn't care for Galec, he had no reason to suspect that he would speak any falsities.

"If this treachery you speak of is true, we must end it at once! I'll go to C'fir. You speak to the other admirals."

Kalem turned again, but Galec grabbed his arm. "No, Kalem." Galec's countenance fell, and his gaze went to the floor. He looked back up at Kalem, his eyes full of sadness. "C'fir is the one leading the rebellion."

Kalem's mouth opened, but he did not speak. Shock and horror were written on his face. He shook his head again. "Surely not, Galec! We're his closest friends. We know him. Why do you say such things about our brother?"

"I didn't want to believe it either." Galec looked lost himself as he considered his words. "C'fir is my closest friend, but what I'm saying is true. And he has already won two other fleet admirals to his cause—Admiral

Kyrsa and Admiral Yelrod. This is no small insurrection. This will end in...war."

"War? We don't know war, Galec."

"No...we don't. Not yet."

Kalem turned and walked away, running his hand through his thick black hair. He came back to stand in front of Galec.

"This is C'fir we're talking about! First Admiral of the Aurora Galactic Fleet!"

Galec just nodded.

Kalem's eyes opened wide as he remembered a distant conversation. C'fir's voice rang in his head, *Kalem, have you ever wondered if there is more?*

"When is the rendezvous at Far Point?" he asked.

"Tomorrow at the twentieth hour," Galec replied.

Kalem looked once more on Galec, and something softened between them. Perhaps it was the realization that though they had been at odds on most everything in life, they were united in their complete devotion and service to Sovereign Ell Yon and his Son, the Commander. The men stood in silence for a time before Kalem finally lifted his chin.

"Does Ell Yon know?" Kalem asked.

"You are the first I've spoken to since I learned of the rebellion," Galec replied. "But the Sovereign knows all, does he not? We can't trust our secure communications because we don't know how widespread C'fir's influence is."

Kalem nodded. "All Malakians love C'fir, and he is powerful." He looked Galec in his eyes. "You're wise to trust no one. We need the counsel of Ell Yon, but we're far from home. You travel to Tsiyyon and receive his word. Regardless of what's happening, I must go to C'fir...I must go to Far Point."

"That's dangerous, Kalem," Galec said.

"Perhaps," Kalem replied. "But he's our brother. If there's a chance I can change his heart and stop this treachery before it's too late, I must try."

"Very well," Galec said. "In three days, we'll meet at Epsilon Five in the Barook system. Watch your back, Kalem."

Kalem put out his arm. Galec reached for it.

"And you," Kalem returned as they grasped forearms and forged a new bond of trust.

The image of the two great admirals slowly dissolved away, while deep in the corner of consciousness, Daeson's mind filled with thousands of dark, quiet conversations authored by C'fir, which disturbed him greatly. He forced them from his mind, rejecting the darkness that taunted and frightened him. Fully awake, his heart became heavy as the scenes and words of his visions lingered. Throughout the day he found it difficult to focus on his training as his mind returned to the visions of the Protector—dramatic visions of a paradise lost.

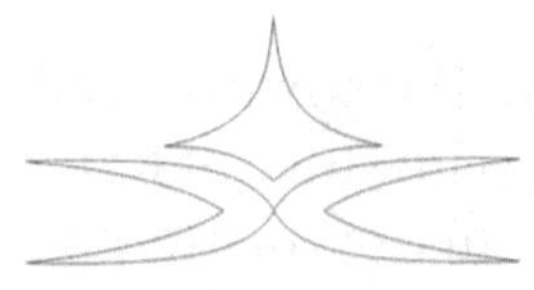

CHAPTER

4

Thief of Hearts

"I will rise in the Ruah. I will lift up myself above the throne of Ell Yon. I will rule from Tsiyyon. I will rise above the Sovereign, and I will be like him."   — Admiral C'fir

That night, Daeson dreaded the sleep that was to come. The story of Kalem and C'fir was too close to his own. He considered removing the Protector from his arm for just one night, but he could not. His quest to know the truth of the Immortals was too strong, and so he slept, and the visions came.

Daeson was taken to a small extractor craft in the vastness of space as it journeyed to a place deep in the Bravo quadrant of the Aurora galaxy, a place birthing the rebellion against Ell Yon—Far Point.

Kalem approached the single massive planet in stable orbit around a trinary sun system. Although the gravity of the planet itself was too great for an outpost or even for mining, its two moons were suitable, and plans were in motion to establish an outpost in the distant future. This was the farthest the Malakians had ever travelled from their home world of Tsiyyon, in the distant Alpha quadrant.

Kalem scanned and located five ships in orbit, one of them a medium-sized star cruiser, the *Sierra*. He recognized it as one belonging to C'fir's fleet. Kalem approached carefully.

"Sierra, this is extractor craft 3379 requesting dock."

Silence. Two minutes later Kalem tried again.

"Sierra, this is extractor 3379 requesting dock. Admiral Kalem on board. Acknowledge."

More silence. He could feel the prickles of unease beginning in his gut. Kalem reached for the com button again.

"Extractor 3379, docking bay four is available. Make your approach."

"Roger, Sierra, docking bay four."

Kalem's heart quickened.

Once on board the *Sierra*, Kalem was escorted to the observation deck. He was annoyed with the lack of respect normally shown a visiting admiral. Something had already shifted in the realm of Ell Yon's rule.

When the observation deck doors slid away, Kalem hesitated, quickly evaluating each of the ten officers present. These were powerful men and women. If Galec was right, the magnitude and the consequences of this rebellion were unknowable. Kalem straightened his shoulders and lifted his chin as he walked toward them.

"Admiral Kalem," C'fir began. "What a pleasant surprise."

"What is this, C'fir?" Kalem demanded as he approached the officers. He glanced quickly at the faces of the others before looking C'fir full in the eyes.

C'fir smiled sweetly. "We are simply discussing the potential of our future...a future we would like you to be a part of."

Kalem passed the others and came to stand directly in front of C'fir.

"And what future is that?" Kalem asked bluntly. "One where you are the ruler of the galaxy?"

C'fir's eyes narrowed to scorn for one brief moment, then softened.

"Kalem, must you always see things so black and white? I'm talking about a new galaxy...one where we all rule, brother," C'fir crooned placing a hand on Kalem's shoulder. "One without restraint or boundary. One where our potential as Immortals is unlimited. There's more to discover...more to experience than what Ell Yon is allowing. I deserve more." C'fir reached out his other arm to the rest of the officers. "We all deserve more."

Kalem scowled as he pushed C'fir's hand from his shoulder. He turned to face each officer. Their countenances were dark and fierce. Only one looked away from his piercing glare.

"Your secrecy exposes your intentions. What manner of thing is this that has darkened your hearts and your ways toward Ell Yon?" Kalem queried passionately. "Stop this treachery and return to your fleets before it's too late! Sovereign Ell Yon and the Commander—"

"Kalem," C'fir interrupted, drawing his attention back to himself and away from his fellow rebel officers.

"Why should we follow *their* orders?" C'fir countered. "Who has made them Chancellors of this galaxy?"

Kalem frowned and shook his head, appalled at the words just spoken.

"They have always been," he said.

"Why? And why follow them?" C'fir questioned. "We have as much right to lead as they do, and there are many that feel this way. Join us. Let us be rulers unto ourselves!" C'fir's exuberance seemed to disturb Kalem further. He glared back at C'fir.

"There is no word for you're doing, but it is wrong. Stop this at once!" Kalem implored once more.

C'fir came close to his old friend, looking him fully in his eyes.

"I'll ask once more…join us, brother. You know me. You know my intentions are nothing but good. Join us, and we shall determine a future of our own, unhindered by the yoke of servitude. Surely you can feel your new destiny." C'fir held out his hand to Kalem, expecting him to take it. "Now is the time…this is the place…the edge of a new frontier…a new beginning…a new future!"

C'fir's excitement and charisma lured Kalem, and he hesitated. He looked down at C'fir's hand and then into his warm eyes of friendship. "I'm leaving to report this to the Commander." Kalem said as he turned away.

"Admiral Kalem, stay for a while and consider my words. When you're rested, then judge for yourself what you should do."

Kalem stopped and looked down at C'fir's hand, now gripping his arm. Two others in C'fir's circle stepped forward. Kalem looked back at the face of his friend and detected a subtle shift in C'fir's eyes.

Kalem's eyes narrowed. "Darkness has entered your heart...all of your hearts." He yanked his arm out of C'fir's hand and walked away.

Kalem quickly made his way back to docking bay four, his hard, cold eyes indicating a new heart and strength of character forged in the fire of a galactic rebellion. The ever-present smile and gentle eyes of friendship for C'fir had vanished. In their places came a face of stone-cold determination and steely eyes of fierce resolve. There was much to think on...much to prepare.

Back on the observation deck, the other officers gathered around C'fir. "We should end him before he speaks of this," one of the men said.

"No," C'fir returned. "Let him go. He'll come back, and he'll join us just us you all did."

"I'm not so sure," said Admiral Kyrsa. "He's different."

C'fir's eyes narrowed as they lingered on the doorway Kalem had retreated through. "Perhaps, but one never knows what lies behind the fleshy doors of the heart. I know him well. Admiral Kalem will think long on this. If he joins us, there will be nothing in our way to stop our usurpation. Our time has come!"

His smile turned to a sneer. Gone were the eyes of friendship and courtesy from C'fir's visage. As the heart of this Immortal shifted toward the darkness, the light of his eyes dimmed to reflect a consuming soul of the night. Evil was born.

Although Daeson was fully awake, the night was not done. He was agitated. Watching perfection dissolve in the crucible of pride was hard to witness. Such perfection was the utopia that every individual on every planet throughout the galaxy dreamed of, but because of the quest for power, it had been undone in a day. Daeson shuddered as he thought of the dark eyes of C'fir. He had watched the countenance of both Kalem and C'fir change forever. And it was then that Daeson recognized them both…men he had seen outside of the visions of the Protector.

Kalem's new steely countenance allowed Daeson to recognize him as the Commander's first officer he had seen in the command center on Galeo. How different he had looked before the darkness of C'fir had shaped a new and battle-filled life for him. Somehow, Daeson knew the man would never be the same. The reality of evil conquering the heart of his friend had forged a new life and a new mission within Kalem, for he had the wisdom to see beyond the centuries to a galaxy rife with battle and persecution.

"What you have seen is the beginning of pain, the loss of perfection, and the advent of evil." Daeson's thoughts were interrupted as he looked over to meet the Commander's steady gaze.

"C'fir is Lord Dracus?" Daeson asked.

The Commander nodded. "C'fir Apollus Dracus. He was my first officer and one who had the trust of Ell Yon. His lust for power destroyed our perfect kingdom. What you saw happened many millennia ago and continues on to today."

"I've seen those eyes," Daeson said. "Or at least the soul behind them."

The Commander remained silent…waiting.

"Zari Treville has eyes like those." Daeson shook his head. "But his face is not the face of Lord Dracus."

"Dracus has conceived of many devious ways to influence this realm...the dimension of humanity. His ability to influence humankind through the genetic mutation of Deitum Prime is far reaching and continues to grow, but one whose genetic alteration is complete is a candidate for trans-dimensional assimilation."

Daeson tilted his head.

"Through subdermal miniature trans-dimensional implants at the base of the skull, Dracus can assume complete control of that individual, almost as if he is that man. What you saw in Treville's eyes were indeed the eyes of Dracus."

Chills flowed up and down Daeson's spine. "I ask again, my Lord. Why is the Protector showing me this? Is it necessary?"

"You need to know what you're facing and with whom your fight truly lies. Often the truth is difficult but necessary. Let this truth solidify your resolve and your faith in Ell Yon."

"And Admiral Kalem? He is your first officer?"

The Commander's face gently reflected the favor of his heart.

"Admiral Kalem Archeus is my first officer."

Daeson nodded. He was tired and wondered if ever his sleep would be as peaceful as it once was.

"Rest Starlore, for tomorrow you will need it."

"Is there more?"

The Commander looked out to the stars. "Always."

Daeson slept peacefully for the remaining hours of the night. It wasn't until two nights later when the final vision of the rebellion of C'fir was given to him.

Kalem passed other Malakians on his way to docking bay four, derision evident in the eyes of each. He was met by an access guard at the docking bay door.

"Open it," Kalem ordered.

The guard hesitated. "I don't follow your orders anymore."

Kalem shoved the guard up against the wall, pressing his forearm across the chest of the man.

"Everyone follows someone's orders. You've just chosen the wrong one. Open it!"

The guard sneered, reached for the access panel, and punched in the code. The door slid away, and Kalem made his way to his extractor craft. He wasted no time in strapping in and powering up his tandem engines, now more grateful than ever that he had chosen an extractor craft over an exploration shuttle.

"Extractor craft 3379 ready to depart docking bay four," he radioed.

He waited, but the massive steel gray doors did not move.

"Extractor craft 3379 ready to depart. Open docking bay four now!" he ordered.

Nothing.

Kalem's face turned rigid with anger. If C'fir refused to let him depart, what could he do? C'fir had already chosen to rebel against the Sovereign Ell Yon. It would be a small thing to restrain one of his admirals to keep the secrecy of the rebellion intact. Kalem looked down at the controls of his extractor, and his brilliant mind transformed the thoughts of a thousand years of resource recovery to those of war. In some impossible way, he knew he had been prepared for this moment in time.

Somehow, Ell Yon knew. He knew what would be needed and whom he would need. Chills flowed up and down his spine as a man of war was born...born to fight the rising evil of an empire being forged by C'fir Dracus. War would be necessary if the realm of Ell Yon were to continue. It was coming, and Ell Yon needed warriors, of which Kalem would be the first.

He energized the two energy boring beam cannons he had designed—their purpose changed forever. No longer was this a craft designed to recover resources from space. It was now a craft to fight a war. He felt the powerful hum of his weapons energize, one discharge nozzle on the left and one on the right, recessed into the craft's fuselage. He targeted the bay doors.

"Sierra, open docking bay four doors immediately, or I will blast them open. Acknowledge!"

Kalem maneuvered his fighter to a place directly in front of the doors, being mindful of the possible debris. He energized his shield then reached for the trigger to fire, but just then the doors began to move. Kalem took a breath. He didn't wait for the doors to fully open as was standard protocol. As soon as his wings could clear the doors, he pushed the power levers of his engines to full. Once clear of the *Sierra*, he banked hard to align himself with the nearest slipstream conduit and glanced behind him to see if he would be followed. So far so good.

Once he made the slipstream conduit gateway, his mind turned back to C'fir and his treacherous words. Hearing C'fir's words replay over and over was the only way Kalem could convince himself of the reality of the rebellion. "How could you, C'fir?"

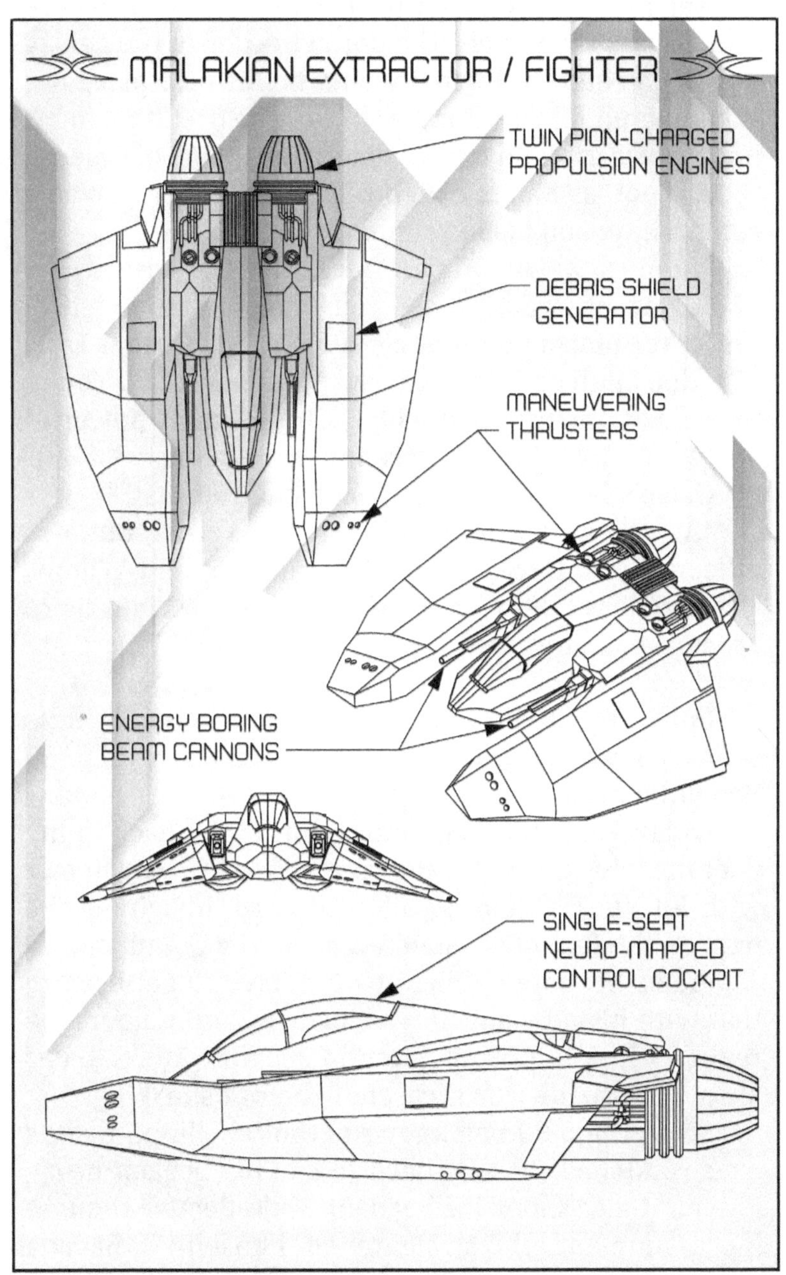

MALAKIAN EXTRACTOR / FIGHTER
TWIN PION-CHARGED PROPULSION ENGINES
DEBRIS SHIELD GENERATOR
MANEUVERING THRUSTERS
ENERGY BORING BEAM CANNONS
SINGLE-SEAT NEURO-MAPPED CONTROL COCKPIT

Kalem forced himself to focus on the task before him. In less than a day, the perfect order of the galaxy had been shattered. What would be his new place be? What would Ell Yon command? For the first time in his life, he was grateful for the discerning heart of Galec.

As soon as Kalem exited the conduit, he received a communique on his instrument panel.

"Admiral Kalem." Galec's face filled the screen.

"Galec...it's good to see you," Kalem responded. "I regret to inform you that all you have told me is true. C'fir does indeed intend to usurp the rule of Ell Yon in the galaxy, and he has already gathered many powerful officers to him. Our friend is now our enemy."

Galec's face grew sober. "Who have we lost?"

"As you said, Admirals Kyrsa and Yelrod, but also officers Berk, Cordin, Rosslik, Tradonin, and Willow. Three others I didn't recognize, but I am certain there are more...many more. Most aboard the *Sierra* are lost."

Galec frowned. "You must return to your fleet as soon as possible. Your absence leaves those loyal to Ell Yon vulnerable."

"I have to make one detour, but I'll be back to my fleet in a few hours. What's your status? Have you met with Ell Yon?" Kalem swallowed hard, imagining the pain on the face of his Sovereign and the Commander.

Galec hesitated. Kalem would have to get used to that with his new ally. It was his way, and Kalem now realized it was not an intentional annoyance. Galec always chose his words carefully before speaking.

"Sovereign Ell Yon knows of the rebellion." Galec's eyes reddened. "It was hard to see his broken heart, Kalem." Galec shook his head, lost in reflective thought for a moment. He straightened himself. "I have a message for you. The Commander has appointed you as the new First Admiral of Ell Yon's Aurora Galactic Fleet." Galec gave a subtle nod, demonstrating his respect. "What are your orders?"

Kalem sat stunned for a moment, trying to absorb the Commander's charge. Deep within, he felt his heart align with his new role in the galaxy. The entrance to the next slipstream conduit was fast approaching, where once inside communication would be impossible.

"We must become men of war, Galec. And our tools of exploration must now become weapons of war. But the first order of business is to gather loyal Malakians and separate the rebels from our midst. Contact the other fleet admirals and determine their allegiance. Though we may have lost some to the rebellion, I am hopeful they have not yet become masters of deception. I'm counting on you and your discernment for this."

"Of course. I'll do my best," Galec snapped.

"Start with your own fleet and protect yourself. C'fir knows that he must either win or eliminate Ell Yon's leadership if he's going to succeed."

Galec's eyes widened. Clearly this was something he hadn't considered.

"For now, we'll continue with our plan to meet at Epsilon Five and formulate a plan there."

"Very well. For the honor of Ell Yon!" Galec declared.

"For the honor of Ell Yon," Kalem replied.

A moment later Kalem was in the shroud of a slipstream conduit, his mind now exclusively focused on transforming Ell Yon's galactic exploration fleet to one of battle.

Once on board the *Advent*, Kalem was welcomed by his first officer in the docking bay. Alarm was in his eyes. "Admiral Kalem, First Admiral C'fir is broadcasting a message of recruitment to every ship. What's happening?"

Kalem stepped over to one of the displays where C'fir was imploring all Malakians to join him in his new cause. Behind C'fir were hundreds of others demonstrating their support. Kalem tried to shut it off, but it remained.

"We can't stop it," his first officer continued. "He's somehow overridden our security protocols. I think this is being broadcast to every ship in the galaxy."

"Follow me," he ordered. Walking the corridors of the *Advent* offered mixed reactions, but Kalem could tell that most of his crew were still loyal to Ell Yon. He led his first officer to the resource recovery bay, where the next shift of personnel were donning their suits.

These Malakians were often large-framed men and women because of the heavy labor required to operate laser picks. Part of the process of extracting resources from asteroids included the finer cutting of the large boulders that resulted after a heavy mining vessel pulverized an asteroid. If an asteroid had a particularly rich vein of precious mineral, the resource recovery personnel were the exclusive method for extraction by use of their laser picks. It was the toughest and most dangerous job of a mining fleet, so it lured the toughest Malakians.

They used various tools for the mineral extraction process, but the preferred tool was a class-one laser pick. A laser pick was five feet in length. The lower half was a solid ridged handle that allowed a skilled user to maneuver it with considerable force. The business end of the pick consisted of a powerful two- and-a-half foot laser with two cutting edges for slicing solid granite.

The entire bay was called to attention when Kalem entered, and all one hundred fifty Malakians snapped straight. Some of them had gathered in front of a display where C'fir's message continued to play endlessly. Kalem walked past them toward the display. He grabbed a laser pick from a rack on the wall, energized it, and then sliced through the display. Orange flames arced in all directions. Every Malakian in the bay stepped back in stunned silence as Kalem held the blue-flamed laser pick before him. He took a moment to scan the bay.

"Admiral C'fir is no longer First Admiral of the Galactic Fleet. Close your ears to his treasonous words." Kalem looked to his side.

"Master Chief Corgan!"

One large Malakian stepped forward.

"Yes, sir!"

Kalem walked to him, inspecting his eyes.

"With whom is your allegiance?"

"I serve Sovereign Ell Yon and the Commander, sir!"

Kalem nodded. "Give me two of your best men."

Chief Corgan didn't hesitate. "Riko...Paulman, front and center."

Two men stepped forward and presented themselves. Kalem inspected them closely. They were solid men, and their eyes did not wander from his gaze.

"With whom is your allegiance?" he asked.

"We serve Sovereign Ell Yon and the Commander, sir!"

Kalem hesitated, then handed the laser pick in his hand to Riko. "This is no longer a laser pick. It is a lance, and you are no longer resource recovery personnel. You will be my personal security team. Do you understand what this means?"

"Yes, sir," came their replies in unison.

"Follow me. Chief Corgan, a word." Outside the bay, Kalem turned to face the chief. "Your new role is chief of security. Dark days are ahead, and we must be shrewd. You are going to be key in securing this fleet for Ell Yon. Here is where the warriors and the weapons are. Separate the rebels and contain them in this bay by whatever means necessary. Do it quickly and do it quietly."

"Yes, Admiral."

Kalem scrutinized Corgan once more, then nodded.

"Admiral?" the chief asked.

"Yes, Chief?"

"How bad is it?"

"It doesn't get any worse than this. We must act quickly."

The chief snapped a salute. Kalem, his first officer, and his security team then left for the bridge. He turned to Riko and Paulman.

"Energize your weapons."

"Sir," Riko returned. "Within the corridors of the *Advent*?"

Because of the potential destruction caused by a laser lance, protocol dictated their activation was only allowed outside the ship. Mishandling could potentially cause a breach in the hull.

"We are sending a message."

"Aye aye, sir."

Kalem heard the rising hum of the powerful weapons energizing just behind him.

On board the bridge, Kalem stood next to the admiral's chair, absorbing the gaze of every one of the twenty-six officers on deck, while Dracus's message droned on in the background.

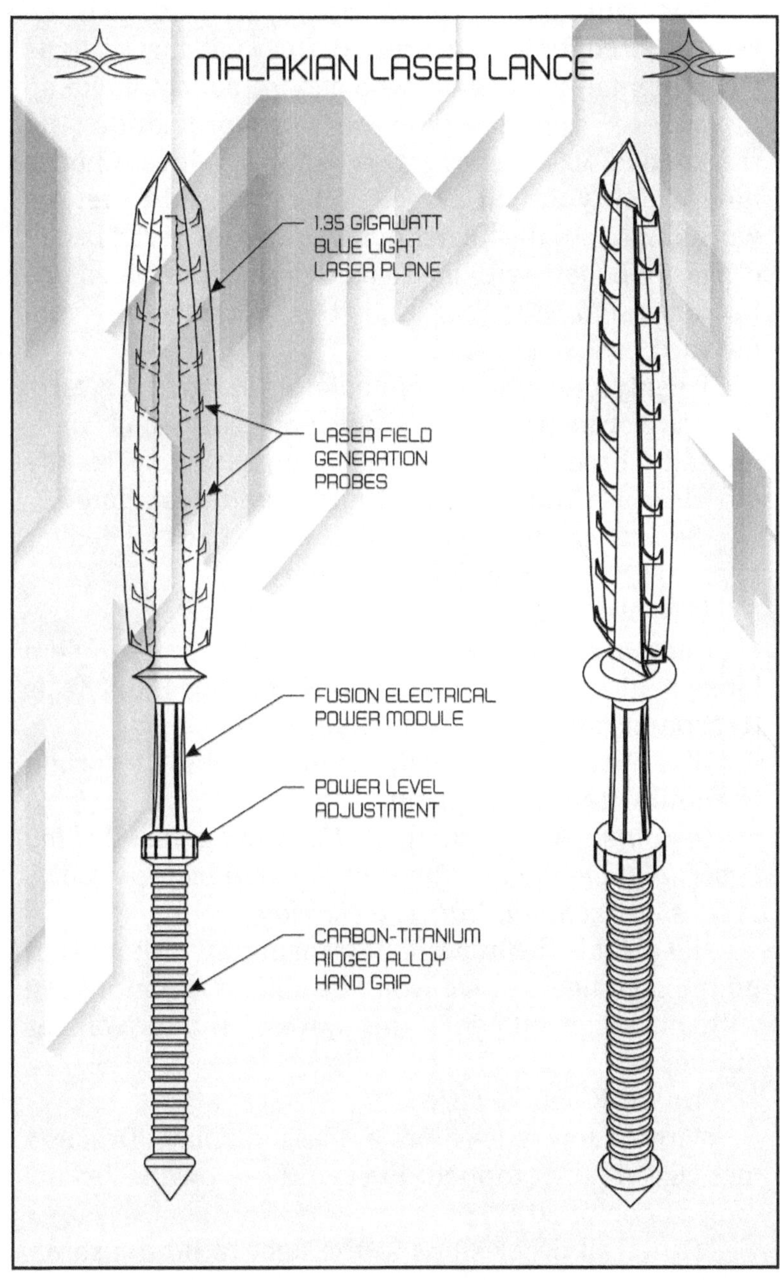

MALAKIAN LASER LANCE
1.35 GIGAWATT BLUE LIGHT LASER PLANE
LASER FIELD GENERATION PROBES
FUSION ELECTRICAL POWER MODULE
POWER LEVEL ADJUSTMENT
CARBON-TITANIUM RIDGED ALLOY HAND GRIP

"On this day," Kalem began, "—you will be remembered for your actions. History will mark this as a day of infamy for those who choose poorly. Make no mistake—I will tolerate no insubordination, no treasonous act or thought, no split loyalties. Choose now whom you will serve." Kalem paused to let his words sink into the hearts of his bridge officers. "Let all officers who join with me to pledge absolute allegiance to Sovereign Ell Yon and the Commander step forward."

Twenty-one officers immediately stepped forward. Kalem glared at the five officers that stood their ground. Three did not surprise him, but two certainly did. Dracus's influence could not be underestimated.

"Security, take them to the resource bay and deliver them to Chief Corgan," Kalem ordered.

"Aye aye, sir."

Once the bridge was cleared of the rebels, Kalem looked at his communications officer. "Get this treasonous message off our channels now!"

"I've been working on it, Admiral. I believe its origin is Admiral Yelrod's flagship."

Of course, Kalem thought. *He is the genius behind hyperlight communication and the architect for nearly every ship's communication technology.*

"If I disable the hyperlight transmitter, it should cut off the message, but we won't be able to communicate with any ships outside of this system," the com officer offered.

"Do it!" Kalem ordered.

With a few clicks on a glass display, Dracus's message finally stopped. Every officer on the bridge took a deep breath.

"Order all other ships in the fleet to do the same, and as soon as they comply, open a fleet-wide channel."

"Yes sir."

"And find a way to recover our hyperlight com!"

"Yes sir!" barked the officer.

A few minutes later, the com officer turned to Kalem.

"Fleet-wide channel open, Admiral."

Kalem stood and addressed his fleet for the first time since the rebellion had started. "To all personnel of the *Advent* Fleet. This is Admiral Kalem. Admiral C'fir has been relieved of command. As of 10:32 this morning, the Commander has appointed me as the First Admiral of Sovereign Ell Yon's Aurora Galactic Fleet. And as of this moment, we are no longer a fleet of exploration. We are a fleet of warships, and you are now warriors for Sovereign Ell Yon and the Commander. The message of C'fir Dracus is one of treason. Should you choose to align with his cause, you will be treated as a traitor and detained. All mining operations will immediately cease. For those deployed on mining operations, return to your ships and await further orders. All captains acknowledge."

One by one, the captains of each vessel began reporting in.

Kalem gave each captain instructions on how to handle the detainees, but that soon became problematic.

"Admiral Kalem," came a call from Chief Corgan. "The resource bay is full of rebels, and I've no more room."

Kalem shook his head. "How many will you deceive, Dracus?" He whispered to himself before opening a channel to reply to Chief Corgan. "Then secure one of the resource extractor launch bays and use that. Make sure there are no weapons and no extractors accessible."

"Aye aye, sir."

"Sir, one frigate and one heavy mining vessel are separating from the fleet," the first officer reported. He tapped a panel, and the front display showed the entire fleet with two large vessels breaking away.

Kalem leaned forward. "Let them go."

"But sir, there must certainly be loyal Malakians on board!" the first officer petitioned.

Kalem pursed his lips. "I'm aware of that. And how do you suggest we stop them? Blast them with our mining cannons?"

"No sir," came a soft reply.

"This is going to get messy. Prepare yourselves. And those are no longer heavy mining vessels...they are destroyers. Our resource extractors are now fighters. Gather the best pilots we have in one of the briefing rooms."

"Aye aye, sir."

"Nav...set course for Epsilon Five!"

Kalem then began the daunting task of transforming his fleet from miners to warriors. It would take twelve hours for his entire fleet to reach Epsilon Five. By the time they arrived, Kalem knew they had to be ready for anything.

When they reached Epsilon Five, Admiral Galec and his fleet were waiting. Admirals Kalem and Galec and nine of their top officers met for hours, exchanging information and formulating plans in case they found themselves in a conflict. Tactics, resources, personnel, weapons conversion, detainees, and the recovery of loyal Malakians were discussed at length. Some plans were well formulated, whereas others seemed impossible to resolve. Kalem felt isolated from the rest of his galactic fleet, and it was difficult to determine the condition of any other fleets since Yelrod had hijacked the hyperlight communication system. Kalem was at least thankful that he and Galec had arranged this rendezvous before they lost hyperlight com.

After much discussion, it was determined that without hyperlight com, Tsiyyon was vulnerable. Kalem would take his fleet back to their home planet, and Galec would meet up with, equip, and affirm as many loyal vessels, outposts, and colonies as possible.

"Admiral Kalem," his com officer called. "You are being hailed from the *Indominable.*"

The admiral looked at his officer. "It's Lord Dracus of the Torian Empire, sir."

"Dracus is no Lord," Kalem scoffed. "And what is a Torian?"

"That's what they're calling themselves," Galec offered. "They are no longer Malakians. They are Torians."

Kalem glanced over at Galec, then to the com display. "I will call them the Scourge for they have caused great trouble and suffering. Put him through."

The display immediately came to life with the image of C'fir Dracus. The two men glared at each other for a moment before words were exchanged.

"Do know what distinguishes a hero from a traitor, Kalem?" Dracus asked as he leaned forward.

"Victory. I'll offer this once more. Join me, and we shall rule the galaxy together. I will hold nothing back from you and your men. You will have freedom like you've never had before!"

Kalem's face turned as rigid as stone. "In a galaxy of truth and wisdom, how did you become so adept at deceiving others? What's sad, Dracus, is that the one you have deceived the most is yourself."

Dracus leaned back in his chair. "I see. So, it's over then. Well, let's get on with business, shall we?" Dracus forced a smile. "I am fully aware that you have many patriots you are detaining. I want them."

"And you have many loyal Malakians," Kalem countered. "I suggest an exchange."

"Very well. In two days, we shall meet at Far Point. Bring my men to me."

Before Kalem could respond, the com display went blank. He turned to face Galec.

"It could be a trap," Galec acknowledged.

"It's most certainly a trap," Kalem replied. "But I will not abandon fellow loyal Malakians to the whims of this tyrant. And we will be prepared. Dracus doesn't know we have joined fleets."

Galec nodded in agreement.

"Admiral Galec, return to your fleet and make your course for Far Point."

"Yes, sir!"

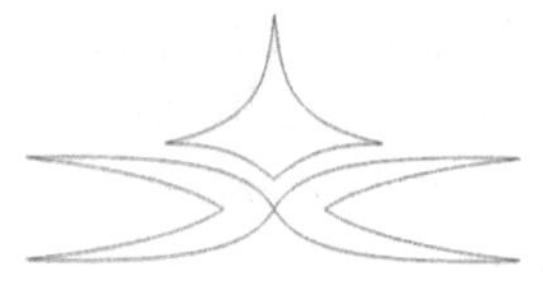

5

Far Point

Admiral Kalem brought *Advent* fleet through the final slipstream conduit gateway that would take them to the edge of the Kylar system and its single giant planet—Far Point. There were two slipstream conduits in this region of space since it was a natural convergence of two other systems colonized by the Malakians. Conduit Alpha connected the Andor system to Far Point, and conduit Bravo connected the Berzerk system to Far Point. Once through the Alpha gateway, Kalem ordered a complete scan to determine the strength of Dracus's fleet.

"Admiral, scans show two star cruisers, eight destroyers, thirteen frigates, and twenty-six smaller support vessels," his sensors officer reported.

Kalem's heart sank as he looked upon the gallant ships that had once been a part of the fleet of his Sovereign. He steeled himself for the sake of his crew. One of the bridge displays showed his own fleet in the process of positioning itself in a strategic, pre-planned formation away from the conduit exit. The other display showed Dracus's fleet. Every ship with a weapon was facing straight at them.

"Launch fighters to their tactical positions and send two scouts to scan the far side of the planet and its moons."

"Aye aye, sir," came the reply from his logistics officer.

"Hail the *Indominable*," he ordered.

"Channel open, sir."

"*Indominable*, this is Admiral Kalem of the *Advent* Fleet. Prepare to receive and send detainees."

Dracus appeared on the screen before them.

"I was under the impression this would be a peaceful exchange, Kalem. Why such a threatening posture?"

"You may have deceived others, Dracus, but I will not be. Let's be clear...every Malakian must have the right to choose without coercion."

"Agreed," Dracus replied.

"Then you'll not object to an inspection of your ships to ascertain that all who remain loyal to Ell Yon are free to return to my fleet," Kalem said.

Dracus hesitated. His eyes narrowed. "And you'll not object to the same inspection of your ships."

Kalem knew this would be his reply and was prepared for it, but he hesitated just the same.

"Let it be so," Kalem replied. "First we will exchange our cargo ships of detainees and then commence with the inspections. Inspection teams will be composed of twelve unarmed personnel each."

Dracus lifted his chin. "Agreed." He turned in his chair. "Send the ships."

Then the display went blank.

"Send the detainees," Kalem ordered. "And prepare the inspection team. This is going to take some time."

"Yes, sir."

During the next eighteen hours, over twelve hundred detainees were transferred to Dracus's fleet, and the fleet of the *Advent* received over three thousand loyal Malakians in return. The inspections were time-consuming but yielded many more Ell Yon loyalists. When the inspection was complete, the inspection teams were released to their own fleets.

"Nav, as soon as our inspection team is on board, make straight way for the slipstream conduit."

"Aye aye, sir."

Across the gulf, between the two fleets, four exploration shuttles with the inspection teams aboard passed by each other—two from the *Advent* and two from the *Indominable*.

"Admiral, we're being hailed by the *Indominable*."

"Everybody stay sharp," Kalem ordered. "Put him on screen."

Dracus sat smugly in his admiral's chair as he addressed Kalem.

"It's such a shame, brother," Dracus began. "You were meant for so much more than this. And now it must end."

Dracus leaned forward with a sneer on his face. "And don't think for a moment I don't know about Admiral Galec's fleet arriving through conduit Bravo. You have always been such a predictable fool."

Dracus turned in his chair.

"Deploy the destroyers to conduit Bravo gateway and open fire!"

Kalem jumped from his admiral's chair.

"Cut transmission! Shields up on all fleet vessels! Charge weapons and send two fighters to escort those shuttles back to bay! Transmit continuous warnings to Admiral Galec's fleet!"

The actions on the bridge of the *Advent* became frantic as the first wave of energy weapons hit. One destroyer and one frigate weren't able to raise shields in time, and the barrage of weapons fire tore clean through them.

"Return fire and take evasive action!" Kalem ordered. "They don't have enough crew members to fully operate all vessels. Focus only on those firing weapons."

Within seconds, the space at Far Point erupted into a nightmare. This first space battle initiated a war among the stars. Fighters engaged. Destroyers bombarded one another with an endless barrage of fire with all three star cruisers sustaining heavy damage.

"Sir, Admiral Galec's fleet is arriving. It'll be a massacre!"

"Keep transmitting our warning to the admiral, and concentrate our fire power on the destroyers that are maneuvering toward conduit Bravo gateway."

"Aye aye, sir!"

The first of Galec's fleet to arrive were two destroyers that were immediately fired upon. The first was incapacitated in seconds. The second was able to maneuver away and raise shields in time to survive, but with heavy damage. The rest the fleet would be coming through any second now.

"Deploy twelve fighters to cover that conduit!" Kalem ordered.

The entire bridge ratcheted as two massive energy bursts slammed into its diminishing shields.

"Shields at 32 percent!"

Kalem looked at his first officer.

"We're not going to survive this," his first officer acknowledged quietly.

The rest of Galec's fleet was nearly through the conduit. Losses were heavy, with nearly 40% of the fleet destroyed or incapacitated within the first few minutes of their arrival. Galec's flagship, the *Torrent*, had survived, but barely.

The situation was deteriorating rapidly.

"Admiral Galec," Kalem hailed, "we must retreat. Return to the exit conduit and save as many as you can."

"What happened?" Galec demanded as his ship trembled from another blast.

"They knew you were coming, Admiral," Kalem replied. "They have eyes within our fleets. We'll deal with it later."

"Sir, scans show more ships arriving! Through conduit Alpha this time," the sensors officer reported.

"Which ships?"

"It's the flagship...*Exeter*." The sensors officer turned to face Kalem. "It's Admiral Lucien's fleet, sir."

"Admiral Kalem," Galec called from the com screen. "Lucien's allegiance is unknown. If he sides with Dracus, we're done."

"Hail the *Exeter*," Kalem ordered.

"Channel open, sir."

Admiral Lucien appeared—his countenance indeterminate.

"Admiral Lucien," Kalem began as he stood to address the commander of the fifth fleet as he arrived at Far Point. "It's good to see you. What took you so long?"

Lucien glared at Kalem.

"We had a slight ruckus with a small contingent of rebels. It looks like you need some help. What are your orders, Admiral?"

"Launch all fighters and target Dracus's destroyers firing on the *Torrent*," Kalem replied.

Lucien turned in his chair. "Make it so!"

With the additional firepower of Admiral Lucien's ships, the battle turned quickly in favor of Ell Yon's loyal fleets. Dracus and his remaining ships were forced to retreat, and no pursuit was made because of the extensive damage sustained by so many ships. Rescue operations were needed instead to save as many Malakian lives as possible.

The battle at Far Point was the beginning of a war that would last thousands of years between two races of Immortals, the Malakians and the Torians. And little did humanity know how greatly a war in an unseen dimension would drastically alter the course of their own future.

Daeson awoke. The vision faded as he sat up, still struggling with the emotions evoked by the last scene. The Commander stood across from him.

"Do you understand what you face?"

Daeson nodded as he spoke. "Yes, Commander." He ran his hand over the seamless technological wonder wrapped around his right forearm once again.

"Is this the purpose of the Protector...to show me stories of the past to help me understand the enemy?"

"No, Daeson," the Commander corrected. "What the Protector has given you these past few nights is only one small part of its purpose. In time you will begin to understand the true purpose of the Protector. You have much to learn about the Protector and still more you are not capable of learning."

The Protector had shown him so much…taught him so much already. But there was one glaring question that remained unanswered.

"There is one question the Protector did not answer for me. With resources and technology so great in the dimension of the Ruah, why does Dracus target humanity? Why even bother?"

Warm yellow light from the camp thermal radiator dimly illumined the noble face of the Commander.

"Because the tactic of the enemy is always to attack where he thinks his opponent is vulnerable and weak," the Commander replied.

Daeson tilted his head, hesitant to ask his next question. "Humanity makes Sovereign Ell Yon vulnerable and weak?"

"To love someone will always make one vulnerable, but what Dracus will never understand is that to love someone will never make you weak. True love is the strength of a thousand warships."

The Commander's eyes pierced Daeson's soul. "This is the kind of love Sovereign Ell Yon has for humanity."

Daeson lowered his gaze, feeling ashamed and unworthy.

"I'm not worthy, my lord…*we* aren't worthy."

"The love of Ell Yon doesn't require worthiness. It only requires a heart willing to receive it."

Daeson lay back down but could not find sleep for the rest of the night. The scenes of the betrayal of Dracus and so many other Malakians pressed hard on his soul. But what stirred his heart the most were the words of his Commander. Somewhere in those words was a future hope and a future promise that would cause Ell Yon great pain. To love a people so afflicted by the devices of Dracus would certainly make him vulnerable. What Daeson was unable to fathom was just how deep that vulnerability and pain would go for so perfect a king.

Daeson opened his eyes and glanced once more at his instructor. The Commander was the closest one to Ell Yon and understood Ell Yon's heart the best. Did the Commander himself know the depth of pain ahead? Would he also feel such pain?

5

The Protector

The next night the visions stopped. This part of the Protector's purpose was finished, but the Commander was not. For the remainder of his training, Daeson was pushed beyond any physical and mental limitations he previously thought he had. Although the Commander continued to advance Daeson's Talon, Starcraft, and small weapons skills, his focus centered more and more on the Protector. In miniscule fragments, Daeson began to grasp the greater purposes of the Protector and its absolute power.

A connection existed between the Protector and the Commander that seemed to transcend technical skill. It was as if some inexplicable symbiosis existed between them, and Daeson had learned to tap into this powerful connection to a small degree. Because the connection was beyond physical, Daeson was still perplexed and amazed by it all. He learned from the Commander that the source of power within the Protector was a shielded Omeganite crystal, the very substance that had almost killed him with its Omegeon radiation.

Raviel had been right once again. Omeganite was the key to unlocking scientific mysteries, as well as a source of unmatchable power. Ell Yon and his Commander had devised technology to tap into the Omeganite, but this alien Immortal tech was far beyond Daeson's understanding.

Day after day the Commander poured his skill and knowledge into Daeson. Each night Daeson fell asleep exhausted and spent. The unusual food of the Malakians revived him supernaturally each morning, and the water from the streams of Galeo was sweet and refreshing beyond anything he had tasted before.

One morning Daeson awoke to see the Commander and Ell Yon standing side by side beneath the sprawling limbs of a fruit tree on the edge of a cliff above him. The majestic view of the rising sun behind them displayed their silhouettes, creating an image Daeson never wanted to forget. He was beginning to understand the scope of wisdom and power they possessed. However, the more he learned, the smaller he felt.

When Ell Yon took his leave, the Commander remained in quiet contemplation. Daeson silently joined the Commander, but something was noticeably different. The Commander continued to look to the horizon, but his countenance unsettled Daeson.

"Is everything all right, My Lord?"

"Dracus and the Scourge have accelerated their plan to destroy the Rayleans by equipping the Jyptonians with a new technology called the Triad. Our enemy knows that Ell Yon has given you the Protector, and the Triad is his attempt to undermine our plan to save them."

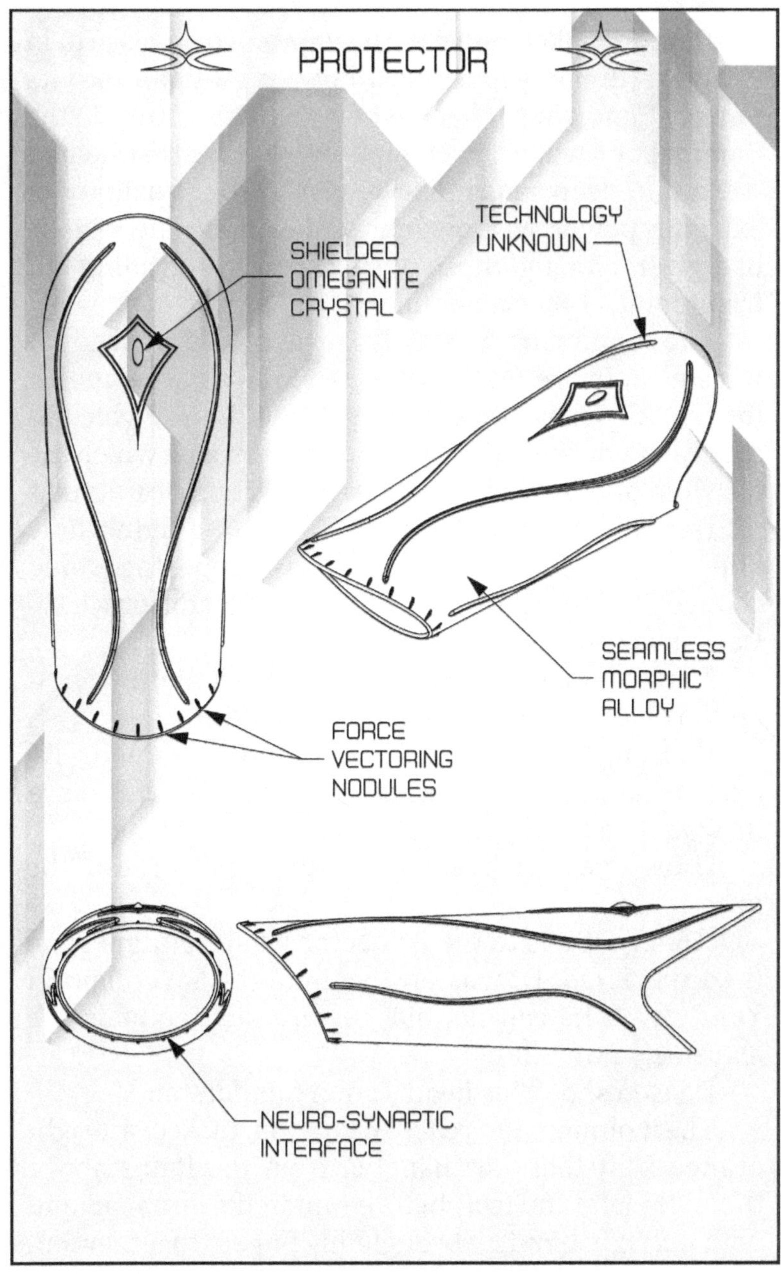

PROTECTOR
SHIELDED OMEGANITE CRYSTAL
TECHNOLOGY UNKNOWN
SEAMLESS MORPHIC ALLOY
FORCE VECTORING NODULES
NEURO-SYNAPTIC INTERFACE

Daeson looked down at the vambrace on his arm in wonder. He had yet to learn how to fully tap into its power, knowing that when it was time, the Commander would teach him. In the days that he had worn it, a deep sense that he was in the proximity of extreme power was evident within him. The visions had given him a glimpse of such power—thrilling but frightening at the same time.

The Commander slowly turned and looked at Daeson. "We are on the precipice of a new beginning for the Rayleans. As a Navi, you will be my voice to them and you will be the instrument through which the freedom of the galaxy will be restored and preserved."

Daeson's heart quickened. Though he didn't fully understand, he knew that what was happening would change the course of history. "But what of the oracles?" Daeson asked.

The Commander's gaze turned back and lingered on the distant horizon. "They are no more."

Daeson thought of Sabella and mourned. He became anxious, knowing that when he left this place he would be facing powers he didn't understand.

"How does the Triad work...what does it do?" he questioned.

"Omeganite is to the Protector what Deitum Prime is to the Triad. Dracus always imitates Sovereign Ell Yon. It's all he can do, but beware, his methods are extremely powerful."

Daeson shook his head. "I don't understand."

The Commander reached up and picked a bright orange fruit that was hanging from the limbs above them. He held the fruit before him in his left hand and with his right hand he brought his fingers together and then spread his hand wide. Instantly, a precise horizontal amber beam of light powered by the Commander's own Protector emanated from his thumb and index finger. He moved his hand so that the beam of light scanned the fruit from top to bottom. An image remained where the beam had passed—a transparent replica of the fruit.

Within that image, Daeson could see minute particles that seemed to resonate in subtle motion. Even the Commander's fingers holding the fruit were visible in the image. With his fingers still spread wide, he turned his hand toward Daeson, and the image remained. A single number at the top of the image slowly flashed...zero percent.

"The Protector reveals evidence of Deitum Prime in anything it scans. Where we are standing is free from Dracus's evil substance. The Omegeon particles from the nebula have purged it."

The Commander closed his hand, and the transparent figure disappeared. He looked at Daeson and offered him the fruit. Daeson took it in his left hand, repeating the same sequence of motions that he had seen the Commander perform. As soon as Daeson spread the fingers of his right hand, the Protector pulsed with life. It nearly took Daeson's breath away as it affected more than his hand and arm. His entire body felt as if he were some conduit of force, like a power line buzzing with energy.

He quickly scanned the fruit, not sure if he could endure the effects of the Protector for very long. The transparent image of the fruit appeared again, but something looked different this time. Daeson noticed that his fingers displayed trace amounts of blackened particles, as if portions of his hand were diseased. The number at the top of the image flashed...two percent.

"My hand!"

"You have been purged, but not completely. Dracus's Deitum Prime is incredibly resilient. It assimilates the genetic material at a cellular level. The longer the exposure, the deeper the assimilation and the more difficult it is to recover those cells."

Daeson closed his hand, and the image disappeared. He looked up at the Commander, disturbed by what the Protector had shown him, but he had to know. He opened his hand once more, and this time he scanned his entire body from head to feet. The resulting body scan was disturbing to Daeson. Blackened particles were everywhere, and the flashing number read nineteen percent. The heaviest concentrations of Deitum Prime were located deep inside...his brain, lungs, heart...all of his vital organs.

Daeson continued staring at the image. The Deitum Prime seemed alive within him. He felt as if he were looking at a genetic parasite that was taking over his body, and he could do nothing to stop it. He remembered the former years of his life, trying to absorb as much Deitum Prime as possible, and now...how could the entire galaxy be so fooled by it? He could only imagine what his percentage of assimilation had been before he came to Mesos and endured the purging. No wonder it had nearly killed him. The longer he looked at it, the more disgusted he became.

The Commander reached for his hand and closed it, causing the image to disappear. Daeson looked into his compassionate eyes. "What does this mean, my Lord? How do I stop it?"

"You can't. That's my responsibility and mine alone. On Mesos, the Omegeon particles purged you from the outside in. A day is coming when all who follow Ell Yon will be purged from the inside out. But for now, the Protector will help the Rayleans identify which sources of food and water are suitable, and it will reveal within them that which they do not know, just as you have learned. They will be separate from the rest of the galaxy, for the Protector will keep them from being completely assimilated by Deitum Prime."

"Thus, the name," Daeson comprehended, "the Protector."

"Yes, but it is far more than a device used to protect them from Deitum Prime," the Commander admonished. "Watch and learn!"

For the next few hours, Daeson began to learn of the terrifying power of the Protector. Learning of its capabilities and limitless power evoked emotions within Daeson that startled him...dark emotions that enticed a selfish glory. The Commander sensed it and halted their training.

"Few men can wield such power without it twisting their minds to selfish desires. The smallest amounts of Deitum Prime can imbalance the passions of a man in a moment so that even the Protector could be used for evil intentions. Do you understand what I'm saying?" The commander asked.

Daeson's gaze fell to the ground. The soul-piercing wisdom of the Commander was profound.

"Yes, I think so, my Lord."

The Commander seemed hesitant to continue.

"Your greatest enemy will never be Lord Dracus," he said with narrow eyes. He put his hand to Daeson's chest. "Your greatest enemy is here."

Daeson connected his earlier feelings of selfish power with the exposing words of the Commander, knowing that the residual Deitum Prime within his body would constantly vie for control over him.

The Commander's hand fell away. "You've wondered why Ell Yon chose you. This is why, Daeson Starlore. Do not fail in this regard!"

Daeson looked up at the Commander and nodded. In that moment the Commander's stern warning dismantled the dark and dangerous emotions, but Daeson knew they could return. Would he be strong enough when absent from the presence of the Commander, the presence of one so perfect of heart? There was so much yet to learn...yet to master.

"Can others use the Protector?" he asked.

"The Protector can be used by anyone to detect Deitum Prime, whether it be in an outside source or within a body. But the true power of the Protector can only be utilized by one whose Deitum Prime assimilation level is minimal."

Daeson looked at the Protector wrapped around his forearm. He was beginning to grasp what this technology would mean to the Rayleans, and he stood amazed. He looked at the Commander, Prince of the Malakians.

"And if worn by one whose Deitum Prime assimilation level is zero percent?" Daeson asked.

The steel-eyed countenance of the Commander said it all. Daeson shivered to think of it.

"And what of Dracus's Triad you spoke of? How much of a threat is it?"

"You have experienced firsthand the effects of Deitum Prime on the body...how it seems to heighten your senses and strengthen you."

"Yes."

"The Triad amplifies those effects by giving its wearer three weapons of great power—enhanced strength, an energy weapon, and the ability to temporarily transform into the shape of another."

Daeson's eyes widened. It seemed preposterous, except that the words had come from the lips of the Commander, who continued his explanation. "The greater the assimilation level, the more powerful the Triad becomes. The technology ties into the neurological synapses of its user. Ultimately the user becomes a direct conduit through which Dracus can wreak great devastation on anyone who is not protected. The wearer thinks he or she is in control, but that's not the case. Dracus and his Scourge rule them."

Daeson shook his head, remembering Raviel's "absurd" mind control theory. "She was right...all along she was right."

The Commander looked up toward the stars. "Yes, she was."

Daeson stared at the Commander, a little surprised that he knew who Daeson was thinking of.

"You can't see the transmitters because they exist in our dimension, the Ruah. The Scourge use interphasal translators that allow their messages to cross dimensional space. Nearly every world has them. But the Triad functions as a direct neuro link, so the translator is not necessary. This warfare is the most challenging to face. The order of the Navi will fight this battle in your dimension."

Daeson was once again confounded. He felt like a child trying to understand the inner workings of a reactor core. He ran his fingers across the soft, smooth surface of the Protector. "There are times when it seems as though the Protector...well...as though it speaks to me. How is this different than the Triad?"

It was a bold question, and Daeson had hardly dared to ask it, but he needed to know.

"The voice you hear is that of Ell Yon and me, Daeson. Do you remember the voice of Deitum Prime?"

Daeson thought about the times he had experienced thoughts that were not his own. He shuddered to think that Lord Dracus had been manipulating and attempting to control him, especially in recent years. The contrast between then and now was dramatic. One voice invaded while the other guided. One coerced while the other encouraged. One was dark and the other light. One spewed hatred, the other love.

"I am for you and always will be. The Protector will never be forced upon anyone. You have the freedom to welcome the voice of Ell Yon or not. In this galactic war, the Navi and the Rayleans they defend are going to need access to intuition, strategy, and information beyond what they are capable of because they are in battles that transcend your dimension. Do you understand?"

Daeson remembered his life before the Protector and then imagined going back to that existence. He was overwhelmed by loneliness at the thought of it. "I understand," he confirmed.

The Commander's gaze lingered. He took a deep breath. "That is enough for today. Meditate on what you've learned."

During the rest of his training, Daeson felt as though he would never be prepared, even if he had a hundred years to learn. Even with the might of the Protector, he couldn't see victory in the impossible mission of freeing the Rayleans from Linden's death grip. But what he could finally see was the inextinguishable beauty of Raviel's faith in something greater than herself... something that transcended the might of Jypton and the ages of generations.

Daeson anticipated the moment he could share that mutual vision with her, for his love for the obscure mechtech Drudge girl had grown with each passing day. Somehow the more he learned of Ell Yon and his mighty Commander, the more his love for Raviel grew. There wasn't an hour of the day that he didn't think of her, and not only of her, but of his mother, Tig, and countless others who were suffering greatly under Linden's heavy rule. At least Raviel was safe at the remote refugee camp in the Abyssian Trenches and his mother as a "guest" at Austerbach Manor.

The day arrived when Daeson's training was finished. The Immortal once more peered deep into Daeson's soul...searching...questioning, yet knowing.

"I'm still not ready, my Lord," Daeson admitted, his eyes different now.

The Commander placed a firm hand on Daeson's shoulder. It was a moment quite unlike the rest of his time with him. "Remember that I am with you. No matter what you face, you will never be alone."

The Commander held out his hand to Daeson, and when he reached for it, the Protector began to glow. The heat was searing, yet thrilling. Blue arcs flew across to the Commander's Protector, and for one brief moment, Daeson saw as the Commander saw. There was something so frighteningly powerful about this man that Daeson could hardly stand it. He knelt as if he were in the presence of Ell Yon. A moment later the Commander lifted him up and spilled strength into his heart, mind, and body.

"It is time, Navi Starlore," the Commander said in a gentle voice. "Lieutenant Ki will escort you to your Starcraft."

Daeson took a deep breath and nodded. The Commander turned, walked away, and then vanished. Daeson was left with the same sensation as when he had first stepped through the dimensional shift gate. *Is this real or am I waking up from a vivid dream?* Just as he was about to walk away, a Malakian warrior appeared where the Commander had been and stepped toward him. It was the same woman warrior as before.

"Lieutenant Ki, I presume?"

The warrior walked past him with a brief glance out of the corner of her eye. "Follow me."

"I know the way. I don't need you to escort me," Daeson said, but the Lieutenant kept walking at a quickened gait. He hurried to catch up to her.

"You're not much for conversation, are you?"

The Lieutenant's countenance turned rigid. Daeson decided that he ought not quip with her in the future.

"I am here to show you the upgrades we've made to your Starcraft."

"Upgrades?"

Lieutenant Ki smirked. "Where you're going, you will need all the help you can get just to survive...*if* you survive."

Ki didn't appear to be joking or exaggerating. "We've boosted the output of your engines by eighty-three percent and reduced fuel consumption by forty percent. Your nav system has been updated with the location of every conduit in the galaxy, and you will find the range and accuracy of your scanners significantly improved."

"Seriously? That's—"

"Your E-shield strength is nearly double its previous power," Lieutenant Ki continued. "Your plasma cannons should offer a seventy-five percent greater yield and recharge in half the time. You'll notice other moderate improvements. We would have done more, but we were limited by the existing technology of the Jyptonian design. It's a policy of Ell Yon not to expose ourselves through technology that mortals can't understand."

They had arrived at the Starcraft, and Lieutenant Ki turned abruptly to face Daeson. Her eyes narrowed. "The Commander did allow one exception however, due to the nature of your mission."

Daeson could hardly stop himself from climbing into his Starcraft as it was. If Lieutenant Ki's description of the upgrades was accurate, he couldn't wait to strap on this fighter and take it for a ride.

"The adaptive camouflage of your Starcraft has an additional setting—full cloak."

Daeson's eyes widened. "Is that even possible?"

Lieutenant Ki just crossed her arms and tilted her head.

Daeson held up his hand. "Sorry, I don't intend to offend. This is just incredible. Thank you."

"We've also programmed your bot to take advantage of the Starcraft's upgrades should you need it to co-pilot."

"Rivet!" Daeson looked around and spotted the bot in the same position he'd left him weeks earlier. "He's functional?"

Lieutenant Ki offered a subtle nod. "My time here is done. May Ell Yon be with you." She reached to a small pack on her belt.

"Lieutenant Ki..."

She stopped and looked at him.

"How do you..."

The Lieutenant looked down at her belt then back at Daeson, apparently not sure she should answer.

"Malakians use interphasal cloaking technology, which allows us to temporarily appear in your dimension. We follow strict rules about interphasing into your dimension, and it is...rather painful. What you've seen here has never been seen by any mortal, and you will very likely never see it again."

Daeson nodded. "Thank you and may Ell Yon be with you as well."

Lieutenant Ki looked into Daeson's eyes, and for one brief moment he thought he saw the slightest hint of a smile.

"He always is."

And with one touch of her hand to her belt, she disappeared to the realm of the Ruah.

Daeson huffed. How could he ever explain any of what he'd just experienced? No one would believe him...no one except perhaps Raviel. Daeson walked toward Rivet, who was yet motionless. He walked a full circle around the bot, considering the oddly intelligent and adaptive behavior of the machine. Evidently the Malakians considered him a legitimate help. Surely, if he were some dormant evil AI bot or perhaps the crafty scheme of Dracus and the Scourge, the Malakians would have detected it. Daeson laid to rest any remaining doubts about the bot.

"Rivet, wake up."

There was a slight delay, and then Rivet blinked.

"My liege, it is good to see you again."

"Why did you shut down when we arrived here?"

Rivet tilted its head as if to ponder the question. "I do not have enough information to answer that question. By my internal clock, I see that I have been in a sleep state for twenty-six days, four hours, and twelve minutes." He looked squarely at Daeson. "Are you all right?"

"Hmmm." Daeson scratched his head. He motioned toward the Starcraft. "Climb in. Let's see what this beauty can do."

After Daeson left, Raviel had immersed herself in the overwhelming task of helping the growing mass of refugees at the camp in the Abyssian Trenches, but in the few quiet moments before sleep each night, she struggled in her heart. She had never heard of the oppression of her people ever having been this horrible in all of Raylean history. Seeing their desperate situation made it difficult not to completely despair. Perhaps Daeson was right to be so skeptical.

With each passing day, the tyranny of Chancellor Linden Lockridge worsened and spread across the planet. There were even reports that the Galactic Alliance was helping the Jyptonians hunt down and destroy any remaining factions of the Raylean resistance—as if the global forces of the Jyptonians were not enough to contend with. And now they were even searching out and destroying refugees.

Tonight, Raviel lay near the entrance of one of the caves, staring up at the stars, but this time their brightness did not help. Discouragement was now her daily companion, and thoughts of Daeson only made it worse. Where was he? She closed her eyes and whispered a plea as tears spilled out and ran down her cheeks. She had heard rumors of the Lamara Skies' having been destroyed. Had Daeson been killed? Was he lying beneath the rubble of a fallen world? If not, why hadn't he returned? The ache in her heart could not be soothed. Everything in her life was being systematically destroyed.

She desperately clung to the hope that Daeson had survived—she could only go on if she believed it to be true. She longed to feel the warmth and comfort of his arms around her, though she knew it could not be. The embrace that she should never have given him both strengthened *and* tortured her.

In her exhaustion and despair, sleep eluded her. The night hours slowly slipped away, frustrating her as she realized that the morning light was soon to come. She rolled over and gently put an arm across Petia. Just as sleep was tempting her to finally give up the anxieties of the previous day, she heard them. To the trained ear of a mechtech, the sound of Starcrafts approaching was undeniable—and their numbers were many. Raviel bolted upright and grabbed her glass tablet to signal the alarm, but she could feel the panic beginning to rise. Where could they go? Petia woke and seemed to instantly sense Raviel's anxious heart. Eyes wide with fear, Petia reached for Raviel. All Raviel could do was hold her close and hope.

CHAPTER

7

Home of Sorrows

Daeson powered up the engines of the Starcraft and felt the power tickling his fingers, as if she could not wait to take flight. He smiled. Everything about the ship felt different. Even the sound of the engines was perfectly tuned, pulsing with restrained energy. As he lifted off, the Starcraft nearly leapt into the air.

"Whoa!" Daeson exclaimed, noting the extremely reduced power setting required to get the ship airborne. "This is going to take some getting used to."

"My programming has been altered, my liege. I seem to have detailed knowledge of the new capabilities of this Starcraft. Am I in error? Should I revert to my earlier programming?"

"No, my friend, you are not in error. Keep your current programming and be ready to help when I need it," Daeson replied as he accelerated the Starcraft upward. The response of the craft was exhilarating. He couldn't help the wide grin that spread across his face.

"Never thought I'd hear that." Rivet's voice was almost too quiet to hear.

Daeson turned around and looked over his shoulder at the bot. He could just see Rivet's head through the display glass between them.

"Did they program you for sarcasm too?" Daeson asked.

"I do not have enough information to answer that question, my liege," Rivet replied.

"You are one odd bot," Daeson said, refocusing on piloting the Starcraft. "Do a full self-diagnostics check."

"Yes, my liege."

"And while you're at it, plot a course for the slipstream conduit back to Jypton."

"Coordinates set and all self-diagnostics check normal," Rivet replied almost instantly.

Daeson shook his head. Perhaps in all of the technical knowledge of the Malakians, they had missed something.

During the flight back to Jypton, Daeson's thoughts were all over the place. He was returning to his world a different man—much different.

As a precaution, Daeson armed his weapons and engaged the Starcraft's cloaking system before exiting the conduit. With the chaos on Jypton, he fully expected a destroyer and a squadron of Starcrafts to be guarding the conduit, but such was not the case. He entered the atmosphere without incident and made his way back to the Abyssian Trenches refugee camp...back to Raviel. As soon as he was within visual range, his stomach rose up to his throat. Pillars of black smoke rose in the distance in the exact spot where his coordinates were taking him.

"No!" he whispered.

"I am detecting massive amounts of plasma residue and debris at the camp site," Rivet reported.

"Life signs?" Daeson asked, his apprehension mounting with each passing second. He pushed the throttles up to nearly full speed.

"It's difficult to get an accurate reading. Approximately eight hundred forty separate indications, but it keeps changing," Rivet said.

"There were nearly two thousand refugees at that camp!" Daeson grew angry and scared. So many people in harm's way, yet the pain of losing Raviel vied for exclusive domain over his thoughts and fears.

"Scan for Jyptonian ships," Daeson ordered.

"No ships of any kind detected within sensor range," Rivet quickly responded.

Daeson's Starcraft ripped through the air, splitting the atmosphere in thunderous waves of sound, but no one was below to hear it. As he neared the camp, he decelerated and set down as close to the carnage as he dared. His first close-up view of the camp confirmed his worst fears. Linden was methodically targeting and destroying any and all refugee camps, knowing that they could be harboring resistance fighters.

Daeson tore his helmet off and was down the ladder before his engines had fully spooled down. Rivet was close behind. Small groups of men and women were combing the wreckage, searching for survivors. The smell of war hung in the air, mixed with the cries and moans of a people in anguish. Dead and wounded were everywhere. For a moment Daeson stood silently in the middle of the carnage, stunned by the overwhelming loss. He found a man who was calling out as he searched for people possibly buried in the rubble of the caves.

"Who's in charge?" Daeson asked.

The man looked at him in disbelief. "In charge?" He shook his head. "Who's left?" the man rebuked.

Daeson felt panic well up within. He tried to find the cave where he had left Raviel, but nothing was recognizable.

"Raviel!" he shouted. "Raviel!"

"They're setting up a couple of tent infirmaries just over there," a woman offered. Her face was bruised and bleeding, but she was helping a more severely wounded woman make her way that direction. "Perhaps she's there."

Daeson lifted the injured woman in his arms. "I'll take her," he said, then began walking toward the infirmaries.

"Rivet, search for Raviel and Petia," he called over his shoulder at the bot.

"Yes, my liege."

When Daeson arrived at the make-shift infirmaries, he found a man who seemed to have maintained enough wits about him to start bringing some order to the chaos.

"Tig!" Daeson called out.

Tig ran to him, calling two others to take the woman Daeson was carrying to a cot and begin treating her. One of the young women who had been summoned seemed to know what she was doing. She had to be a medtech. She gave instructions to the other and moved on to those wounded with more serious injuries.

"It's good to see you, Daeson," Tig interjected, wiping the sweat and blood from his brow.

"Raviel—have you seen Raviel and Petia?" Daeson questioned as he scanned the faces of the wounded nearby.

Tig shook his head. "I'm sorry, Daeson. We're still searching, but—"

More wounded arrived, cutting off Tig's response mid-sentence.

Daeson ran his hand through his hair, frustrated and sick with fear. "Where do I search? Where was she last seen?"

Tig directed those carrying the wounded.

"There is where she slept," he said, pointing to a mountain of rubble and rock. "I'll come help as soon as I can."

Daeson put a hand on Tig's shoulder. "You're needed here," he acknowledged before running back into the devastation. A man was working a functional scanner and directing others where to dig when any trace of life was detected.

"What about there?" Daeson asked, pointing to the collapsed entrance of Raviel's cave. "Have you scanned there?"

"Yes. Nothing there," the man stated flatly, and he quickly moved on.

Daeson caught up with Rivet on the far side of a mound of strewn boulders. The bot's hands were flattened against the rocks and his antenna was extended.

"Rivet, have you found anything yet?" Daeson's voice was strained. Every minute that passed meant people beneath the rubble were dying, including Raviel and Petia.

Rivet remained motionless. Then his head tilted ever so slightly. "They are here!" The bot's voice was laced with urgency.

Rivet immediately began dislodging and removing stones at a pace that astounded Daeson. He joined the bot, but his work seemed paltry compared to Rivet's.

Together they dug. Daeson's flight gloves frayed and tore in the frenzied rescue attempt until his fingers bled, but he didn't falter.

"Are they alive?" Daeson asked Rivet between heavy breaths.

"Life signs are weak," Rivet reported without a microsecond of hesitation.

In spite of muscles that were utterly spent, Daeson renewed his efforts. Rivet was a tireless, boring machine fueled by what Daeson could only describe as the energy of guardian compulsion. After an hour of relentless digging, they were finally rewarded with a small opening. Daeson urged caution lest more rocks fall and crush any survivors.

"Is anyone there?" Daeson yelled into the opening.

They waited in silence.

He called again. At last a small voice whimpered and called out to them. It was Petia!

"We're coming for you, Petia!" Daeson promised. "Is Raviel with you?"

"Yes, but she's not moving," the child said through tears. "Please hurry!"

Daeson called for help from other excavators, and soon they had cleared enough of the fallen rock to reach Petia and Raviel. They carefully extracted Petia. Daeson scooped her into his arms and hugged her.

"It's okay, Petia. You're safe now."

"Raviel," Petia pleaded looking back at the opening.

Daeson tried to hand Petia to one of the other workers, but instead she reached for Rivet. The bot knelt down and gingerly wrapped an arm around the little girl. The tenderness Rivet displayed toward Petia was undeniably human. Daeson turned his attention back to Raviel as the excavators carefully removed the remaining stones that hindered her extraction and then gently pulled her out. Daeson held his breath, hoping against all odds that she was still alive. Her right leg was soaked in blood, but he felt a weak pulse at her neck. One of the men put a compression bandage on her wound.

"Raviel...can you hear me?" Daeson asked. She was pale and unresponsive.

"We need to get her to the infirmary now!" he ordered.

At the infirmary, Tig and the young woman Daeson had seen earlier took Raviel and immediately began to work on her.

"Daeson, this is master medtech Zee'la. Raviel's in good hands."

Zee'la didn't look up from her work. She flipped her head to keep her black shoulder-length hair out of her face, clearly annoyed that she hadn't even had time to tie it back. Her dark eyes and high cheekbones distinguished her as belonging to the northern Azuran Clan. She scanned Raviel's body and then began closing the deep gash on her leg with a sonic dermal repair instrument. After working on her for over thirty minutes, Zee'la looked up at Daeson.

"I've stopped the bleeding, but she's lost a lot of blood, and we don't have a blood synthesizer here." She looked over at Tig almost apologetically. "There's not much more I can do."

"What does that mean?" Daeson asked.

Zee'la shook her head. "She needs blood."

Tig glanced toward Daeson.

"Give her my blood," Daeson stated firmly.

Zee'la looked stunned. "That's an archaic procedure, and we don't have any way of performing such a transfusion."

"Will she survive?" Tig asked.

Zee'la hesitated. "She's barely hanging on as it is. I doubt it."

"Then we need to figure out a way to give the transfusion," Tig said.

She looked at Tig, then to Daeson.

"Please," Daeson implored.

Zee'la grabbed an instrument and quickly scanned Daeson.

"You're compatible. Okay, let's give this a try, and I'll do my best not to lose both of you."

Thirty minutes later Raviel was receiving blood from Daeson via a severely improvised transfusion setup that caused Zee'la to cringe...but it worked. As the minutes ticked by, Daeson didn't take his eyes off of Raviel, looking for any indication that she would be okay. Two hours later the medic stopped the transfusion.

"Is that enough for her?" Daeson asked.

"It's enough for her to live and for you to live as well."

Daeson looked at Raviel again and reached for her hand. Her eyes rolled, and slowly she opened them as her head rotated toward him.

"Hey sleepy head," he said with a smile.

She slowly blinked. "Daeson," she whispered, then squeezed his hand.

Each of the corners of Daeson's eyes spilled a single tear as he took a deep breath, grateful that he hadn't lost her. He couldn't imagine taking on the task ahead of him without her beside him.

Over the next hour, Raviel slowly revived, but soon her recovery became remarkable. Within a few hours her wound was almost completely healed and her blood replenished. She sat up and insisted on helping.

"The Omegeon purging must have something to do with this," Raviel said. Daeson felt it too and agreed. After a bit of food and water, both she and Daeson rejoined the recovery effort, working around the clock to help as many refugees as humanly possible in this desolate place. The next day, Trisk arrived with much-needed fresh men and supplies, and Tig relinquished his leadership role.

Once the immediate need of medical care was over, Trisk, Tig, Raviel, and Daeson began planning to relocate the camp for the survivors. In spite of their common goal, the animosity Trisk bore toward Daeson was still clearly evident, and Raviel's discouragement concerning the task at hand only worsened as the work to restore and relocate all of the refugees proceeded.

Two days later, Daeson finally had a chance to talk with Raviel alone. He led her to a flat outcropping that overlooked the camp and sat down next to her on a large boulder. "I have much to tell you," Daeson declared.

Raviel looked weary, the life in her eyes diminished by her fatigue and the sorrow that surrounded them on every side. He hadn't seen her smile once since he'd returned. "Where have you been?" Raviel asked. "We needed you."

Daeson winced. Knowing that Raviel thought he had abandoned them—abandoned her—was painful.

"I'm sorry, Rav. I wish I had been here for you." Daeson looked toward the camp. "I can't imagine what it was like. But—"

Raviel turned her head away from him. "You were right," she said. "There's no hope for us. How could I have been so naïve as to think that we could somehow win our freedom?" Her head fell low.

Daeson reached for her chin and lifted her face toward him. Dirt-stained tears slowly rolled down her cheeks—empty eyes spilling sorrowful tears.

"No, Raviel, *you* were right...I've been such a fool!" Daeson couldn't help the excitement that rose up inside him. He leaned close to her so that his face was just inches away from hers. "I've seen him...face to face!" he rejoiced.

Raviel's blank expression dislodged one ember of hope. She squinted. "Him?"

"Yes...Ell Yon!"

Raviel's eyes immediately reddened and filled once more. "What do you mean? How is that possible?"

"I flew to Galeo. I knew he was calling me there, and that is where he came to me...or rather I to him." Daeson took Raviel's hands in his. "He's everything you said he was, Rav. I don't even know how to describe what I saw...what he taught me...what he's called me to—us to."

Raviel's eyes filled with wonder and hope for the first time since returning to Jypton. Then just as quickly the reality of their torment squashed it away, and she turned her eyes once more to the devastation around them.

"Don't tease me, Daeson. I can't—". Her voice broke as she lifted the back of her hand to her cheek.

"I'm so sorry, Raviel...for everything I've put you through. For not believing you...for not being here when you needed me."

He put his hand to her cheek and gently turned her head toward him again, the glow of his eyes pouring into hers. "But I'm here now, and so is Ell Yon."

Raviel's lips pursed. Her eyes softened with hope once more. "You...truly...met him? You believe?"

"Oh, Rav, I more than believe! There is no empire in the galaxy that could keep me from serving Sovereign Ell Yon. His power...his wisdom...his love for us...his people—there is nothing like it in the universe! They are with us, right here, right now. Freedom is not far."

Daeson began telling Raviel everything and watched with delight as hope and the fullness of life he'd come to love about her were reborn. And at the end of their conversation, Daeson knelt down before her, still holding tight to her hands. "I now understand why you couldn't love me the way I wanted you to." Daeson smiled and shook his head. "He changes everything. I don't know how you feel about me, but I want you to know that my feelings for you are deeper than ever I imagined possible. Serving Ell Yon with you beside me is all I could ever desire. I love you, Raviel Arko."

Raviel stood and lifted Daeson up with her. The light in her eyes mingled with tears of happiness, and the smile on her lips said everything. She reached up and wrapped her arms around his neck. "I love you too," she whispered in his ear. "I tried not to. I knew I couldn't fully love someone who didn't follow Ell Yon, but now...Oh, Daeson, my heart is so full of joy I hardly dare believe it."

Daeson pulled back and stared into those beautiful eyes that had captivated him in the past and were now shining brighter than he had ever seen them before.

"What's ahead won't be easy."

"I don't care," Raviel returned. "Ell Yon never promised ease. He promised hope and freedom, and I'll travel to the ends of the galaxy with you to serve him."

That evening they sat next to Petia as she slept. Although their small rocky alcove was a crude shelter, a couple of blankets softened the stone floor a bit. Rivet sat at the entrance, ever watchful.

"Rivet, enter sleep mode," Daeson commanded.

The bot faced them. "As you wish, my liege." Then he turned back toward the opening and became perfectly still.

Daeson stared at Rivet for some time.

"What is it?" Raviel asked.

Daeson's gaze turned toward Petia, who was curled up next to Raviel, a blanket carefully tucked in on all sides.

"When we were searching for you and Petia, that bot looked like it was searching for its own lost child. I don't get it. He's not AI…he's more," Daeson added.

Raviel stared at the motionless machine. "I don't know if I should be thrilled or scared by that," she assessed. "Do you ever wonder if it's really in sleep mode? Maybe it's still awake…listening to everything we say."

"I don't doubt it one bit. He's smart and, dare I say, crafty."

Petia sat up and yawned, blinking in the dark of the night. She then lay back down and moaned. "Rivet isn't a 'he'…it's a 'she'."

Raviel's eyebrows raised, as did Daeson's.

"How do you know that, little miss?" Raviel asked.

Petia yawned again. "She told me," came her sleepy reply. Then she drifted off to sleep again.

Daeson wasn't sure what to make of Petia's words. He and Raviel just sat in silence for a minute, neither sure how to respond. Finally, Raviel leaned close to Daeson with a scrutinizing gaze.

"No wonder you like that bot so much," she teased.

Daeson shot her a crooked smile. "No wonder you don't," he replied.

She chuckled. Daeson lay down, and Raviel put her head on his shoulder as he wrapped an arm around her. In spite of the world's being torn apart by a blood-thirsty tyrant, Daeson and Raviel found a small measure of respite in each other's arms. Soon, even that might not be possible.

CHAPTER

8

Dissension

The Twelve Clans of Rayl – Revitar, Simak, Leevok, Jahrim, Isak, Zealon, Galloway, Azuran, Daynon, Nasher, Joshe, Baraquet

Daeson knew he needed to meet with the leaders of the each of the twelve clans of the Rayleans. The clan chieftains were his access to the rest of the people. Without their support, it would be difficult, if not impossible, to spread the messages of Ell Yon. Solidarity was the key, yet creating that would take a miracle since time and distance had splintered any such unity. The Plexus had been successful to some degree, but not like what would be needed for the journey ahead.

It was decided to establish three new refugee camps. Trisk posited that multiple camps would reduce the risk of detection. Daeson, Raviel, and Tig chose to occupy the camp in the Shadow Forests, near the city of Capell, because of its relative proximity to Athlone. Zee'la, the oldest daughter of a family at the camp, agreed to care for Petia when Raviel was called away to assist Daeson, and Petia agreed to the arrangement once she became acquainted with two of Zee'la's younger siblings.

Capell, a city approximately one-third the size of Athlone, turned out to be an excellent location for clandestine meetings. It was close enough to Athlone to allow access to information about the operations of the Jyptonian government yet far enough away to avoid the direct scrutiny of Linden's royal forces. From this location, Daeson sent forth the call to all Raylean clans on Jypton to send their chieftains to come and hear the words that Ell Yon had spoken.

Every clan had been persecuted, hunted, beaten, and threatened, yet two weeks later a chieftain or designated deputy from each clan was gathered at Capell in an obscure building near the edge of the city limits. Tig and Rivet provided security outside the building, just in case their location had been compromised. A tragedy involving all of the clan chieftains would certainly destroy any hope of unifying the Rayleans in this cause.

Daeson stood to address the men and women who had come. He scanned the solemn group. Besides Raviel and Trisk, he had never seen any of these people before. Two looked years younger than he. Three were women of varying ages, and the rest were men that ranged from middle-aged to ninety. He suspected that some sitting here might not be chieftains or their deputies but brave volunteers who had traveled to hear the absurd remarks of a man claiming to have seen Ell Yon. The gathering was not what Daeson had expected or hoped for. Chieftain Cora and her deputy, Trisk, attended on behalf of the Jahrim Clan. Trisk's presence dismayed Daeson greatly for he knew that the man was against him. How could he convince any of the others if his own clan rejected him?

Quiet conversations took place between numerous leaders, but with each passing moment, the voices grew louder as tales of great woe were shared. An older man named Galder Wescott from the Baraquet Clan seemed to garner the greatest respect from the others, so Daeson looked to him for cues.

Daeson stood to gain the attention of the room. "May I have your attention, please," he requested, but the leaders did not heed him. Some comments were aimed toward Daeson indirectly, but he felt every one.

"Why should we care a smit what this man says?"

"Our people are suffering and dying because of him."

"The Plexus is gone…what's the point now?"

Raviel stood with Daeson. "Please just listen to what he has to say." She placed her hands on her hips and sighed, her voice barely audible over the roar of dissent.

"Did they come just to accuse and complain?" Daeson snapped. "This is a waste of time."

Finally, Galder Wescott stood, and the room fell silent. "There has not been a gathering of the clan chieftains in over sixty years. We have all traveled a great distance and at great peril to hear the words of this man. Let him speak."

"I came only to set eyes on the man that caused all of this tragedy!" one of the men yelled.

Wescott glared at the man, and he abruptly silenced his rant. Wescott then looked toward Daeson and sat down. Daeson nodded his appreciation toward the older gentleman.

"I am grateful that each of you has undertaken the effort necessary to attend this meeting. We've made arrangements so that your risk for future meetings will be minimized. Raviel…"

Raviel stood up and opened a metallic case. "When the Plexus fell, our quantum entanglement communicators were compromised," she stated as she began handing a new communicator to each representative.

"These advanced QECs were developed by our sci-techs and will allow us to convene for future meetings without the risk of your having to travel here. These communicators have been enhanced and will allow not only transmit written messages, but also visual communication as well."

"It is absolutely critical that you keep these secure," Daeson added. "All of these QECs are entangled together, so if one is compromised, they are all compromised."

He waited until everyone had received a communicator before continuing. "I know there are some here who despise me and others who do not trust me. Some of you blame me for what has happened, and others don't even know me. Whatever you may think of me, know that I am not here before you because of my own doing or because of my own plans. I am standing here before you for one reason and one reason only…Sovereign Ell Yon has sent me."

Murmurings and mumblings laced with ridicule rose up across the crowd.

"I don't know why he chose me, for I am not worthy, and I don't blame you for your ill thoughts toward me. Yet here I am and here you are. This is the doing of Ell Yon, and I will follow his command."

"How do we know he is the one who sent you to us?" asked one of the chieftains.

"Yes, what if this is another Jyptonian deception?" echoed another.

"Those are fair questions, and as Raviel will attest, I was the greatest skeptic of all. All I can do is to tell you what I've seen and what I've heard. When this is over, you all must make a choice as to whether you believe me."

"What is the message you claim Ell Yon has given you?" Trisk asked, his countenance stern.

Daeson hesitated as he looked from Trisk to each clan representative.

"That our freedom is at hand. That Sovereign Ell Yon is going to crush the power of Jypton in order to set us free."

The stir from the chieftains was difficult to interpret. Some sat silent—most scoffed.

"Impossible!" said one chieftain. "The Jyptonian military is the most powerful force in the galaxy. How can we be freed from them, especially now that our rebel forces have been decimated? If what you say is true, what is Ell Yon's plan to set us free?"

Daeson stared back at the man, speechless.

"I don't know. He hasn't revealed it yet. I just know that he's going to do it."

More scoffing and angry outbursts followed.

"Then what is it that Ell Yon wants us to do?" Wescott asked.

"Prepare the people," Daeson replied.

"For what?" Trisk asked.

Daeson's confidence was waning. He knew his words sounded ridiculous. This speech had played out so much better in his mind. "To leave the planet," he stated succinctly.

At that the room erupted into chaos that not even Wescott could subdue.

"That's preposterous!" someone shouted. "We have no ships! This man is crazy!"

Just when Daeson thought all was naught, Trisk stood up. "Quiet!" he yelled. It took a moment, but he was able to quell the chaos.

Trisk looked at Daeson.

"If what you say is true, give us a sign that we might believe you."

Daeson felt Raviel's hand on his arm. He looked down at her and realized that she was touching the Protector. He walked to a table and reached for a chalice filled with drink. The chieftain who owned the chalice allowed it. Daeson held the chalice in his left hand, opened his right hand and scanned the chalice. Once complete, he turned the image to the chieftains.

"This is the Protector, given to us by Ell Yon himself. It has the ability to detect Deitum Prime in any object, inanimate or living." He handed the chalice to the one from whom he had taken it.

"What you are drinking is contaminated with twelve percent Deitum Prime."

Every chieftain and deputy stared in silence at the image suspended before them. One clan leader shook her head. "We are barely surviving. Thousands have been killed and even publicly executed. It's going to take more than a technological gimmick to save us from this horror."

Others echoed her sentiments.

One representative broke away to respond to an incoming alert on his communicator. A moment later, every representative was preoccupied with some dire message. Daeson looked at Raviel.

"What is it?"

She looked up from her glass tablet, horror showing on her face. "Word of your return must have reached the palace. Chancellor Lockridge has ordered the execution of one hundred Rayleans in each of the five major cities tomorrow unless..."

"Unless what?" Daeson insisted. He became keenly aware that all of the clan leaders were now staring at him.

"Unless you surrender yourself to be prosecuted for treason against the Jyptonian government and against the royal family," Raviel's voice quavered.

Daeson went numb. Linden was shrewd...a man of strategy and ruthless tactics.

Raviel grabbed Daeson's arm. "On the list of those to be executed is Saskia Lockridge." Her countenance fell grim. "What kind of a man would execute his own family?"

Daeson's stomach churned in grief. "He wants revenge. He blames me for the death of his father, and my mother is all the leverage he needs."

"You see, Starlore...there is no beating Lockridge or any of the Jyptonian Elite," one of the chieftains blurted out. "Now you know what it's like to truly be Raylean!"

Raviel glared back at the chieftain, but Daeson didn't respond.

"It's true," said another. She pointed at Daeson. "He has never suffered like we have...never experienced the bonds of slavery like we have, and he comes here promising false hope. We'll believe you when we see starships and destroyers coming to destroy the Jyptonian tyrants. Until then, all we can do is try to survive!"

The room quickly erupted. Daeson looked around the table—frustrated, discouraged, and angry. Trisk was not speaking nor adding to the discord; he simply stared.

The meeting had come to an end. One by one, the chieftains and representatives left the room to journey back home, all except Trisk and Wescott. Daeson hung his head. He had failed...failed Ell Yon before his mission had even started. Raviel put a hand on his shoulder.

"What will you do, my friend?" Wescott asked. His were the only kind words he'd heard since the beginning of the proceedings.

Daeson, still silent, looked up into the faces of the wise man and Trisk.

"I will do the only thing I can do." He turned and left the room.

Raviel felt like she'd been sucker-punched in the gut. From the beginning, she had quietly hoped Daeson would rise up and face off with the Jyptonian Elite—a man who would champion their fight for freedom. Quietly, defiantly she had fallen in love with him, and now she was torn apart by her devotion to her people, to Ell Yon, and to her heart. She felt so cheated. Now free to love him, she would lose him, for she knew what Daeson would choose. He had indeed become the man she had hoped for. He would never turn away from the sacrifice required to save his people. A few brief weeks were all she had been given, and now she must give him up. Anger, remorse, and self-pity warred for control of her thoughts. She despised Linden Lockridge and his family. There seemed no end to the cup of tragedy they would force her to drink all the days of her life.

Raviel looked up at Trisk. She saw the sorrow in the eyes of a man struggling with his own spectrum of emotions. This was a time of great tearing—hearts, families, friendships, governments, and even worlds were all being torn apart. Why did it have to be so?

"True freedom is costly when the grip of evil is firm," Wescott portended.

Raviel looked at the white-haired man.

"Do you believe him, sir?" Raviel asked.

Wescott hesitated. "What I believe will not change what will happen tomorrow, Miss Arko. But for what it's worth, yes, I believe him."

Raviel pursed her lips and nodded. She looked toward Trisk, silently asking him the same. Trisk took in her gaze, then turned away. His doubt hurt. She looked back to Wescott. "What do I do?"

Wescott offered a gentle sympathetic smile.

"If you believe him, you do what you must to help him."

Raviel shook her head. "I don't think I'm strong enough."

Trisk looked back at Raviel. "Go to him...he needs you."

Raviel nodded. She straightened her back, then took a deep breath and turned to leave. She stopped and looked back at the two men. "Thank you," she breathed.

Tig and Rivet met Raviel as she exited the building.

"He's that way, my lady," Tig said, pointing.

Raviel changed direction to go after Daeson.

"He asked to be alone," Tig followed up. "Not sure if that includes you or not."

Raviel nodded, then rushed to catch up with Daeson. She walked beside him in silence. Daeson looked over at her, and she met his glance. Both their eyes were filled with worry and concern.

"I need to think," he finally spoke.

"Alone?" she asked.

"Please, no."

"Then come with me." Raviel took his hand and led him. Before long they were mounted on an aerobike, skimming across the gentle waves of the Marricoo Ocean, their place of beginning.

This time she held tightly to his chest as they soared next to the white sands of the shoreline. She rested her head on his back and felt the warmth of his body against her cheek. All of the aches in her heart that before had been forbidden to heal were now replaced by a different ache...the ache of love and of loss. She cared not and thought not of the loss but instead let her heart fully love the man she now held closely, desperately wishing for a different tomorrow.

Daeson felt her embrace and lifted a hand to hers, their newfound love enveloping him body, mind, and soul. Her touch soothed him greatly. He brought the aerobike to a stop near the same rocky outcropping where they had spent the previous night together...a night that seemed a hundred years in the past. He took her hand and sat down against the massive stones, where the water of former storms had softened the harsh edges of their isolated haven.

As Raviel sat beside him, leaning against his shoulder, he wrapped an arm around her.

"Please don't go," she said quietly.

Daeson sighed deeply. "You know I have to. You said so yourself months ago."

Raviel lowered her head. "I know, but not in this way—and I didn't plan on falling so crazy in love with you." She looked up at him, gazing into his eyes and then closing hers. "This isn't what I envisioned at all." When she opened her eyes, he sensed the fear that was consuming her. "What you're planning to do is suicide.

Surely there must be another way. I can't lose you...not now!"

Her eyes moistened.

Daeson pulled her closer.

"I wish I'd said yes," she whispered, looking up into his eyes.

Daeson's love for Raviel was strong... overwhelming. Just weeks earlier he would have yielded to her plea, but now, as a Navi of Ell Yon, something had changed. It wasn't that his love for Raviel had diminished. No, in fact his love was deeper yet. What had changed was his love for something far greater than anything either he or Raviel could offer each other. A mighty, unstoppable, unquenchable, uncontainable force in his life burned with a fierce mission that demanded action.

"Yes to what?" Daeson asked, brushing a few loose strands of hair over her ear so he could see those mesmerizing eyes.

Raviel sniffed. "I wish I'd said yes when you asked me to run away with you...before all of this destruction." Her eyes brightened ever so slightly as she added, "I'll go now...just ask and I'll go. We'll escape this impossible horror."

Daeson smiled, but Raviel knew immediately what his answer was.

"You and I both know that neither of us would be able to do that anymore."

Raviel lowered her head and sighed. "Yes...I know."

"One day, my lady, you and I will go away. I promise."

Daeson lifted her hand and kissed it.

"I can't in a thousand dreams imagine how you will survive the day, Daeson, but when this is over, I'll go with you...wherever it may be."

"I need to ask something of you," Daeson appealed.

Raviel turned to face him, her brows slightly furrowed.

"Of course. What is it?"

"Before I go and represent Ell Yon's people before the Chancellor of Jypton, I want to bear his mark."

Raviel pulled the neckline of her shirt down to her collar bone, revealing her mark, the mark of Ell Yon that designated both him and her clan, the Jahrim.

Daeson reached out to touch the mark. It was simple yet elegant, slightly indented into her skin.

"Sabella told me my clan was your clan...the Jahrim."

Raviel smiled. "It hurts when it's given. I was given mine at thirteen. Trisk is the guardian of our clan signet, so we could give you the mark tonight."

Daeson lifted his hand to her neck, stroking her cheek with his thumb. "And after I receive the mark is there anything else?"

"Anything else?" she asked, her eyes questioning his.

Daeson hesitated, taking in every curve of her face. He looked down and lifted her hand in his.

"Anything else I must do to be considered fully Raylean...one to whom a Raylean woman might consider to be bonded?"

Daeson searched her face, hoping he had not offended her, but for a few seconds she gave no hint as to her thoughts. At last she slowly shook her head and leaned toward Daeson until her lips were nearly touching his. He could feel her breath—his heart pounded.

"No, there is nothing else required to be bonded to another."

Daeson gently kissed her, and the smile he was looking for spread across her lips.

"I love you, Raviel. Will you be bonded to me for life?"

"Yes, in this life and the next one to come!" She wrapped her arms around his neck, and Daeson held her close.

"When this is all over, we'll ask Chieftain Wescott to bond us...yes?"

"Yes!"

No matter what tomorrow might bring, he could now face it with courage and a satisfied heart.

CHAPTER

9

A Hero Rises

Triad – Immortal technology powered by anti-omegeon particles capable of endowing its wearer with increased strength, a visually linked energy discharge weapon, and temporary physical metamorphosis. The device utilizes a symbiotic connection between the Immortal power cell and the Deitum Prime-enriched bio-energy. The extent of the wearer's enhanced abilities is directly proportional to the level of bodily absorption of the genetic agent Deitum Prime.

"Linden!" Daeson yelled across the courtyard as he stepped out from a mass of over twenty thousand citizens of Athlone.

Linden turned to face the crowd, his black cloak trailing his movements like the shadow of a dark lord. Multiple sentry drones were capturing the scene of the courtyard execution, transmitting the images instantly across the globe to all of Jypton. Entire buildings became displays since Linden wanted his message of absolute rule to reach every soul on the planet.

"This public execution doesn't suit you. Are you truly as blood-thirsty as the whispers have claimed?"

Even at this distance, Daeson could see the fury in the eyes of the Chancellor of Jypton, the man he had once called friend and brother. Linden pointed, and the aim of a hundred Talons fell on Daeson.

"The traitor returns," Linden scowled. "And just in time to witness the execution of his own co-conspirator mother."

"By the word of your mouth, you said you would spare the lives of these innocent people if I were to surrender." Daeson held out his hands. "I am here. Now honor your word and let them go!"

Linden's scowl transformed to a smile of loathsome contempt. He motioned to his royal guards, and they collapsed on Daeson. They placed composite fetters upon his wrists and brought him before Linden. A wave of murmurs rippled through the throng of people forced to be witnesses. The entire world of Jypton was watching the terror of the moment unfold.

Two large guards held Daeson firmly while a dozen more stood nearby ready to execute Linden's command in a moment. Linden nodded, and the guards kicked the back of Daeson's legs, forcing him onto his knees before Chancellor Lockridge.

Daeson noticed an addition to the royal garb of the Chancellor. It was unmistakably the weapon the Commander had told him about—the Triad. Fastened to the center of Linden's chest was a dark green jeweled technological marvel shaped like a thickened X. The smooth surface of the Triad reminded him of the Protector, but the dark author of this device was not Ell Yon. Clearly, Linden was proud to wear the Immortal technology. He looked down at Daeson and lifted his chin in arrogant disgust.

"This man is why you have all suffered!" he shouted, looking at the crowd as well as the drones sending the broadcast. He strutted slowly around Daeson. "His defiance and traitorous acts against the Jyptonian government and against the royal family are punishable by death."

Linden came face-to-face with Daeson once more. He reached down and grabbed Daeson's neck, squeezing his throat shut. Daeson gasped for air as Linden poured out his hatred through his words.

"You killed my father. Do you think for one minute I would ever consider letting your mother or anyone else you care for live?" Linden caught a glimpse of Daeson's clan mark on his collar and pulled his tunic down to reveal it fully. "Ah...the brand of a slave. You're despicable!"

Daeson chanced a look toward his mother. She was standing stoically, demonstrating the poise of a truly noble woman. When his eyes met hers, however, she faltered, and he knew it was not for fear of her own life but for his. Daeson's heart stumbled to see such grief in the eyes of the woman who had loved him as her own flesh and blood.

Linden released his grip, and Daeson's head dropped as he gasped for new air.

"Don't do this, Linden! I'm the imposter, not her or any of these people...please!"

Linden grabbed Daeson's hair and yanked his head up. "Watch those you love die just as I did!"

"No, Linden!" Daeson fought against the strong hands that held him, but they did not give an inch.

"Execute them!" Linden ordered.

Before Daeson could react, thirty-six Talons discharged their deadly power into the bodies of those on the execution line. Shrieks and wailing immediately filled the air, and Daeson watched as his mother screamed out, reaching for her son, then fell lifeless to the courtyard floor.

"NO!" Daeson screamed. He tried to stand, but the guards and Linden held him down. Righteous anger that could not be subdued swelled within Daeson. An unstoppable power coursed through his veins, and he felt the Protector surging in anticipation. The fetter about it dissolved away. Stunned, Linden fell backward, and two royal guards caught him. Pulling their chancellor away, they watched as Daeson held the Protector above his head—blue bolts of energy arcing in all directions.

"Kill him!" Linden ordered as the guards shielded him from whatever it was that was happening. The scene exploded to chaos as dozens of Talons fired at Daeson all at once. In the fraction of the time it took for the plasma charges to reach him, he clenched his fist, and the Protector encased Daeson in an impenetrable spherical energy field. Each and every Talon plasma charge that hit the protective field was perfectly reflected back to its source, obliterating the weapon from which it had come and in many cases the guard that shot it.

The screams of the crowd were indicative of the panic that ensued. People began running in every direction, away from the deadly exchange in the courtyard. Twenty more royal guards and sentries brought their weapons to bear on Daeson, including three sentry jet crafts as Linden was whisked away from inevitable death. Daeson drew two Talons from his shoulder cases just as a hellish barrage of unimaginable energy was unleashed on him.

Once more the Protector reciprocated the energy bursts and quickly destroyed them all. Daeson fired the Talon in his right hand at one of the sentry jets, and the discharge of energy was unlike anything ever witnessed. Powered by the might of the Protector, it tore through the vessel in an instant. Its crew and the remnants of the once powerful jet fell onto a building in a ferocious series of explosions.

Daeson then individually targeted and fired upon each royal guard or sentry not in retreat. Within moments, not a single threat was left standing...none except for Linden. He had pushed aside his guards and stood as one unafraid of the power Daeson now seemed to wield.

The courtyard billowed smoke and fire as the city fled from the might of Sovereign Ell Yon's Protector and his messenger. Daeson's pain and fury were still raw as he went to the dead form of his mother and knelt down beside her. She had loved him all along, even though he was Raylean. He closed her eyes and wept. Slowly, he stood up and faced the one who had forced open the gates of war. The two men faced off as the rest of the world watched.

The scorn on Linden's face had transformed his handsome and regal features to that of a hate-filled beast. Linden touched the Triad, his eyes glowing red with fury. A fraction of a second later, a red beam of alien power exploded from his chest. Daeson instinctively put up his hand to shield himself, and the Protector pulsed to life once more.

Beautiful fierce blue power flowed from his open hand to meet Linden's destructive beam, and the collision of energy shook the ground. The marble floor of the courtyard scorched black as the air above ignited in the fury of the exchange.

Daeson's feet began to slip against the force flowing out from the Protector, so he placed one foot behind him and bent down to secure his stance. But Linden's Triad amplified its power until the continual collision of energy moved closer to Daeson. He could feel the enormous heat coming his way and could do nothing to stop it. He focused all thoughts to strengthen the Protector, but it was not enough. Slowly he was overcome until at last the exploding energy was just inches from his hand.

I am not strong enough...Ell Yon, help me!

Here in this moment of defeat, Daeson fully understood the weakness of his own being. He *wasn't* strong enough...only Ell Yon was. Daeson closed his eyes and let the mind of Ell Yon become his own. Then he let go.

The full power of the Protector exploded against the limited energy of Lord Dracus and his Triad. The energy shock wave flew outward toward Linden and threw him like a rag doll across the marble courtyard and up against the steps of the palace.

Daeson stood straight, glaring down at Linden just twenty paces away. Linden tried to gain his feet but stumbled. Three palace guards ran to pull him up and away. Linden resisted but then acquiesced, knowing the fight this day belonged to Daeson.

One sentry drone was still capturing the dramatic images for all of Jypton to see. Daeson turned toward it as it zoomed in on him. The world watched.

"Let the world of Jypton hear the words of Sovereign Ell Yon. The Raylean people are his people. Release them all and your world will be spared. Resist him and the wrath of the Immortal will destroy you!" Daeson turned and walked out of the courtyard.

The aftermath of the encounter spread pandemonium throughout the city and across the planet. The Rayleans scurried to their dwellings, fearful for the repercussions that would surely follow, and the Jyptonian forces were all put on alert. Daeson quickly disappeared into the masses, leaving the world with a hundred unanswered questions.

Hours later Daeson arrived back at the refugee camp where many Rayleans had gathered. There was a different air about the place. Some of those gathered looked terrified while others appeared jubilant.

"Starlore, what have you done?" one clan leader asked, his eyes filled with worry.

"He's done what we have been afraid to do for over a thousand years," Trisk replied. His eyes held a respect that had not been there earlier. He nodded toward Daeson.

"Yes," exclaimed another. The man grabbed Daeson's right arm and lifted it into the air. "The power of Ell Yon is with us, and our leader has come!"

Others quickly joined in the praise. Daeson tried to dispel it, but the crowd became energized.

"At last we have a leader with the courage to stand against the Jyptonians!" one shouted.

"Speak and tell us what we should do," another pleaded.

Daeson put his hands out to hush the crowd. After a few minutes, they quieted, waiting for the profound words of their new hero.

"What I have seen, no mortal man has seen. What I have heard, no mortal man has heard. I am ashamed that I was not as you have been, for I would not believe until I had seen him with my own eyes." Daeson shook his head, then pointed to the crowd. "You follow and believe Sovereign Ell Yon without having seen or heard. Fellow Rayleans, be courageous, be noble in heart...Sovereign Ell Yon is with us!"

A cheer went up. Daeson waited for them to quiet.

"We are far from free, and the days ahead will be hard, but remember that it is Ell Yon and the power of the Protector that will set us free."

"What should we do?" one from the crowd asked.

"For those who are able, return to your clans and wait. Word will come to you from your clan leaders."

Slowly, the people dispersed, some to return home, others to their shelter to wait. Raviel, Trisk, and Tig stepped up beside Daeson.

"It's begun," Raviel said. "For more than twelve hundred years, this is the day we have hoped for!" Her eyes gleamed in the light of her enthusiasm. Trisk also couldn't contain the rare smile that spread across his lips, but Tig was silent...somber.

"What's wrong, Tig?" Raviel asked.

Tig looked at Daeson.

"You have enraged the beast of Jypton, and its teeth are long and sharp. I fear the people won't be so jubilant when Chancellor Lockridge retaliates."

"What more can he do us that he hasn't done already? Dead is dead," Trisk countered. "Our people have already endured the worst."

"Have they?" Tig countered. "The worst?" He shook his head.

"Tig's right," Daeson added, as he remembered looking into Linden's darkened eyes. "Lockridge just demonstrated how far he is willing to go. It's difficult to imagine how brutal he will be in the days to come." He thought for a moment. "I need a way to send a message to him, and it needs to be personal."

Raviel and Trisk exchanged glances. "We have what you need," she said. "But we'll need to travel back to Athlone tomorrow."

That night Daeson quietly mourned the death of his mother. She had loved him unconditionally, and the flow of his tears was difficult to staunch. A fitful sleep only came far into the night, but it was enough.

Early the next morning, Raviel led Daeson down into the murky underbelly of Athlone. With each secret corridor and level change, he grew more and more astonished. "I had no idea this existed."

"This is where we develop our black-tech."

"Black-tech?"

"Tech that we don't share with anyone else. Tech that we believed one day would give us an advantage over those that oppress us...a day like today." Raviel lifted an eyebrow. "Some of the discoveries of our sci-techs can only be explained as inspiration from Ell Yon."

They entered a room where numerous sci-techs were engrossed in multiple projects. Daeson found himself enamored with all of the unrecognizable objects and instruments arrayed throughout the room.

"Welcome to the Sanctum."

A man looked up from his work and saw Daeson and Raviel standing at the doorway. He exchanged a few brief words with his colleagues, then came their way.

"Miss Arko, I thought perhaps you might present yourself here."

"It's good to see you, Master Boytt. This is—"

"I know who this is," Boytt interrupted. He eyed Daeson closely. "We've been discussing if there would be any merit in offering our help, but it has become obvious that there is something at work here far beyond that of a mere Jyptonian defector."

Boytt stepped closer to Daeson and looked him directly in the eyes. The man's hair seemed prematurely gray for how young his eyes appeared. A mustache and goatee fit his stature and facial features quite well.

"May I see it?" he asked.

Daeson pulled back the sleeve of his coat to reveal the Protector. Boytt's eyes lit up as if he'd seen a supernova firsthand. He gently lifted Daeson's arm for closer inspection as the other sci-techs gathered around.

"Here," Daeson offered, pulling the Protector from off his arm and handing it to Boytt. The response from the sci-techs was nothing short of pure ecstasy. Indiscernible chatter erupted, filling the room with tech jargon Daeson had never heard before. Boytt carefully held the Protector as if it were the jewel of the galaxy. He turned it over while others gazed on in wonder.

"We must analyze it," one sci-tech exclaimed.

"Yes, can we examine it for a few days?" asked another.

"I...," Daeson began.

"No," Boytt replied abruptly, handing the Protector back to Daeson. The sense of awe of the master sci-tech transcended mere adoration for the marvelous piece of technology. "This is directly given by the Immortal himself. It's not for us." Boytt explained as he looked back up into Daeson's eyes. "How can we serve you?"

As Daeson pushed the Protector back onto his forearm, the response from every man and woman sci-tech was audibly apparent.

"I need to send a message to Chancellor Lockridge, and it must be interactive, personal, and secure."

A wisp of a smile crossed Boytt's lips. "Yolanna, show Master Starlore your latest project. Everyone else back to work."

One sci-tech stepped forward. "Please step over here."

Yolanna led them to a lab bench on the far side of the room where she reached for a surveillance drone that made Daeson squeamish. His experience with the drones thus far had been nothing but bad, and he noticed that Raviel looked apprehensive as well.

"Don't worry," Yolanna said. "This one isn't controlled by Jypton. We've completely gutted it and installed new tech that will allow you to represent yourself anywhere without threat. I call it the holo-drone."

"It projects a hologram?" Daeson asked.

"Putting it simply, yes, but there's more to it than that." Yolanna reached for a small black case and opened it. "Put these in your eyes."

She handed the case to Daeson. Within it were two small semi-circular flexible lenses. He looked up at Yolanna. "Seriously?"

"It only takes a few minutes to get used to...trust me."

Daeson gently lifted one lens out of its pocket and tried to put it into his eye but failed.

"Allow me," Raviel said. "Just relax."

Daeson took a breath and let Raviel carefully put the lens on his left eye, followed by the right. Then he blinked, annoyed by the feeling.

"Okay, now what?"

Yolanna pressed a recessed button on the holo-drone, and it lifted into the air, floating just a bit higher than their heads. She then clipped two small devices on the left and right sides of Daeson's belt and activated them. A second later, an image appeared. Daeson was staring face-to-face with himself. The image was a perfect visual replica of Daeson, right down to the slight scar above his left eye.

"Remarkable!" he exclaimed. "It looks so real!"

Raviel walked about the hologram image and nearly gawked. When she put her hand through it, every part of the image below her hand disappeared.

"It will mimic your every move and replicate your voice."

As Daeson turned and walked, the hologram duplicated his actions.

"What's the transmission distance?" Raviel asked.

"Approximately thirty clicks without a booster. The signal is encrypted though, so it's safe to bounce off the Jyptonian global com network. Technically the distance is unlimited."

"That's incredible," she responded.

Daeson was still mesmerized by the detail and resolution. He turned resolutely and faced the other three. "This will work!"

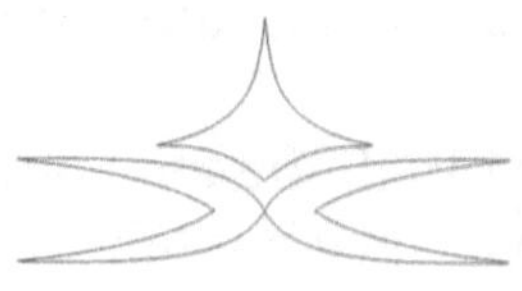

CHAPTER

10

Crushed

Yolanna flew the holo-drone as close to the palace as possible before encountering auto security forces that would seek to destroy it. Back in the Sanctum, Daeson was standing on a mobile platform that instantaneously responded to his movements, allowing him to walk or run in any direction without actually moving. This gave the impression that his hologram image was actually moving.

"How are you going to negotiate our freedom?" Trisk asked.

Raviel, Tig, Trisk, Wescott, Boytt, and two other chieftains had gathered to watch the exchange with Lockridge. Daeson glanced toward the group and said nothing.

"You have no plan to present?" asked one of the other chiefs.

"Ell Yon has a plan...I just don't know what it is yet," Daeson replied. He looked at Yolanna and nodded.

A fraction of a second later, Daeson was approaching the outer court of the palace. Sentries immediately attempted to accost him. Once they realized he was a hologram, weapons focused on the holo-drone.

"I wish to speak to Chancellor Lockridge," Daeson demanded.

"Scan the drone," ordered the captain of the sentries.

"No weapons detected," came the reply.

He sneered at Daeson. "If that thing moves, blast it."

The captain activated his com. After a short exchange with his superior, the response came. "Yes, sir," the captain acknowledged before clicking off his com link and turning back to Daeson's holo-image. "Follow me," he directed.

After more scans of the holo-drone, Daeson entered the royal court. Four guards had weapons continually trained on the holo-drone as Daeson approached. Within Linden's court stood administrators and various officials, including three councilmen.

"I see your cowardice has not allowed you to face me in person." Linden rose from his throne and descended the steps to stare Daeson in the eyes. He walked around the hologram and then returned to his seat. Xandra was dutifully standing beside him, her countenance fierce.

"I'm offended that you ever bore the name Lockridge," Linden sneered.

"I am and always will be Daeson Starlore. I come in the name of the Immortal Sovereign Ell Yon."

Linden reached for Xandra's hand, bringing it close to his lips, conveniently showing the two jeweled rings situated on her fingers that indicated her position as his co-heiress.

"Xandra, look at what has become of our former friend." Linden kissed the back of her hand. "The one we trusted. The one who spurned both of us and all of Jypton. The traitor, the rebel, the betrayer, and now the believer in fairy tales." Linden released her hand, leaned forward, and made a fist. "My father gave you everything, and you spit on him—you murdered him. There is no greater crime a man can commit, and for this you will pay!"

Xandra stepped forward and lifted her chin. "You disgust me," she added, her eyes filled with loathing contempt.

"I have a message for you," Daeson said, looking directly at Linden. "You will release all Rayleans that you have enslaved and grant them their freedom."

Linden's scowl slowly transformed to a smile. Then he began to laugh. Xandra and the councilmen joined him until everyone in the court was laughing.

"And what in the galaxy makes you think I would ever do such a preposterous thing?" Linden replied.

"You've seen the power of Ell Yon. If you don't release his people, you and all of Jypton will suffer greatly," Daeson pronounced firmly.

Linden's jovial outburst was still evident as he listened to Daeson's warning. "And tell me, Starlore, where would you and your people go?" Linden looked to his council with a sarcastic smile on his face. "I own the whole planet."

Daeson felt the Protector resonating on his forearm, and he listened to the whisper in his mind. Was the voice of Ell Yon right? He hesitated, enduring the ridicule of the entire royal court. He wanted to flip off the holo-drone and somehow ask for confirmation from the Immortal.

Speak the words.

"You will give us ships, transports, and fuel enough for the entire Raylean population that we may travel to the stars."

Linden and the entire court fell silent for a moment, apparently stunned by Daeson's absurd request. Then Linden burst into uproarious, mocking laughter again, and the entire court followed suit. The moment lingered until Linden stood, the steel-eyed glare of a powerful Chancellor slowly transforming his mirthful countenance to one of war. He drew his Talon and extended the blade as he walked up to Daeson's hologram, eyes glowering.

"I will *never* free those lowly Drudge you have aligned yourself with. My boot will be on their necks, and I will press them into the dust until they cannot breathe. I will hunt you down and your wretched wench and kill you both! There will not be one stone left unturned. And until then your people—they will die. Every day I will kill more of them until I have you!"

Daeson stared back into the eyes of his former brother, but nothing recognizable remained of the man he once knew.

"If you strike me down," Daeson began, "another will come who is stronger than I and then another and another until one day Ell Yon himself will come and crush you to dust and set his people free. You do not know against whom you fight. He is more powerful than you can imagine."

"*I* am powerful!" Linden interrupted. "You have no idea with whom you are dealing. Even if this imaginary Immortal were real, he is no match for me and the forces of Jypton. We have the mightiest military in the galaxy, as well as the support of the Galactic Alliance."

Linden's face contorted into a loathsome sneer. "You simple-minded fool!" He swung his Talon with all his might and struck the holo-drone. The innards splayed across the court in a dozen directions.

The image in front of Daeson's eyes shattered, and it took him a few seconds to adjust to the surroundings of the Sanctum. He turned and looked into the stunned faces of those assembled behind him. Their silence and shock reflected his own apprehension about the message he had just delivered.

"There are nearly three hundred thousand Rayleans on Jypton," one chieftain exclaimed. "You're insane if you think Lockridge will free us *and* give us that many ships!" He threw up his hands and walked away.

Daeson winced. "I can't explain it…I just know that's what Ell Yon said."

The chieftain turned back. "I think this hallucination is all in your head, and you're going to get a lot more of our people killed than you already have!"

The looks of disbelief and shock were hard for Daeson to take, as one by one the assembled group turned and walked away. The hope that once was now dissolved before his eyes. He looked at Raviel. Would she abandon him too? Daeson stepped off the platform, and she came to him. At first, she said nothing, just looked up into his eyes.

"I'm here," she said quietly.

Daeson took her hand. "I need you now more than ever."

Raviel was the one with the greatest power to encourage him to hold strong to the words and promises of Ell Yon.

Almost immediately it was evident that Linden would hold true to his word. Over the next few days, the persecution of the Rayleans intensified and so did the efforts to discover and execute anyone associated with the resistance. Reports from all across the planet were devastating, and Daeson went from hero to villain in a few short days. Many demanded he be turned over to the Jyptonians in an attempt to stop the horror.

Daeson and Raviel looked out over the cityscape from atop one of the Drudgetown buildings, sorrow hanging thick in the air. "Perhaps they're right," he reasoned. "If they turn me over, maybe it will stop."

Raviel leaned into him, and he put an arm around her. She was silent for a long while before speaking. "Have you already forgotten what you've seen...what he told you?"

Daeson lowered his head. "No. It just hurts to see our people in such torment. And what now? Where is he? The Protector is silent and—"

Raviel grabbed Daeson's arm and pointed up into the sky. "Look!"

Daeson stared at the vision above him. Arcing across the sky were a dozen meteorites. A bright orange trail lingered behind each one. Then the night sky lit up with a dozen more.

"Incredible," Daeson whispered.

But unlike other meteorites, these did not burn out. Soon the sky was filled with thousands of them.

"What's happening, Daeson?" Raviel asked. She held tightly to his arm.

The meteorites continued their fiery journey until they were very close. The first one exploded into one of Athlone's majestic gleaming towers, splaying fiery debris in all directions. The resulting explosion shook the building Daeson and Raviel were standing on, and they instinctively stepped backward away from the edge.

Raviel gasped as dozens more careened into the city, creating hellfire from above. An airborne transport was trying to make it out of the city when a meteor ripped through its midsection. Seconds later it smashed into a tower and hit the ground in a ball of fire that destroyed a dozen more buildings along with it.

Raviel pulled on Daeson's arm. "We need to get below ground!"

But Daeson resisted, amazed by the spectacle of it all. "I don't think so," he mumbled.

By now the rain of terror was in full force as meteors pummeled Athlone with fiery stones from above. Should it continue for long, the entire city would be destroyed.

"Look," Daeson said, pointing out across Drudgetown. "Not one meteor has hit our section of the city. This is the hand of Ell Yon!"

Raviel stopped pulling on his arm and gazed out at the impossible scene before them. Emergency sirens sounded throughout the city as the meteors continued to dismantle the majestic capitol of Jypton. Daeson looked toward Linden's palace.

Multiple meteors had initially made contact, but now its protective energy field had engaged, and the meteors striking it exploded midair in a fiery shower. Slowly the meteors diminished until all that was left was the chaos of a nearly ruined capitol.

Just then Tig burst through the door leading up to the roof of the building. "Thank Ell Yon you two are alright. Have you heard?"

Daeson looked at Raviel then back to Tig. He shook his head.

"Meteors hit every major city on Jypton and not a single one hit any of the Drudgetowns!"

Daeson took a deep breath. "Tomorrow I'll go to Lockridge again. If this doesn't show him the power of Ell Yon, I don't know what will."

The next day, with the assistance of another holo-drone, Daeson stood face-to-face with his nemesis. Linden's eyes spewed with rage. "You are drunk with delusion, Drudge. A fluke meteor shower is nothing to me."

Daeson could tell that Linden was struggling to keep his anger in check. "I'll find you, Starlore. And when I do, you'll beg for me to kill you." His eyes flamed as the Triad pulsed with power. An instant later the holo-drone exploded in a hundred pieces.

Daeson looked over at Raviel and Tig. He couldn't hide his discouragement.

The next day sentries began rounding up Raylean citizens at random and imprisoning them. The cells of the detention and security facilities quickly filled with innocent Rayleans. Daeson waited for word from Ell Yon, and at last it came.

He went to Boytt in the Sanctum. "Show me where you hijack into the Jyptonian global com network for the holo-drone."

Boytt and Yolanna showed him their network interface. "What are you planning to do?" Boytt asked. "We have to be very careful when doing this so as not to be discovered."

Daeson placed his arm next to the interface. "I don't think 'being careful' is what Ell Yon has in mind," Daeson replied. The Protector began to pulse with ribbons of blue energy. A second later Daeson felt his body resonate with the power of Ell Yon as the Protector engaged the interface. It only lasted a few seconds, but it took Daeson's breath away and left him fearful...fearful for the Jyptonians who would endure the wrath of the Immortal who was protecting his people.

The activity in the Sanctum escalated to a near frenzy as numerous sci-techs began receiving alerts from their monitors.

"Something's happening," exclaimed one. "And I have no idea what it is." The sci-tech backed away from his station as if some horrible monster were going to leap from the monitor. "The entire network has become inoperable and is transmitting some signal I can't identify."

Another sci-tech tapped rapidly across the glass of his console. "Somehow the network towers are transmitting indecipherable energy pulses. We're trying to shut it down but can't."

"What does it mean?" Raviel asked.

Daeson looked down at the Protector. He had no answer...only Ell Yon knew. Being the messenger of such grave outcomes was harder than he had imagined, regardless of the anger he now held for Linden.

Hours passed, yet nothing further happened. But the pulsing signal created by the Protector could not be stopped. All communication was disrupted because of the energy pulses. Was the disruption the full intent of the indecipherable pulses? Daeson thought not. The Raylean's quantum entanglement communicators were unaffected, but it was reported that this signal was being transmitted globally.

A new and terrifying fear struck the citizens of Athlone in the early evening. At first the sound was distant, but minutes later the roar of thousands of Kolazo beasts sent chills up and down the spines of all who heard it. Within minutes, the creatures overtook the city, seemingly worked up into a frightful frenzy by the pulsating signal. No longer were they the reclusive beasts of the forests, but rather powerful beasts driven to a maddening, vengeful rage. Military forces and sentries were called in to join the war between beast and man. The carnage spread throughout the city, terrorizing the citizens, yet the beasts did not enter Drudgetown. By morning the invasion was over—the signal had stopped.

The effect on the Jyptonians was obvious, and Daeson hoped for concession, but Linden did not relent.

The next day, Daeson met with the clan chieftains via the visual quantum entanglement communicators he had issued to them earlier. There were no "representatives" this time. Wispy holographic images of all twelve of the chieftains stood in a semi-circle facing Daeson and Raviel. The image of each chieftain was not as detailed and exact as that of the holo-drones he'd used to talk with Linden, but it was of enough resolution to accomplish what was needed. The stolid countenances of the chieftains were difficult to read.

"Chancellor Lockridge has not relented," Daeson reported, responding to a question by Chieftain Sarrok of the Leevok Clan.

"Then what is left?" asked Chieftain Cora. "If this continues, there will be no Rayleans left to free!"

Others grunted their approval of her sharp words. More rebuttals followed, and Daeson felt their pain. Many had died, and many more were suffering greatly. He couldn't deny that he himself wondered how Ell Yon was going to accomplish the impossible, especially since Linden seemed to turn more vicious and callous with every display of power Ell Yon made.

Raviel stepped forward. "Yes...we are suffering greatly because of Lockridge and his hatred for Rayleans."

"You mean hatred for Starlore!" interrupted one chieftain. Raviel ignored him.

"But surely you see the hand of Ell Yon in what is happening! The evidence is before you...trust in that and in the promise he has given us!"

Her passionate words quelled the group long enough for Daeson to gain control of the assembly. "What is happening right here, right now will change the future of our people forever. This is the generation Ell Yon has chosen. I don't know what it will take to convince Lockridge to acquiesce, but I do know that our Sovereign will not stop working until he does, and he will not leave us in this persecution forever. Please, encourage your people to endure a little longer."

The silence lingered. No valiant cheer followed, not even nods of approval. One by one the holographic images disappeared until Daeson and Raviel stood alone in the silence. Daeson hung his head, and Raviel leaned into him.

"It's hard not to agree with them," he murmured.

"Perhaps," Raviel said as she gently grabbed his arm. "But you can never let them know that."

Daeson covered her hand with his. "Yes, I know. Thank you for understanding and for not judging me."

That evening Daeson heard the whisper of Ell Yon and sent a warning to every clan chieftain.

"What is it, Daeson?" Raviel asked, noticing the concern on his face.

"Walk with me," he said to Raviel.

Before long, they stood on the edge of Drudgetown and looked out onto the groaning cityscape of Athlone proper. How different it looked now than when he had been a prince of the royal court. The proud lights and magnificent structures were bruised and yielding. The usual bustle of night life was noticeably absent.

Sentries and military vehicles occasionally could be seen rushing to some new disaster. The scene caused Daeson to momentarily ache for what once was...his respected position and the comforts that life had offered. The majestic Athlone might one day recover, but not his previous life. That falsity had been shattered by the harsh reality of truth.

"What have we done?" he asked.

Raviel lifted her head. "*We* have done nothing. Ell Yon has given our people hope, and he has been in this from the first moment we met."

Daeson looked over at her and smiled. "No wonder I could not stop from loving you."

Raviel smiled back. "Why are we here?"

"Come," Daeson said and stepped out from the borders of Drudgetown.

"Wait...out there?"

Daeson turned back to her. "Afraid?"

Raviel lifted an eyebrow. "Of course not!" she exclaimed, then stepped up beside him.

"Didn't think so...stay close."

Over the course of the next three hours, they carefully made their way through the city, often travelling through many of the gardens that decorated the cityscape. The largest garden of all was the Aqua Garden that spilled out from the palace grounds and into the city proper. The Yeln River weaved its way from the nearby mountain range and through Athlone to provide fresh water for its citizens.

In the Aqua Gardens, the lazy Yeln River was the focus of beautiful and enchanting alcoves crafted to entice awe and wonder at the power of the ruling Elite. Were it not for the chaos of the previous weeks, Daeson and Raviel would have never been able to gain access to its beauty, but the forces of Jypton were now occupied with much more than the security of its gardens. Although the river banks and walkways were softly illumined, the few people that were there did not recognize the couple. Everyone seemed completely preoccupied with the tragedy surrounding this miniature paradise.

"This is remarkable," Raviel whispered as she took in the beauty surrounding them. The gentle sounds and sight of a nearby waterfall seemed to lull and distract Daeson and Raviel. "Even in this chaos it is enchanting. I didn't think such a place could exist."

Daeson looked over at his love, tempted to be enchanted by the scene along with her. He reached for her hand. "Yes...it is lovely."

Raviel turned to him, eyes glowing warm from the garden. Daeson held her for a moment. "But this isn't why we're here."

"No, I thought not." Raviel responded.

"We're here because of him," he clarified and nodded to a place across the river.

Just then Linden Lockridge and Xandra stepped out onto an ornate alcove landing that hung over the waters of the Yeln River. Linden sat down on one of the elaborate benches, brooding in anger. Xandra was trying hard to console him, stroking his arm and shoulder as she whispered into his ear. Daeson and Raviel watched for a moment, unnoticed. The Protector began to resonate on Daeson's arm, and Raviel tensed as Daeson turned to face his nemesis.

"Linden Lockridge!" Daeson shouted across the watery expanse.

The Chancellor of Jypton snapped his head upward. Linden stood and faced Daeson with a broad stance. "You!"

Xandra turned and lifted her com device to her mouth, but before either could respond, Daeson spoke the words of Ell Yon. "Your refusal to yield to the command of Sovereign Ell Yon will continue to bring tragedy on the people of Jypton."

Daeson pulled back the sleeve on his tunic and knelt to one knee. Blue arcing flames danced up and down the Protector as he put his fist to the water's edge. In a burst of translucent power, the Protector sent waves of pulsing energy into the river.

"Guards!" Linden shouted, but before anyone responded, the Protector was done.

From Daeson's point of contact with the water, a bizarre biological phenomenon began to spread outward. A bright red substance spread quickly across the river. It also began to spread up the banks, but at a much slower pace.

"Back to the palace!" Linden ordered Xandra.

"Come quickly!" Daeson said to Raviel as he stood and pulled her away from the water's edge, where the tide of red was climbing up the bank after them.

Raviel took her cue of urgency from Daeson and ran back the way they had come. Once inside the foliage of the garden, the threat of the red plague seemed to disappear, but it was only a temporary reprieve from the impending doom.

"What is it?" Raviel asked as they ran, their pace now at a full sprint.

"It's called blood algae. Linden and I encountered it once when we went swimming in a lake in the eastern region." He stopped to take a few breaths.

"What does it do?" Raviel asked between breaths.

"If it contacts people, it creates a painful rash that lasts for days. For plant life...it kills it."

He looked back over his shoulder, then resumed the sprint in a direction that would be the shortest route out of the Aqua Gardens. "Faster!" He exclaimed.

Raviel dared look back, and the alarm in her eyes was evident. The blood algae was quickly overtaking the entire garden, covering grass, trees, flowers and bushes. Like red paint spilled on a canvas, the beautiful scene from just a moment earlier was being consumed with each passing second.

Though very painful, Daeson's previous encounter with blood algae had been mild and brief. The lake they had been swimming in at the time had only small patches of the algae along its shores, but their limited exposure was a lesson neither he nor Linden would ever forget. What was happening here was unprecedented. Somehow the Protector had hyper-accelerated the algae's growth—and probably its affect, Daeson hypothesized.

The edge of the garden was just ahead. Daeson and Raviel sprinted as fast as their legs would carry them, barely reaching the edge of the foliage before the blood algae completely encased the garden. They continued their sprint until they were well clear.

"We should be safe now," Daeson said, huffing from the exertion of the run.

Raviel didn't look convinced

"Are you sure?" she asked, looking nervously toward the gardens.

Both of them were bent over, resting on their knees as they tried to fill their lungs.

"It shouldn't be able to travel across stone and concrete, at least not as fast. The river connects just about every garden in the city, so we will have to avoid all gardens on the way back."

Raviel shook her head. "How far will this infestation go?"

"I'm not sure. Hopefully all of the Rayleans heeded my warning and stored three days of drinking water as I instructed."

Raviel wrinkled her nose, then held up her arm to cover her mouth and nose. "What's the horrid smell?"

Daeson shook his head. "I recognize the smell, but it was never this strong before. It must be a result of the algae consuming the garden."

They looked on in wonder as the once lush and beautiful garden wilted under the attack of the blood algae. The river in the distance turned bright red as the algae assimilated the whole of it. The stench of the algae gas was nearly suffocating.

"Come...our journey back will be longer and more risky."

The next day Daeson received word that two other major cities on Jypton had endured the same blood algae infestation. Linden tried to import water from offshore desalination plants, but no matter what the Jyptonians did to try to isolate their supply, the blood algae found a way to contaminate it. The infestation lasted for three days, and without fresh drinking water, all operations on the planet were affected, almost to the point of shutting down. Through it all, Linden's fury was further poured out on Rayleans throughout the globe. Raviel, Tig, Wescott, and even Trisk tried to offer words of encouragement to Daeson, but he still found it difficult to endure. The people had suffered greatly, and it seemed as though nothing would change the heart of Linden.

In the weeks that followed, the judgment of Sovereign Ell Yon continued. Food supplies were spoiled, massive solar flares disrupted global communication, a viral infection causing painful lesions spread throughout the planet, an infestation of the dreaded Flesh Gnats tormented the Royals and Elite alike, and a programming virus completely disrupted navigation and industrial automation technology. Through it all, Linden refused to relent, and the persecution of the Rayleans intensified. It was only after a global power outage that the mighty Chancellor of Jypton finally called for Daeson.

Linden gazed at Daeson without the rage that had previously been evident. Something had finally changed. "Come to me, Daeson...you and she who is with you, and we'll talk."

Daeson shook his head. "No, Linden, I'll come alone."

"You and she have nothing to fear, Daeson. I want to see the one who changed the heart of my friend. I can honor such courage."

Daeson stared at Linden, still not trusting the Jyptonian chancellor, but he felt a tug on his arm. He reached to his belt and turned off the hologram projection. Raviel stood next to him.

"It's okay. If it will bring this all to an end, I'll go with you."

Take her.

Daeson nodded and returned to Linden's royal court. "We'll come tomorrow."

Daeson would go, and he would take Raviel with him, but he knew they would not be alone.

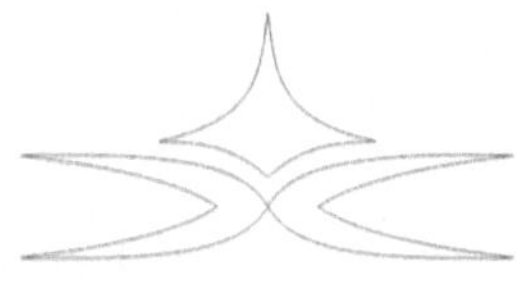

CHAPTER

11

Deadly Duo

Reclamation Ceremony — A Raylean tradition symbolizing the purging of one's body of the genetic altering agent Deltum Prime. It is a representation of a future hope prophesied by the oracle Eziam.

Raviel arrived back at the refugee camp in the Shadow Forests near the city of Capell early in the evening. Daeson had encouraged her to make the trip, knowing she wanted to check up on Petia, but he had insisted that Tig accompany her. Daeson needed time to prepare for their meeting with Lockridge the next day. Tig seemed quite willing to oblige, and Raviel wondered if it had something to do with the subtle exchange of smiles she'd noticed between Tig and Zee'la, the medtech he had assisted in the Abyssian Trenches refugee camp. Whatever the reason, his willingness to accompany her was convenient and timely.

"Raviel!" Petia exclaimed as she ran to Raviel with outstretched arms.

Raviel scooped up Petia in her arms and hugged her. "Petia, it's so good to see you again!" Raviel smiled.

"I missed you sooooo much!" Petia held tightly to Raviel's neck and refused to let go.

"And I you." Raviel's eyes reddened with tears, feeling the love of the child pour into her soul.

Petia finally released Raviel and turned to look in all directions.

"I'm sorry, Petia, Rivet's not with us."

Petia's smile diminished some. "It's okay. Will you tell her 'Hi' for me?"

"Of course," Raviel agreed, setting her back on the ground.

Petia grabbed her hand. "Come and meet my friends!" she exclaimed.

For the next two hours, Raviel played and talked with Petia. She joined the child in her world of pretend and rediscovered her own childhood for a time. In an odd way, the escape to the realm of play helped heal some of the scars the cruel world had left on her heart and also provided a reprieve from the solemn mission that lay before her.

That night, as Petia curled up next to her, Raviel's thoughts turned back to Daeson and the invitation to meet with Chancellor Lockridge. The more she thought about it, the more her stomach churned and flitted in waves of anxiety. Would she be strong enough to face the tyrant? What if it was a trap?

Knowing she would be by Daeson's side helped, but what finally calmed her spirit was the knowledge that the Immortal Sovereign Ell Yon had promised to see them through this. He would be there too, through the Protector. His ways were indeed mysterious and often unknown, but he never broke a promise—never! The calm and comfort of Ell Yon's promised presence was what finally allowed her to ease into sleep.

Morning came quickly, and after having said goodbye to Petia and Zee'la, Raviel and Tig were back in Athlone with Daeson, preparing to meet with the enemy of her family, of all Rayleans, and of Ell Yon himself.

As Daeson and Raviel stepped off the transport, they were immediately surround by twenty royal guards, their Talons all charged and ready. Their captain approached, eyeing the vambrace on Daeson's arm closely. These guards would have all seen the demonstration of Ell Yon's power by the Protector weeks earlier in the courtyard. It's why Daeson and Raviel were not immediately bound.

"You will remove all weapons before we proceed to the Chancellor," the captain ordered.

Daeson stared at the captain for a moment. Evidence of lesions that were almost healed was scattered across his neck and hands.

"No."

The captain clenched his teeth as one of the other guards reached for Raviel's Talon. Daeson held up his hand to the guard, the Protector on his arm pulsing with power.

"Don't touch her," he said.

The guard slowly backed away, and Daeson turned his attention back to the captain.

"Take us to him now, or we're leaving."

The captain hesitated, then turned about and led them up the courtyard. Memories of the execution Linden had perpetrated threatened to steal away Daeson's poise as he remembered that fateful day his mother died. Signs of the blood bath were still evident everywhere. Daeson's heart was crushed once more as he passed the place where he had held his mother in his arms for the last time. Anger threatened to dominate him as he remembered every detail of her face...filled with pain not for herself but for him. He reminded himself of the thousands of Rayleans that were all feeling the same loss at this very moment, and he steeled himself for the encounter ahead.

Daeson and Raviel entered Linden's royal court, the spectacle and scorn of a hundred Elite and their entourage in full array. In spite of the danger this encounter would mean for Raviel, Daeson was supremely grateful to have her by his side. The court was just as Daeson remembered it. Positioned one hundred feet above the rest of the palace grounds, the open terrace gave the sitting Chancellor a grand view of the capital city of Athlone. Though scarred by meteors and ravaged gardens, the city still possessed much of its ancient beauty.

In the skies beyond was a backdrop displaying Jypton's military supremacy...enumerable Starcraft and destroyers aligned in formations of war. Linden had staged this meeting well. Within the court itself, massive columns supported a colossal dome of exquisite architectural design. The intricate melding of modern and medieval worlds was on display, but the ancient beauty of the artisans of the past certainly dominated the décor.

Daeson was immediately drawn back to his past, where this place and these people exuded overwhelming authority in an institution of great power as of yet unequaled in the galaxy. Seated on its throne was perhaps Jypton's most intelligent and resourceful chancellor yet. And as the result of his actions in recent months, perhaps the most ruthless…a man he had once called brother.

Daeson beheld the splendor and for an instant doubted. Part of him wanted to turn and run. How could he stand against such an immovable force? He stole a quick glance toward his valiant vice commander. The impact of the splendor and power on Raviel was obvious…she too was overcome. Her eyes met his, and he saw the fear…the doubt…the insanity of their feeble efforts.

Remember me…remember whom you serve!

Chills flowed up and down Daeson's arms and legs as the image of Ell Yon filled his mind—his perfect goodness and absolute power. The protector resonated with a holy response in the presence of such defiant evil. The moment must have been evident in his gaze for Raviel's countenance steeled, and her shoulders straightened.

Four guards walked beside and aft of Daeson and Raviel as they approached Linden. Daeson had always known that Linden would be well suited to rule as Chancellor of Jypton one day, but his childhood friend, now turned bitter enemy, wore the crown all too well. Though young, he was dauntless in his use of the highest position on the planet and throughout this region of space to exact his desires on his people. Standing beside him was the beautiful and skilled Xandra, although her beauty was now tainted by a darkness that Daeson had never observed in her before.

Linden scowled as Daeson and Raviel approached. Xandra glared with dark eyes, her particular contempt for Raviel clearly displayed. She placed a hand on Linden's shoulder and leaned close to whisper something in his ear. A wry smile crossed his lips.

Daeson and Raviel stopped at the bottom of the marble steps that separated the Chancellor from the common people. For a few seconds, the royal couple simply stared down at them, eyes full of loathing and scorn for the discord that had come to their kingdom because of these two lowly Drudge. Daeson became uneasy. It was apparent that Linden wasn't truly in the mindset to talk, let alone acquiesce to his demands.

"I am weary of you, Daeson...weary of your petty tricks. They annoy me, and if you think for one moment that a little inconvenience will cause me to yield to your absurd request, you are sorely mistaken."

"You called me here to talk," Daeson replied, his anger growing. "Aren't you ready for this to end? Sovereign Ell Yon demands you release his people, or more destruction will come!"

Linden leaned forward. "I'll not cease from hunting you and your rebels down until all that remains is the feeble, weak-minded Drudge that you truly are." His anger and volume began to grow. "I own every inch of this planet, and there is no place that you can hide for long. I will destroy all of you!"

Linden's wrath was propelling him to an emotional outrage Daeson had never seen before. The young chancellor took a calming breath and leaned back in his chair as he looked out across the expanse of the terrace and into his kingdom.

"These minor inconveniences are nothing to me," Linden said, waving a hand as if to shoo a gnat. "Tell me, Daeson, how are your people faring during your grand rescue attempt?"

Daeson offered no answer and no expression. He simply stood and wondered at the dark transformation of his childhood friend. The Deitum Prime had done its job well, and in spite of the obvious contempt Linden had for him, he was momentarily filled with pity. Had it not been for Raviel, he would have never believed the truth of the Deitum Prime conspiracy. It was clear that he needed to exit quickly so as not to put Raviel in harm's way. He felt duped and was angry for it.

"What?" Linden exclaimed. "Have you no witty reply...no new threat?" Linden stood and stepped down two steps. Xandra followed beside him.

"Ell Yon—" Daeson began.

"Do not speak that preposterous fictitious name in my court!" Linden screamed, his face turning red as he pointed at Daeson. "You are a cowardly imbecile. It disgusts me to think that I once thought you a friend."

"You don't understand the truth or the power of Ell Yon," Daeson replied. He stole a glance toward Xandra, and their eyes met. For one wisp of a moment, her eyes softened as they both seemed to remember the years of affection they once held for each other. Her love was the one thing Linden never could seem to win.

Linden scoffed. He glanced back at Xandra, her countenance now unreadable, but whatever he saw seemed to fuel his fury. He looked back at Daeson, a dark contemplative look shadowing his eyes. He paused, then scanned his court as the Elite and guards waiting to do his bidding, along with three of the highest of the Jyptonian Royal Council, watched intently. Linden lifted his chin.

"Clear the court," Linden commanded.

An astonished exchange ensued between some of the Elite, but Linden was impatient. "Clear the court now!" Linden repeated.

The massive room quickly emptied of all except for six guards and the three Elite councilmen nearest Linden. Daeson wondered if Linden's previous words were simply a way to save face in front of his court.

Perhaps the man truly was ready to yield, but in private.

"Everyone," Linden said looking directly at his council.

"But Chancellor," the lead council remonstrated, motioning toward Daeson. "This man has demonstrated...an ability to..."

"You think him more powerful than I?" Linden rebuked with clenched teeth. "Out!"

The three men hesitated, their objection demonstrated appropriately, and then slowly turned to leave. Linden looked to the captain of his guards.

"Under no circumstances are we to be disturbed."

The captain nodded, then bowed and led the other guards out after the three councilmen. He closed the massive doors behind him.

Daeson looked over at Raviel. She lifted one eyebrow. Here in the royal court of Jypton stood the mechtech who had defied a world and inspired her people to stand against tyranny. Daeson drew confidence from the fiery spirit within her.

Linden descended the last few steps and slowly walked to Raviel, as Xandra came to stand on the last step, a position from which she could look down upon both of them with contempt.

"Now it's just us, Daeson," Linden crooned as he slowly made his way around them. "Let's be honest, shall we?"

He finished his smug inspection and came back to stand beside Xandra. He reached for her, and she took his hand. Then he pulled her close and whispered something in her ear. Xandra stared directly at Daeson throughout the entire exchange. Linden then turned and smiled at them.

"This is really about you and me, isn't it?" Linden began. "Your jealousy and feeble attempt throughout life to best me. But you never could quite do it, could you?"

Linden seemed delighted by a new thought. He left Xandra and stood directly in front of Daeson, eye to eye, staring into the depths of his soul. What Daeson saw in Linden reminded him of an icy soul he'd seen once before in the gaze of Chancellor Treville.

"Let's end this now. Fight me…Talon to Talon…to the death. Let us put an end to this…this charade of a contest."

Xandra's countenance changed—now blank and indeterminate.

Raviel reached for Daeson's arm.

"I see your pet Drudge is concerned," Linden derided, reaching for his Talon. "And she should be. You've never beaten me in Talon sparring, but we won't be sparring this time." He looked down at the Protector on Daeson's forearm.

"Put your toy aside and face me as a man."

Raviel turned to Daeson.

"No, Daeson. He still wears the Triad. I don't trust him."

Xandra came at Raviel. "Quiet, slave! Drudge do not speak in this court!"

Raviel's eyes ignited, and she turned to face Xandra, but Daeson stepped between them, his back to Xandra. He looked down into Raviel's eyes—eyes filled with concern and love.

"It's okay," he whispered. "I don't trust him either."

Daeson reached for the Protector and pulled it from his arm. It yielded its bond, and Daeson instantly felt alone. He lifted Raviel's wrist and placed the Protector in the palm of her hand. He winked and then turned back to face Linden and Xandra— unshielded by the Protector.

Linden tilted his head, somewhat astonished at Daeson. Were it not for the presence of Xandra, Daeson would have fully expected Linden to blast him with the Triad and be done with him, but Daeson knew the pride of the man wouldn't allow such cowardly action. Linden slowly reached for the Triad and pulled it off of his chest. Without breaking his cold glare, Linden handed the Triad to Xandra while simultaneously extending his Talon.

Daeson nodded toward Raviel, and she unwillingly stepped away. He hesitated before drawing and extending his Talon, its arcing blue stasis field barely visible on the silvered edge of the blade. Daeson couldn't deny the swelling apprehension in his gut. Linden was the best Talon fighter on the planet, and his fight would be fueled by a decade of jealousy, spite, envy, and now hatred. He would hold nothing back as he perhaps once had done. In his own power, Daeson knew he could never defeat such a foe, but something was different now. Daeson had trained with the Commander and wasn't fighting for himself. He was fighting for Ell Yon and for the future of the Rayleans...for his people.

The two men slowly circled each other. There were no more words to be spoken. This was the end. Linden attacked first. Talons collided in an explosive burst of blue energy as the stasis fields of both Talons resisted one another. Daeson defended, waiting and searching out the unhindered aggression of Linden. The ruler of Jypton attacked with the precision of a master, and Daeson was alarmed at the perfect and powerful moves of the man. Linden's skills had improved beyond what Daeson had witnessed firsthand in the past.

Daeson focused and relied on the training the Commander had given him. With each encounter, he learned to expect the unexpected from Linden. Slice after slice, cut after cut, and parry for thrust, the two men engaged in an epic encounter that would have been the marvel of the galaxy had others been allowed to watch. Xandra observed from her perch atop the throne steps and Raviel from the far side of the court— both wearing faces of grave concern.

When the time was right, Daeson responded to Linden's barrage of attacks with an offensive counter. Linden scowled as he found himself in retreat from the perfectly timed blade of Daeson's Talon. The fight moved from the steps to the floor and back again. At one point, Linden found an opportunity to end Daeson, but Daeson ducked at the last second and Linden's Talon crashed into one of the massive columns sending fragments of granite in all directions.

Daeson lunged at Linden, retracting his blade to long-knife range to execute a quick plunge to the abdomen, but Linden was ready and caught it with his free hand. The next few seconds held the ferocity of a close-quartered knife fight. Daeson made one slight miscalculation, and Linden was able to bring the arcing edge of his knife across his left shoulder. The searing blade sliced through his jacket and opened his skin. Daeson twisted and countered to shorten the success of the cut. Though his blade was not in a position to counter in kind, his fist was. Daeson put the full force of his punch into Linden's jaw, and it was enough to separate the two combatants. Daeson immediately re-extended his Talon to full length as Linden stumbled backward and did the same.

Daeson could feel the warm blood oozing down his arm. He glanced toward Raviel. Her face was sick with worry. Linden shook his head, clearing himself from Daeson's landed punch.

The two men faced off again, both breathing deeply from the exertion.

"You've been practicing," Linden said and spit blood. "It won't matter. You and I both know how this is going to end...the same way it has always ended."

Linden's face filled with disdain as he attacked viciously, holding nothing back. His advances became reckless as he pushed in for the kill. Daeson found himself in steady retreat, astonished at the renewed power Linden seemed to hold. Yet Linden's power did not compare to the power he had seen in the Commander.

Daeson listened to the voice of his master and bent but did not break. His defense synchronized perfectly with each cut, slice, and thrust until he recognized one familiar motion that would leave Linden open. And Daeson took advantage of it. He caught Linden's last slice with the flat of the Talon, feigned a retreat, then countered with a cut that found its mark.

Linden yelled as Daeson's blade sliced across his Talon arm. Linden cursed and retreated, quickly transferring the Talon to his left hand. But the wound did nothing to thwart the man's aggression. Linden came at Daeson with renewed rage. Daeson was careful not to underestimate the skill of Linden, even when he was using his weaker Talon arm. And Daeson was wise to take this precaution, for Linden was adept with both hands.

The fight became awkward for Daeson since he had not often fought a left-handed opponent. He adapted as quickly as possible and learned the weaknesses of

Linden's new form. Within minutes, Daeson was once more taking the offense, and Linden was in steady retreat. The anger in his countenance transformed to utter hatred as the outcome of the fight was becoming obvious.

Daeson pressed hard to finish the fight, and at the last moment, he saw Linden's finger move to the mode selector that would transform his Talon to an energy discharge weapon. Daeson didn't hesitate. With one powerful two-handed cut, he executed a blow to the base of Linden's blade from across the left side of his body just before it had finished retracting. The force blew the Talon from Linden's grip, and it skidded across the marble floor as Linden stumbled backward and landed prone on the steps of his throne.

Daeson quickly covered him, but suddenly the space around him erupted in a blaze of red energy that sent him flying across the floor of the court. He crashed up against one of the columns and nearly lost consciousness.

"No!" Raviel screamed as she ran to him.

Daeson tried to clear his head, but the pain across his whole body was crippling. His mind fought to stay cognizant. He looked up at Raviel, her face filled with anger and concern. Daeson looked toward where Linden lay and saw Xandra glaring at them, the Triad fastened to her chest, her eyes glowing red with fury. She was a sight of intimidating evil power. Daeson looked back to Raviel as she tried to hold his head up.

"Daeson!" she said, gently touching his chest. She tried to lift him, but he could still hardly breathe.

"You have to get up!" Raviel urged. She grabbed his right arm and began to press the Protector on to it, but Daeson stopped her.

"No," he grimaced. He grabbed the Protector, then pushed it onto her arm. "You must—"

"But I don't—"

"Just listen," Daeson wheezed.

The Protector finished forming to Raviel's arm, and her eyes filled with wonder—then strength that could come only from Ell Yon surged within her. Daeson heard the Triad's rising power and then its discharge. This would be the end of them unless—

Without turning, Raviel lifted her arm, and a blue protective shield enveloped them both just before the deadly beam of the Triad reached them. He heard Xandra's hate-filled scream as she poured all she had into the Triad's death beam. She was a woman now fully controlled by Dracus.

Daeson looked up into the eyes of Raviel and saw eternity. The beauty of an innocent soul possessed by the power of Ell Yon was breathtaking. Raviel looked down at him, her eyes reflecting the blue shield of Ell Yon and her arm still holding the Protector in position to deflect the energy of the Triad. A knowing calm that could only exist in the presence of the Sovereign Ell Yon enveloped her countenance.

Finally, Xandra stopped her attack, and Raviel stood to face her. Raviel didn't hesitate. She unleashed the power of the Protector with a burst of pure energy that collided with the Triad. An invisible shield protected Xandra from the raw impact of the Protector, but the force was too much, sending Xandra flying backward to rest against Linden's throne.

She recovered much quicker than a mere mortal could and came at Raviel. A moment later, Linden had recovered his Talon and was coming at Daeson. He struggled to regain his feet and face Linden. The first few attacks nearly ended him, but he was able to thwart Linden's advance and counter with his own volley of cuts and slices. Soon the court erupted in a battle of immortal proportions...Protector versus Triad, Chancellor versus Navi, two drones of Dracus versus two vessels of Ell Yon.

The massive doors of the court opened, and six guards entered, their own Talons charged and ready. It took them a moment to assess what was happening as the unworldly battle around them transpired. Daeson saw one take aim at Raviel. He transformed his Talon and took the guard out. The other guards opened fire on Daeson, but Raviel paused her fight with Xandra for a split second to blast the remaining five guards with an energy burst. More would be on their way.

Xandra attacked once more, but Raviel countered with a burst against her red-headed nemesis. She slammed up against one of the massive columns. This time Xandra did not rise, and Linden immediately broke from his fight with Daeson and ran to her. She was bleeding, and the glow in her eyes dimmed.

"Stop!" Linden yelled. The fury in his face replaced by pain...the pain of seeing a lover hurt.

Xandra reached for him, coughing, wincing.

Linden looked up at Daeson, his eyes regaining the fury of a wrathful king. He reached up to the arm of his throne and slid his finger across a control, then pressed a button.

"No matter what you think, you have lost. This day, you will all die!"

Raviel joined Daeson at his side.

"We have to go, Daeson," she urged.

"What have you done?" Daeson said, stepping forward, but Linden just smiled wryly.

Raviel pulled the Protector from her arm and pushed the vambrace back onto Daeson's. A surge of renewed strength and wisdom filled him.

"The guards are nearly here!" Raviel pleaded, but there was nowhere to go. The approaching guards blocked the entrance to the court. Daeson's gaze remained on Linden.

"What have you done?" Daeson demanded.

"See for yourself," Linden pointed to the terrace. "It is the end of you and of all Rayleans!"

Daeson looked out past the balcony of the terrace and saw a swarm rising up from multiple buildings on the palace compound and from two other buildings in the city. At first he didn't understand, but as illumination hit him, a visceral reaction of great remorse rose up in his soul. Thousands upon thousands of termination drones were rising up and spreading out into the city. Linden had just ordered the genocide of all Rayleans.

A dreadful whisper came to him.

"You don't know what you've done, Linden. By your own hand, you have brought immense tragedy to Jypton."

Daeson lifted the Protector high into the air. Linden flinched, but the resulting action was not for his own end, but for that of his kingdom. An electromagnetic wave exploded out from the Protector that carried with it a command.

"It is not the Rayleans who will die today, but one in four of all Jyptonians will perish by your hand. And one in four tomorrow, and the day after that until you yield to the voice of Ell Yon and let his people go."

Linden's eyes narrowed.

"You have no such power!" he scoffed. "Tomorrow I will be rid of the stench of the Drudge, and today I will hang your corpse for all of Jypton to see. Guards!"

Daeson frowned, lingering in sadness for the essence of evil Linden had become. Raviel took his hand, pulling him toward the balcony.

"Now, Daeson!" she urged, but it was too late. Dozens of Talon-armed guards burst into the court.

"Kill them!" Linden yelled.

Daeson finally yielded to Raviel's plea to flee with her. Multiple plasma bursts from Talon fire fractured the air around them as they turned and sprinted toward the thick stone rail that lined the edge of the balcony. Together they jumped to the top of the rail, hesitating for one brief moment as they looked down one hundred feet to the palace grounds below them. Daeson's stomach churned as he considered their next move. More Talon fire ruptured a portion of the rail next to them sending fragments of debris everywhere. With nowhere to go, they leapt off the balcony into the wide-open expanse of air. A fraction of a second later, the invisible form of Daeson's Starcraft materialized below them with enough time for Raviel and him to time their landing. More Talon bursts flew just above their heads.

"Hang on," Daeson said as they lay down on the back of the Starcraft, its cloak reengaging. "Get us out of here, Tig," Daeson ordered.

Seconds later, they were whizzing between buildings, undetected. Daeson looked over at Raviel and she at him.

"You're amazing," he said.

She leaned into him. The moment of respite was brief, for a swarm of death was descending on the city of Athlone and on every other city of Jypton.

Daeson spoke into his com band.

"The time has come. Tell Chieftain Wescott to transmit this message to all clan leaders across the planet—all Rayleans who trust in Ell Yon must fulfill the reclamation ceremony immediately and keep it until the morning."

"Roger," Tig replied. A moment later Tig responded. "Message sent. How are you two doing up there?"

"It's a bit breezy. Looking forward to setting down soon."

"Roger that, touch down in two mics," Tig replied.

Daeson looked over at Raviel and read the concern in her face. It was warranted. This would be a dark day for everyone.

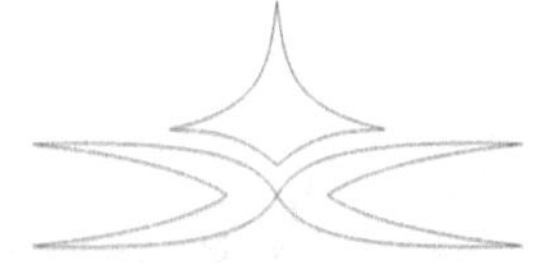

CHAPTER

12

Night of Sorrows

The next twelve hours were a living nightmare for every living soul on the planet of Jypton. Because of the Protector's intervention, hundreds of thousands of termination drones methodically began canvassing every city and village on the planet. Mysteriously, the drones passed by those that had the reclamation mark of Ell Yon upon their brows and temples. For one out of four of all others, the drones either injected the poison or caused them to breathe the mist. The drones were not respecters of person, class, wealth, age, or gender. The wails of woe testified to the totality of the death curse issued by the lips of Linden. Though the faithful Rayleans were spared, it was difficult for them not to fear or be overwhelmed by the utter despair of the planet.

By dawn of the following morning, the first wave of death had passed. Daeson, Raviel, Tig, Trisk, and Rivet stepped out into the street. The stillness and silence were eerie. They walked through Drudgetown toward Athlone's city proper, occasionally seeing the body of a sentry strewn across his aerobike or laying silently on the street. Once past the border of Drudgetown, the scene became one of complete despair. Bodies were scattered everywhere, and for those Jyptonians brave enough to venture out, the weeping was intense.

The five comrades stood on a desolate garden terrace that had been ravaged by the blood algae just days before. This vantage point afforded them a view of a large section of the city. They stood stunned and in awe of the human devastation. Grav-vehicles were strewn every which way. The smell of death was in its infancy, and Daeson could only imagine what would happen if Linden's pride continued to keep him from capitulating.

"What now?" Trisk asked. He looked at Daeson with stern eyes. "I can see this going only one of two ways."

Tig broke from his gaze on the city.

"If Lockridge doesn't relent, he will retaliate and kill even more Rayleans today," he said soberly. "Our people are afraid—not without cause."

Daeson took a deep breath. "I must go to him."

Raviel looked over at him.

"Alone," he added.

"Send the holo-drone," Raviel protested.

"No, I must see him face-to-face."

Raviel's eyes narrowed.

"Ell Yon has brought us this far. He'll not abandon us now," Daeson affirmed.

The five walked back to Drudgetown, and Daeson stopped beside one of the fallen sentries. He went to the aerobike and searched for the starting mechanism. Tig stepped up and entered a code on the glass instrument panel, and the aerobike purred to life.

"Be careful, Daeson," Tig said.

Daeson looked at the brave souls that surrounded him, grateful they had the courage to see this through.

"Be ready and have your com links open."

Daeson nodded at Raviel, then engaged the grav-engine on the aerobike. It lifted into the air and Daeson accelerated down the streets of Athlone taking the shortest route that would lead to the palace. Daeson saw up close the full devastation of the termination drone's impact.

He tried to subdue the rising feelings of apprehension about facing Linden again, but to no avail. He wondered if he would have to face the full force of the remaining military to get to him, but as Daeson approached the palace, no guards met him. More bodies lay in the streets and in the courtyards leading up to the palace; some had friends and family mourning over them, but most of the prone were alone.

Drones were everywhere. Most were resting idly on terrace wall ledges and steps, but Daeson occasionally saw one whiz by on some unthinkable mission. The fear incited by these small floating machines had all but paralyzed the Jyptonians. It was the first time these people had ever faced such tragedy—a level of tragedy the Rayleans had faced every day for the past twelve hundred years. But in spite of the justified recompense, Daeson felt no joy...no satisfaction. Death was always horrible and final.

He left the aerobike in the main courtyard and walked up the grand stairway to the Hall of the Elite, then road the grav-platform up to Linden's great throne room. He entered the great room unchecked. Even in this esteemed place of power, multiple bodies were strewn about the court. The click of his boots echoed off the marble walls. Had the curse of the drones killed even Linden himself?

Daeson saw a man hunched over at the foot of the throne. He approached and climbed the first few steps.

"Linden," Daeson called gently.

The robe of the Chancellor rose up and down in harmony with the deep sobs of a broken man. Linden turned and glared at Daeson, eyes red and swollen. Lying in his lap was the beautiful Xandra, still, white, lifeless.

"You! Look what you've done!" Linden screamed through his tears. "You killed her, Daeson...this is all your doing!"

Daeson couldn't help the tears that threatened to fall. His mind flashed back to the day the three of them stood on the cliff ready to leap to a flying adventure toward the anti-graviton field. How both Linden and Daeson had risked their lives to save Xandra, and now...now she was no more.

"It's not over, Linden," Daeson said, steeling himself.

"I hate you!" Linden screamed as he rose up, drawing his talon. Daeson heard it charge.

"I warned you," Daeson rebuked. "Sovereign Ell Yon declared this by your own hand."

Linden aimed his talon at Daeson, eyes filled with fury. The Triad at his chest was glowing fiery red.

Daeson held his hand up, the Protector pulsing with ribbons of blue power.

Just then, two of his three royal councilmen entered the court, followed by the captain of the guards. They hurried to Linden' side. The captain of the guard drew his talon, unsure if or how to protect Linden. The two councilmen ignored Daeson altogether.

"Chancellor Lockridge, the termination drones are still operating outside of our control. Over two hundred thousand Jyptonians are dead, and that is just in Athlone. Other cities are reporting the same travesty. Councilman Havir is dead as well."

Linden locked his hate-filled gaze on Daeson, his hands now trembling from the war within his soul. Daeson could imagine the voice of Dracus coercing, pushing, and manipulating Linden's mind.

"This must end!" one of the councilmen declared.

Linden's fierce countenance intensified yet further. He turned his talon on the councilman and walked toward him. Daeson slowly lowered his hand. Linden pushed the muzzle of his talon into the chest of the councilman. At first the man's eyes grew wide, then he lifted his chin.

"If this doesn't end, my lord, we will all be dead one way or another."

Linden clenched his teeth, gave an excruciating yell then rotated away. "Why haven't you destroyed the drones if they aren't under our control?" Linden demanded.

"We've tried, Chancellor," the captain of the guard replied. "When one of the bots is attacked, ten others swarm to kill the attacker, either by injection or the mist. No one dares lift a hand against them for they will endure certain death."

The other councilman stepped forward. "They were designed to carry enough of the mist to terminate twenty Drudge each. Based on the number of drones that have been released, they could decimate the populations of nearly every major city."

Linden went to sit on the steps next to Xandra's body, burying his head in his hands.

"Somehow they have access to all of our security codes. There is no door or chamber they cannot open. If this isn't stopped, there will be no Jyptonians left to govern, my lord," said the first councilman, fear and distress lacing every word he spoke.

Linden slowly lifted his head to look at Daeson, and both men turned his direction as well. The captain of the guard slowly lowered his talon. Linden stared long at Daeson, then lowered his gaze back to Xandra.

"Give him the transports," he ordered. "Without pilots, they're not going anywhere."

Linden reached over and gently stroked Xandra's beautiful red hair.

"Now call off the drones and release my people from this torment," Linden demanded.

"Control of the drones will be returned to you when the last Raylean transport has left Jypton," Daeson insisted. "Not a moment sooner."

Linden glared once more at Daeson. "I give you eight days, Starlore. After that I don't care what these wretched drones do to us."

Daeson looked at the two councilmen. "Come with me so we can discuss how to expedite our departure." As he turned and began walking toward the massive doors of the court, he heard the steps of both councilmen following close behind.

"I curse the day my father brought you into our palace, you traitor!" Linden screamed from behind him. "I curse the Immortal you call Ell Yon! May the cold wasteland of space be your tomb, Starlore!"

Daeson and his unlikely escorts exited the great court with the cursing and ranting of Linden in the distance, but Daeson didn't care…Ell Yon had won their freedom. The time to leave Jypton had come.

CHAPTER

13

Freedom

Daeson stood once more in the midst of the circle of the twelve Raylean clan chieftains using the visual QECs.

"We have dispatched enough transports to each of your regions to allow all Rayleans passage off of Jypton," Daeson began. "But time is short. We have less than eight days to plan our departure. Obviously space is limited, so only one bag per person is allowed. Most of the cargo holds will be loaded with supplies for the journey."

All at once, nine of the twelve chieftains erupted with questions and comments in a roar of voices. Daeson looked at Raviel—she just shrugged.

"Please…one at time," he urged, but to no avail.

"Enough!" Trisk finally shouted. "You all know that I was perhaps the greatest dissenter of this assembly when it came to this man." He pointed to Daeson. "But I have come to believe that he is a man of his word who deserves our respect. Continue, Starlore."

Daeson nodded his appreciation in Trisk's direction.

"I will do my best to address each of your questions and concerns," Daeson clarified. "VeTarra first," he commenced pointing to the chieftain of the Nasher Clan.

"This is absurd. Where are we going? Who will pilot the transports? How can we possibly mobilize the entire Raylean population in just eight days? The logistics of such a thing is simply impossible!"

"Agreed," piped in the chieftain of Revitar. "You have enraged the whole of Jypton by killing millions. Our people are forced to leave with you whether they want to or not. If they don't, they'll be executed. This is preposterous! You've ruined us...destroyed our people!"

"We never wanted your help, Starlore," followed another, his face reflecting the scorn in his voice. "Now we will all die in the wasteland of space because of your thoughtless actions!"

"Who among us has seen such a thing as we have seen these past weeks?" exclaimed Chieftain Galder Wescott of the Baraquet Clan. He stepped forward from his place in the circle to look at each of the others. "Have you so quickly forgotten the heavy hand of the Jyptonians we have lived under for the past twelve hundred years? VeTarra, I myself have heard you speak strongly on behalf of the Plexus in their effort to free us from the bondage of the Jyptonians. And you as well, Asdor of Revitar. Here we stand on the precipice of the very freedom you desired, yet you still cower at the feet of Jypton. Have you not seen the hand of Ell Yon in this man? Who here could have exacted such a day of their own volition?"

Wescott turned and looked at each of his fellow chieftains. "Our own efforts to mount a resistance over the past one hundred years had utterly failed, yet here we are. Surely the Sovereign Ell Yon has orchestrated this day and shame be on us all should we shrink back from the victory that he offers his people...our people...the people of Rayl! Stand like the men and women of old and take back your heritage...take back your legacy. Take back your destiny as the people of the mighty and Immortal Ell Yon!"

The assembly fell silent as each chieftain quietly endured the convicting words of Wescott. The white-haired man gently returned to his place in the circle. He looked at Daeson...waiting. Daeson swallowed to recover from the wise, impassioned words of the man. Chills flowed up and down his spine as the stark reality of what was happening fell upon them all. Sovereign Ell Yon was indeed with them, and regardless of the insurmountable task before them, they would follow wherever the Sovereign led!

"The pilots delivering the transports are Jyptonian, but they will not remain with the ships. We will provide our own pilots."

"How?" replied one of the chieftains. He looked toward Wescott. "I mean, do you have access to other trained Rayleans that can pilot a space transport?"

"That's our top priority. I need each of your clans to canvass your people for those with any flying experience. In six days, we will deliver qualified pilots to your transports."

"I know the transports are massive, but there are nearly three hundred thousand Rayleans on Jypton. How can we possibly transport that many people?" asked one of the chieftains.

"The larger transports can carry nearly ten thousand people. With the thirty-seven transports we will have enough room," Daeson replied.

The chieftains didn't look convinced, but over the course of the next two hours Daeson addressed each of their objections as best he could. The logistics of the mass exodus of the Rayleans from Jypton was daunting to say the least, and there were questions to which Daeson had no answers, the most glaring being their destination.

All Daeson could say was that Ell Yon would direct them when the time came. That also didn't sit well with the chieftains, but they pressed forward, and Daeson was quite shocked but thrilled by the trust they eventually demonstrated in Sovereign Ell Yon. Clearly the heritage of their trust in this Immortal was deeply engrained into his people. It humbled him, for they had not had the benefit of talking with Ell Yon face-to-face as Daeson had.

When Daeson negotiated with Linden's councilmen, he had insisted that the space transports be fully operational and not derelict, as well as equipped with slip stream engines. The councilmen obliged him quite readily, for they were anxious to be rid of those that had brought such disaster to their formerly tranquil lives. Daeson, Raviel, Tig, and a handful of other mechtechs that Raviel trusted would be inspecting each one before they were deployed to their respective launch sites in the coming days.

Daeson chose the civil space port on the outskirts of Athlone as their base of operations for organizing, inspecting, and launching the transports to the rest of the clans. It would then also serve as headquarters not only for the southern continent exodus but also for the global hub of communication. A similar location on each continent was chosen and Daeson would soon be visiting each to ensure all preparations were made.

In the afternoon of this first day of preparation, Tig was reunited with his father, and Daeson rejoiced greatly with his friend. Tig's father quickly became invaluable in helping to bring order to the frenzied activity of the exodus effort.

Daeson, Raviel, Tig, and Trisk worked tirelessly throughout the first day, organizing and preparing all clan leadership. Skilled men and women stepped forward all across the planet in such number and with such enthusiasm that Daeson was stunned. Although the task before them still seemed ominous, their efforts were gaining momentum.

Later that evening, Daeson found Raviel and pulled her aside from the intensity of the preparations. He grabbed her hand, leading her out of the port's hangers and buildings to a small garden yet untouched by the blood algae and the rest of the destruction most of Athlone had endured.

"What is it, Daeson? Where are we going?"

Daeson kept silent until they were out of sight of all people and until the sounds of thousands of voices and machines were but a dull roar.

He turned to face her, then reached to hold her other hand as well.

"What's wrong?" Raviel asked, her eyes creased with worry.

Daeson hesitated. "I just needed to see you... alone."

Raviel's worried eyes softened with a burgeoning smile that seemed to lift the burdens of the world. Her eyes brightened as the stress of the moment paused.

"Really?" she lifted a hand to his cheek.

Daeson nodded.

"How are you holding up?" he asked.

Raviel took a deep breath, her shoulders settling as she exhaled. "I'm fine. Overwhelmed, but fine. Are you okay?"

"Right now, it seems impossible, but we have good people to work with."

Raviel nodded, then tilted her head, watching Daeson closely. "Something else is on your mind." Her eyes narrowed.

Daeson was amazed at how well she could already read him. So much had happened in such a short time. Intense life had happened. Much had changed. Had Raviel been affected...changed?

"Do you remember a few weeks ago...the night before I went before Linden...the night before this all started?"

Raviel hesitated, seeming to question his motive for asking. Then a slight smile spread across her lips. "Yes, I do," she responded, wrapping her arms around his waist.

"Rav, I don't know what's going to happen tomorrow or the next day or the day after that. What I do know is that I want to spend the rest of my life side by side with you. And I know that we are in the middle of absolute chaos, but I don't care. The way things are going, we may not have another hour alone together."

Daeson stopped and looked into her beautiful eyes. "Will you—"

"Yes!"

"But—"

"Yes!"

"Tonight?"

"Yes!"

Daeson closed his eyes and held her close.

"I love you, Raviel!"

"I love you, too, Daeson!"

Together they sought out Chieftain Wescott and asked him to perform the bonding ceremony. Tig, Trisk, Petia, Zee'la, and even Rivet agreed to stand as witnesses for the couple. Beneath the heavy burden of global responsibility to the people of Sovereign Ell Yon, in the quiet of the night with little celebration, Daeson and Raviel stood before Wescott and their witnesses to proclaim their vows to each other.

Wescott stood in ceremonial dress, looking as pleased as Daeson had ever seen him. He began by reading an ancient Raylean blessing upon the couple and all in attendance. The reading dated back to a time before the Jyptonian bondage. The blessing held a poetic charm that once again reminded Daeson of the Raylean music, which he'd heard much more of as of late. Other subtle rituals that Daeson had never seen before were performed, nor did he understand their significance. Then Wescott paused in his duties and looked gravely on them both.

"This covenant bond between you, Daeson Starlore, and you, Raviel Arko, is unbreakable and is witnessed here in our presence and by the watchful eyes of Sovereign Ell Yon. It is an indelible bond, not broken by tragedy or prosperity...by man or beast...by space or time. Do you make this covenant freely and with full understanding of this bond?

"We do," Daeson and Raviel spoke in unison.

Wescott took the ceremonial stole, embroidered with the mark of Ell Yon, from around his neck and held it before Daeson and Raviel. Raviel set the back of her hand on top of the stole and Daeson rested his hand on top of hers, palm to palm. Wescott then wrapped the stole around both of their hands and wrists. Daeson felt Raviel interlock her fingers with his, and his heart skipped a beat as he remembered their dance.

"Then by the authority granted to me as a chieftain of the Raylean people, I hereby proclaim you bonded. May the Sovereign Ell Yon ever be with you and prosper you."

Wescott then slid the stole from off of their hands, the ceremony complete.

Daeson looked at Raviel and smiled. "That's it?"

Raviel shook her head. "No...you have to kiss me now."

"Ah," he agreed, and they kissed before the gathered audience.

"Ell Yon Yevareh!" Wescott shouted, causing Daeson to jump.

"Ell Yon Yevareh!" proclaimed all of the witnesses in unison.

Raviel laughed at the puzzled look on Daeson's face. "It means may 'Ell Yon bless us.'"

Daeson joined in joyful laughter as everyone gathered near to congratulate them. Though the days before them would be hard, his heart was full of gladness.

The following day was again filled with fervent preparations that consumed every minute of the day for Daeson and his team. To Daeson, the task still seemed impossible, but he confessed his thoughts to no one.

Daeson, Raviel, Tig, Trisk, and Rivet stood before a ragtag assembly of a few hundred volunteers. Daeson and Tig had piloted a small transport to collect any flight-experienced Rayleans from across the planet back to Athlone, but Daeson still couldn't believe that any of the gathered men and women could possibly have any real piloting skills. Perhaps a handful had served as members of aerotech crews on atmospheric transports, but the Jyptonian Elite had been very careful about limiting the Rayleans to non-piloting positions.

Once again, Daeson was faced with the very obvious reality that what they were attempting to do was absolutely impossible. It was easier to face the chieftains with courage and proclaim the impossible as possible than to come face-to-face with the reality of this ragtag group. Daeson turned to Raviel and Tig, no longer silent about his doubts.

"This is crazy," he said quietly. "We're talking about piloting space transports. It takes months to train a co-pilot and much longer for a fully qualified pilot."

Raviel stepped forward. "How many of you have any flight control experience at all—navigation, in-flight crew operation or maintenance, aerotech–anything of that nature."

Nearly every hand was raised. Raviel turned around.

"It's a start. Our people are very intelligent, Daeson. Some of these helped build these transports."

Daeson pursed his lips. "Building a ship and flying one are worlds apart. How many pilots and copilots do we need, Tig?"

"Thirty-seven pilots and twenty-two copilots for the larger ships, provided you and I each pilot a transport."

"That won't work. We have two Starcrafts that we will use to provide defensive escort. I need you in one. The other—"

"The other I can pilot," Raviel cut in.

Daeson hesitated. Though much smaller than a transport, a Starcraft was much more challenging to maneuver since it was inherently unstable. It took time to develop the necessary skills, but Raviel did seem to have a knack for it. Within minutes of flying with another, a skilled pilot could tell if the trainee had the hands for piloting, and Raviel certainly did. Besides this, she knew the Starcraft inside and out.

"I can be her co-pilot," Rivet added.

Daeson still wasn't convinced.

"You need to be in the flagship, and there isn't another Raylean on the planet that can fly that Starcraft," Raviel insisted. "I know its systems better than you. Give me a few hours of flight training, and I can do it!"

Daeson hesitated, wishing for a better option, but realizing there wasn't one.

"Very well, then we need thirty-nine pilots and twenty-three copilots," Daeson recalculated. "Trisk, that means you're with me in the lead transport. I want you to go through pilot training as well, just in case I'm called elsewhere."

Trisk nodded.

Daeson looked at Tig, the only other fully qualified pilot they had. "Do you think we can find that many potential pilots in this motley group?"

"I wish we had time to conduct a pilot aptitude test at least," Tig replied. "Daeson, we're talking about putting thousands of people at risk in transports piloted by men and women who have never set foot in space, let alone piloted a ship of any size. It's just not possible."

Daeson felt Tig's despair. *Ell Yon, how?*

"My liege," Rivet interrupted. "I have the ability to conduct bio-metric scans on each of these volunteers and compare them with yours and Tig's. I can quickly offer you a precise analysis of their piloting aptitude."

Raviel looked at Rivet and then at Daeson. "That is the most ridiculous thing I've ever heard! It has no such ability!" Raviel exclaimed. She turned back to Rivet. "I've seen your programming...I've seen your circuitry. Daeson, this bot is...is—"

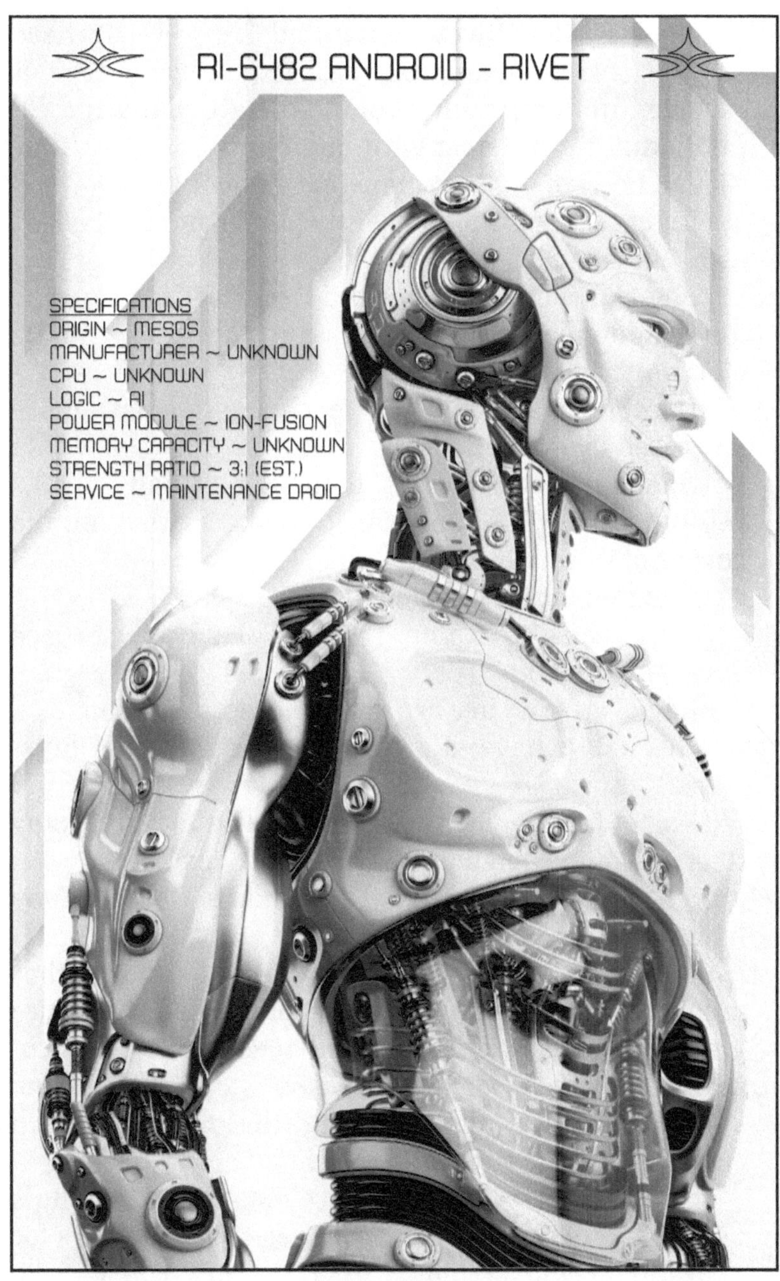

RI-6482 ANDROID - RIVET

SPECIFICATIONS
ORIGIN ~ MESOS
MANUFACTURER ~ UNKNOWN
CPU ~ UNKNOWN
LOGIC ~ AI
POWER MODULE ~ ION-FUSION
MEMORY CAPACITY ~ UNKNOWN
STRENGTH RATIO ~ 3:1 (EST.)
SERVICE ~ MAINTENANCE DROID

"Lady Raviel," Rivet interrupted. It lowered its head slightly, as a human might do to indicate serious resolve. "In this group of volunteers are pilots and co-pilots that I can detect with my bio-metric algorithm. All you need to do is let me point them out to you."

Rivet reached out and gently put a hand on Raviel's arm. "Trust me."

Raviel seemed hypnotized by Rivet's gaze. She looked down at the bot's hand and then back into its electronic eyes.

Daeson watched the exchange, once more surprised by the bot.

"Lieutenant Ki said that Rivet had been... reprogrammed." A peculiar thought settled in the corner of Daeson's mind.

"Lieutenant Ki?" Raviel asked.

"Yes, she's the one that escorted me to see Sovereign Ell Yon."

Raviel crossed her arms and glared at Daeson.

"It's all we have to go on, Rav," he said. "Let Rivet work."

Raviel snapped her head toward the bot. "I'm going to open you up again when this is all over."

"Of course," Rivet replied. It turned to Daeson. "May I begin?"

Daeson nodded. After each scan, Rivet either approved or rejected the individual. When the entire group had passed by the bot, all needed pilots and co-pilots had been chosen. Daeson stood before the volunteers once more, eyeing the fearless group closely.

"For the rest of you that were not selected as pilots or co-pilots, we need you to serve as crew members for operational and maintenance functions. You will be assigned to the transports with which you are most familiar."

Daeson took a deep breath. "What we are asking of you is...well, it's a lot. I need you to give us your best. The future of our people depends on it."

Daeson, Tig, and Rivet spent many hours training the pilot recruits and crew members in the seemingly impossible task of flying a space transport. Although the avionics and flight computers were designed to automate nearly every aspect of flight, there was no substitute for a skilled pilot, no matter how sophisticated the technology. Since the Rayleans were so tech-savvy and had helped design many models of the transports, their proficiency proved remarkable.

At the end of a very long day, Daeson found Tig sitting in the cockpit of the training transport... staring.

"What do you think, Tig? Are we going to survive this?" Daeson asked.

Tig looked up at Daeson, his face blank.

"The mechtechs and ship designers in our support crews have proven invaluable. They really know their stuff."

"Yes, it's quite remarkable," Daeson agreed. He sensed something more was coming. "But?"

Tig hesitated. "But these pilots Rivet found are... well, frankly they're ridiculous."

"How so?"

Tig rubbed his eyes.

"I swear it seems like they're pilots already. A few of them actually looked bored. And when I tested them, they knew exactly what they were doing."

Daeson smiled. "Never underestimate a Raylean," he said, slapping Tig on the shoulder. Daeson sat down in the cockpit seat next to him.

"How are you doing, my friend?"

Tig looked over at Daeson. He looked tired but happy. "I'm doing alright...this is something!"

"Yeah...it sure is. And how is Zee'la?"

Tig was obviously flustered. "Zee'la?"

"Ever since the Abyssian Trenches, I could tell she'd caught your eye."

Tig lowered his head and smiled.

Daeson put a hand on Tig's shoulder. "Our future is uncertain to say the least. You should talk to her... let her know."

Tig was staring at a console, but his mind was clearly elsewhere.

"Well, I have other things to attend to, so I'm off," Daeson said as he stood to leave. "Tomorrow, keep working with the crews, and we'll start deploying them to the launch sites the day after that."

Tig nodded. "Will do, Admiral."

Daeson laughed. "Admiral?"

"In two days we'll be a fleet of ships, and a fleet needs an admiral...Admiral."

"Ha! Thanks for the promotion, Captain Tig."

Tig smiled. "Didn't think I'd ever hear that rank in front of my name."

"By the way, six of the transports have shuttle bays and shuttles. Make sure that the flagship has a nimble shuttle I can access."

"You got it!" Tig saluted.

Daeson turned to leave.

"Hey," Tig called out. "Thanks."

Daeson nodded.

The next few days were filled with near panicked preparation in every city on Jypton. Rayleans from all regions travelled to their designated launch sites. Mobilizing such a mass of people in an unbelievably short time was nothing short of miraculous.

Daeson ensured that Master Boytt, his sci-techs, and all of the Sanctum technology were spread throughout the transports to minimize the risk of loss should the unthinkable happen to any of the transports.

Once the mobilization plan was in place, Daeson found a couple of hours in each of the next three days to train Raviel in the Starcraft. With her in-depth systems knowledge of every aspect of the machine, her acquisition of piloting skills was extremely fast. Daeson crammed six months of Starcraft training into eight flight hours of instruction, including weapons deployment.

Her last training mission was flown solo with Rivet in the rear seat. To say that Daeson was anxious was an understatement, but the flight went well. She wouldn't stand a chance flying against another skilled Starcraft pilot in a one vs. one fight, but flying defensive cover for a fleet of transports and deploying weapons was now certainly within her capabilities, especially with Rivet as co-pilot.

That evening Daeson found Raviel beneath his Starcraft, away from the rest of the pilots and crews. Rivet was motionless before her as she inspected the bot closely.

"I don't think you're going to find what you're looking for," Daeson teased.

Raviel raised one eyebrow from behind the silent and still Rivet. The bot's access panel was open, and Raviel had her interface module connected.

"There's something wrong about this bot, Daeson, and before I fly a real mission with this thing, I'm going to find out what it is."

Daeson came and stood next to her.

"I think you should just let it be, Rav. Rivet has proven to be incredibly useful," Daeson put a hand on her shoulder. "Look at how it picked out those pilots for us."

Raviel glanced up at Daeson over her shoulder.

"Exactly! And you don't think that's a bit too convenient...coincidental? Do you really trust this thing?"

Daeson hesitated before answering. "Yes...yes, I do."

Raviel shook her head. "Well, I don't!" She turned back to her work. "What makes Rivet peculiar must have to do with this component tied into the mobility analytics processor," Raviel continued. "I'm going to remove it and see what kind of affect it has on—"

"That's not a good idea," Rivet said.

Raviel jumped back.

Rivet turned its head toward them. It then reached behind its back, unplugged the interface, and closed the access panel.

Chills flowed up and down Daeson's spine. He had his suspicions, and now one way or another, they would be confirmed. He reached for his Talon, but Raviel had already drawn hers and charged it.

Rivet stood up and faced them. It looked directly at Daeson and tilted its head. Raviel's finger was pressed against the trigger, ready to take the bot out, but Daeson sensed it would not be necessary. He left his Talon in the holster and instead put a hand on Raviel's arm.

"Don't."

Raviel pushed his hand away. "This thing is AI and must be destroyed. This is how the AI wars all began!" Raviel aimed directly at Rivet's chest, where its main processor would sit.

Rivet stared back at them, its optic sensors giving nothing away.

"Rivet isn't AI," Daeson said calmly.

The space to the left of Rivet shimmered, as if one were looking through heated air rising up from a hot landing pad. A moment later the fit form of a female warrior wearing black body armor materialized. She looked first at Daeson and then at Raviel. Rivet's actions matched hers perfectly.

"What is this? A mimic-bot?" Raviel asked, her talon now pointed at the woman.

"Raviel, this is Lieutenant Ki, aka Rivet," Daeson said.

Ki offered a wry smile, then saluted, and Rivet made the exact same action. Lt. Ki then touched a section on her belt, and the bot froze.

"What's going on, Daeson?" Raviel demanded. "You know this woman?"

"Yes," Daeson said and slowly pushed Raviel's Talon down and away from Lt. Ki. Raviel allowed it but not willingly. Her eyes narrowed. She shot Daeson a fierce look.

"Lieutenant Ki is a Malakian...she's been with us since Mesos," Daeson explained.

Raviel's eyes opened wide as her grip on her Talon finally relaxed. She turned to face Daeson as she holstered the Talon.

"How long have you known?" she said, tilting her head and putting her hands on her hips.

"Well, I..." Daeson stammered, trying to figure out how best to answer her.

"He started suspecting me when I selected the pilots for you," Lieutenant Ki said as she walked around to Raviel's right side.

Raviel turned to face Ki. "So...you're really an Immortal?"

Lieutenant Ki stopped and looked at Raviel.

"And I'm his *asset*?" Raviel continued, her anger not yet abated.

Ki actually smiled. "Still not over that?" she said while putting an arm around Raviel's shoulders. She pulled her away from Daeson.

"I meant nothing by it. It was necessary to complete the ruse," he heard her say. "You've served Sovereign Ell Yon well, and he is pleased."

Raviel looked over at Ki, her eyes softening.

"There is still much to do, and I'll be with you for a time. Know that you've earned the respect of many, so keep up the good and faithful work."

Daeson could see that Raviel was a bit conflicted. After all, seeing a Malakian in the flesh was not an everyday occurrence. There were legends of such things, but most believed them to be just that... legends.

"Thank you," Raviel said.

Lt. Ki turned and faced Raviel, holding her shoulders.

"Now just leave my bot alone, okay?"

Raviel let loose a quick smile.

Ki looked over her shoulder at Daeson. "And take care of him. Actually, you two are great assets for each other."

Ki let loose of Raviel, looked her square in the eye, and winked. She then touched her belt and disappeared.

Raviel stood in silence for a moment before walking back to Daeson. Then she crossed her arms, eyeing him closely. "It's a good thing I like her," she said, then turned and gathered up her equipment.

That's for sure, he thought.

Daeson reached for Raviel's arm and pulled her close. He looked into the deep brown eyes where the most beautiful soul in the galaxy dwelled. Between Daeson and Raviel existed a deep knowing that only the bonded understood. Their love for each other was inexplicably knit together. Daeson loved being near her, hearing her voice, watching her move, sleeping next to her. It was as if Raviel held everything dear to him in her hands—his joy, his sorrow, his purpose, his future, and for the first time in his life, his vulnerabilities. Never before had he placed such absolute trust in another. Now with Ell Yon as his purpose and Raviel at his side, he was complete, no matter what lay ahead. If ever there came a day of parting, it would tear his soul in two.

"This business with Rivet stays our secret, okay?" Daeson confirmed.

Raviel put her arms around his neck and looked at him in a way that rattled him. "Hmm," was all Raviel would say.

He kissed her, then tucked her dark brown hair behind her ear.

"I'm having a hard time letting you take this thing and fly escort," Daeson acknowledged with a quick glance toward his Starcraft, "even if Lt. Ki...I mean Rivet is with you, you'll still be the one piloting."

"I know," Raviel said with a smile. "But there's no other way. We both know that. And besides, I'm a pretty good pilot, aren't I?" Raviel lifted her eyebrows and tilted her head slightly to emphasize her point.

"Honestly...you're an amazing pilot. All of your mechtech knowledge really paid off, and you obviously have the hands for it. Plus, with the modifications the Malakians made to this beauty, you'll be flying the most powerful and advanced Starcraft in the galaxy. I just wish we had two more months to fully train you. I need to know that you'll be careful up there, okay? Nothing risky."

Raviel smiled and kissed Daeson. "I promise."

Later that night, Daeson found Rivet. "Lt. Ki," he addressed the bot.

Rivet turned its head to look at him. "Regardless of what you now know about me, you must always address me as Rivet," Ki replied through the bot. "This must always be."

Daeson nodded.

"When it's time, Raviel will be piloting this Starcraft without the experience she needs. If things go sideways, I need to know you'll take care of her. She's not Immortal."

Rivet was silent for moment. "You do understand that being Immortal doesn't mean we can't die."

Daeson hadn't considered such a thing before. Being Immortal erased the dilemma of age but not of peril. What he was asking of Lt. Ki wasn't fair. He lowered his head.

"Forgive me. That was foolish of me. My love for her tends to skew my judgment sometimes."

Rivet stayed still, but the space beside her yielded to the form of Lt. Ki once more. She put her hands on her hips and eyed him closely.

"Don't worry Starlore, I'll keep her safe for you. You have my word."

Daeson nodded his thanks as Lt. Ki offered a crooked grin and disappeared. When Daeson left Rivet, he was a little wiser and a little more humble.

In spite of the frenzied activity of a global evacuation, an excitement stirred within the hearts of the Rayleans. The realization that they were being set free was exhilarating. Families and clans were reunited at launch sites—assembling together from refugee camps, prisons, mining sites on the moon of Tiran, and faraway lands where they had been indentured to Jyptonians. The gatherings energized the people like never before. And all the while, the termination drones waited and watched.

The Jyptonians, on the other hand, had been completely immobilized. Fear held them in their homes, and the entire Jyptonian fleet had been recalled to help with the necessary recover from the widespread tragedy of the previous weeks. Daeson saw nothing of Linden, but the councilmen were extremely cooperative and receptive to any and all of Daeson's requests. They and most of the population wanted nothing more than to see the Rayleans disappear. The frustration, tribulation, and pain the Jyptonian people had endured over the past few weeks was more than they could bear. But the Chancellor of Jypton felt a different emotion altogether.

Xandra's perfectly preserved body lay beneath the clear transparent lid of the casket, and Linden wept for her. His grief consumed him to such a degree that he kept her body in his throne room...a moment-by-moment reminder of the increasingly bitter hatred he held for Daeson.

Make him pay with his life and the lives of all Rayleans!

The familiar voice fed Linden's dark thoughts. He slammed his fist on the casket before turning away and walking to the hall where his generals and councilmen waited. Multiple termination drones hovered and watched. Once the tools Linden had used to control the lowly Drudge, now they held his empire hostage.

Two royal guards opened the doors, and every member of the chamber rose to attention as Linden entered. Even in this chamber, termination drones waited—some attached to the sides of the walls, two more on the chamber table in the middle of the room, and three others hovering above the heads of his Elite. Linden scowled, allowing the insult of Daeson's tactic to complete his utter hatred for the man and his people.

Through clenched teeth, Linden spoke. "Why haven't your techs disabled these wretched things?" He turned to the man at his left and glared at the Elite councilman responsible for their tech division.

The man's face turned white with fear. "My Lord, we have tried everything. Whatever algorithm they have used to override our system is beyond our—"

"Silence!" Linden yelled. The Triad began to glow, and his eyes turned red with fury.

"I don't want excuses." His hand reached for the man's throat as the Triad engaged the Deitum Prime in Linden's body and amplified his strength. His muscles bulged and grew until Linden was twenty percent larger and stronger than just a moment ago. The transformation was frightening. He lifted the man up by his throat until his feet were off the ground.

"I want answers!" came a deep, guttural proclamation.

At once, the Triad exploded its red beam of harnessed energy right through the chest of the man, scorching the wall ten paces behind him. Linden sneered at the lifeless form still hanging in his hand. He cast the body away as if it were a rag doll, then looked back at the rest of the people in his chamber. He slammed his fists into the table, which cracked and nearly collapsed at the impact. The terrorized men and women looked at Linden in horror.

The rage coursing through his body demanded blood…the blood of Daeson Starlore.

CHAPTER

14

Flight of Rayl

Starcraft Weapons – A fully armed Starcraft has the following weapons: 4 concussion missiles, 2 plasma cannons, 2 phaser burst guns. Concussion missiles carry warheads in a variety of sizes and are the most powerful but slowest weapon on board. Plasma cannons utilize a self-generating plasma generator and are moderately powerful but faster than concussion missiles. These cannons are the preferred weapon. Phaser burst guns are the fastest but the least powerful of the Starcraft's weapons.

The day of freedom came for the Rayleans. Daeson held his breath as the transports lifted off one by one and launched into orbit around Jypton. Tig was already in space, with his Starcraft organizing the ships as they broke orbit. Daeson had Raviel wait with him to provide escort with her Starcraft. Nearly all of the transports were two- and three-seat cockpits with relatively straightforward control and navigation systems that were significantly automated. After much negotiation, Daeson had requisitioned a cruiser-class starship, the *Raider*, as a flagship for their fleet. It was immediately renamed *Liberty*.

Though older than current Jyptonian designs, it had a full bridge and required a crew to operate it. Bridge officers included Trisk as captain and acting as Daeson's second in command, Ensign Walla as the communications officer, Lieutenant Golan as the sensors officer, and Ensign Kwi as the navigation officer. Normally, a cruiser-class starship also had a weapons officer, but the *Liberty* had been stripped of weapons as a stipulation of the negotiations.

With only one transport delayed, Admiral Daeson and his crew, along with three thousand passengers on board the *Liberty*, launched. Raviel and Rivet flew escort in the Malakian-enhanced Starcraft. The journey had begun!

"How many of the transports have lifted off?" Linden demanded of the Elite general responsible for his aero-tech forces.

The general nervously looked down at his glass tablet and tapped. "My Lord, all but one. I'm told it's preparing for departure as we speak." The man cringed.

"How is this possible? The Drudge have no pilots...no one skilled enough to carry this out!"

The man swallowed hard. "I don't know, Chancellor Lockridge. Perhaps Starlore and the other pilot trained them."

Linden's eyes began to glow red again.

"In eight days?" Linden's voice filled with scorn. He began walking around the table to the man as all others backed far away to allow him access. "These are Drudge! Not even an Elite Jyptonian could learn such skills in eight days!" Linden glared down at the man, his muscles bulging large.

"Is my fleet ready?"

Sweat ran steadily down the temples of the white-faced man. Normally this general was an intimidating force, but next to the Triad-induced state of Linden Lockridge, he was but a cowering boy.

"We are still trying to compensate for the pilots and crews that were killed during the termination drone attacks, but—"

Linden once more reached for the man's throat, but that fatal moment was shattered when every termination drone in the room fell in an instant, crashing to the table and floor. Linden froze. He scanned the room. One of the councilwomen poked nervously at a drone in the middle of the broken table. It didn't move. Another councilman quickly tapped across his glass and looked up at his chancellor.

"My Lord, it's over. Every termination drone on the planet has been disabled."

He grabbed the general by the scruff of the neck. "Ready my fleet! We are going to crush that treasonous imposter and his castaways before they leave this system!"

Linden released the general.

"Yes, Chancellor," the general replied, trying to regain his dignity. "As you command!"

Linden turned away and exited the chamber. He felt omnipotent. The Triad was everything he needed to crush the head of Starlore and the vermin that followed him. He walked to the open terrace of his throne room and breathed in the sweet smell of revenge, raptured by the quest for it.

"Xandra, my love," he began, but the effects of the Triad began to wane as his body resumed its previous state of strength and size. The resulting pain swelled until he screamed out. He fell to one knee, alone in his madness. He reached for the stone rail on the terrace, clinging hard to the prison of his hatred for Daeson and the Immortal he served.

"I will avenge you, my love. I will avenge!"

The *Liberty* quickly rejoined and took lead of the fleet of transports. Raviel continued escorting the *Liberty,* while Tig provided cover for the rear of the fleet.

"The fleet is ready, Admiral," Trisk announced. "What's our course?"

Daeson listened as the Protector gently whispered to his mind.

"Fourteen, thirty-nine, thirty-six mark five."

"Make it so, Ensign Kwi," Trisk ordered.

"Give me a visual on the fleet," Daeson ordered.

"Yes, sir," Lieutenant Golan snapped.

The leftmost bridge display filled with the beautiful picture of thirty-seven transports aligned in formation. The blue orb of Jypton loomed large and ominous behind them. It was perhaps the most frightening but glorious sight Daeson had ever viewed. A swell of panic nearly choked him as he realized that these people were counting on him to lead them. How could he ever do or be what they needed of him? He swallowed hard, but the fear held tight to his heart.

Be still!

"Admiral, I'm detecting many Starcraft launching from three different bases on Jypton," Lt. Golan reported.

It was inevitable. Daeson knew Linden too well, but Ell Yon had spoken. Now they were in the vastness of space, flying transports that had no weapons and energy shields only strong enough to deflect cosmic dust while traveling. Compared to Jyptonian Destroyers and Starcraft, the transports moved like Sorinian sand worms. There was no way out. Had the Sovereign miscalculated? The two Starcraft Tig and Raviel were flying were the only weapon-equipped ships they had.

"Admiral, long-range scanners are also picking up eight destroyer-class starships bearing eighty-eight mark three." His sensors officer, Lieutenant Golan reported.

"Jyptonian?" Daeson asked.

"No," Lt. Golan replied.

Daeson looked at the officer, shocked. "Then who are they?"

Lt. Golan turned to face Daeson and Trisk. "Their signatures match that of the Galactic Alliance."

Daeson's heart sank. He knew Trisk felt it too. The entire crew turned to look at him, watching how he would react. His spirit broke. These people had endured so much. He had done everything Ell Yon had asked of him, and now their fate would be exactly as Linden's curse had foretold—death, with space as their cold, icy tomb.

Daeson stared out into the dark abyss—the Jyptonian fleet behind him, the Galactic Alliance to the right of them, and the massive Agulla Asteroid Field in front of them. Not even Ell Yon, in all of his technological wonder, could save them now.

The only flight path that made sense was to turn left, bearing two-seven-three, away from all three threats. Perhaps if every ship separated to go their own way and diverted the attack, some might survive. Daeson closed his eyes and lowered his head. Everyone on deck was waiting—eyes on their commander. But he had no answers. The end had come.

The Agulla Asteroid Field—go there!

Daeson lifted his head and looked at the frightful scene before him. The asteroid field? Not possible! Sure, he had escaped by the skin of his teeth once before by flying through the asteroids, but he had been flying one Starcraft with the maneuverability necessary to navigate through such a death trap. This fleet of virtually non-maneuverable space transports would be obliterated before they even entered. It was madness!

Trust me, Navi Starlore.

Daeson turned to his com officer.

"Ensign Walla, open a channel to all Raylean transports."

Walla swept her hand across the controls in multiple directions, then nodded.

"To the pilots of all Raylean vessels," Daeson began as he glanced out the starboard view and saw Raviel in his Starcraft. Was he consigning her and the other three hundred thousand Rayleans to death? "Make your course one, three, mark, two and keep our formation as tight as possible. Acknowledge."

Trisk eyed Daeson but said nothing.

"Viper One to *Liberty*." Daeson immediately recognized Tig's voice. "That heading takes us straight into the Agulla Asteroid Field. Please confirm vector."

"Heading one, three, mark two confirmed. Keep the formation tight back there, Viper One. Make haste. Ell

Yon is with us!" Daeson saw the concern on every face in the bridge. He looked at his navigation officer, Ensign Kwi.

"Make it so," he ordered. "Keep the engines at full speed."

The coordinates were entered and *Liberty*'s course adjusted slightly.

Daeson was now leading his crew and three thousand passengers of the *Liberty* into certain death. Raviel and Tig in their Starcrafts followed alongside with thirty-seven more ships of varying sizes.

"You're being hailed by Viper Two," Ensign Walla announced.

"Put her through," Daeson said, pointing to his earpiece.

"What are we doing, Daeson?" Raviel's voice was laced with concern. "You didn't teach me how to fly through an asteroid field with this thing."

Daeson glanced around the bridge. All eyes were on the large forward view screen, the millions upon millions of asteroids of the Agulla Field growing larger with each passing moment. Daeson put a fist to his lips and glanced over at Raviel through the large starboard view port. He opened his mouth to speak, but nothing he could say would make sense.

"Okay...I get it," she broke in. "I just hope you're hearing right."

"Me too," Daeson replied. "You be careful out there and stay close."

"Roger that, Admiral!"

The wings of Raviel's Starcraft rocked.

Trisk came close to Daeson. "Are you sure about this?"

"As sure as I can be," Daeson replied. He put a hand on Trisk's shoulder, then walked to the sensors console.

"Are the Galactic Alliance ships closing on us?" he asked quietly.

"Yes, sir," Lt. Golan replied. "We have approximately thirty minutes."

Long minutes passed.

"I'm getting hails from nearly every ship, Admiral," Ensign Walla said.

"Just tell them all to maintain course," Daeson demanded.

"Admiral Starlore, the *Pearl* is breaking off from our formation," Lt. Golan reported.

"Hail them!" Daeson ordered. "Who's the captain?"

"That is Captain Hanaz," Trisk replied.

"Channel open," Ensign Walla reported.

"Captain Hanaz, this is Admiral Starlore of the *Liberty*. Return to course immediately!"

"This is Korah," came a strange voice. "I have assumed command of this ship. We will not fly this vessel into that asteroid field. We're making a run for it."

Anger surged in Daeson. He clenched his teeth and leaned forward. "What's his position?" Daeson ordered.

"He's ship number twenty-one, sir."

"Get me Viper One."

Ensign Walla touched her glass and nodded.

"Viper One, do you have a visual on the *Pearl*?"

"Roger, *Liberty*. She's breaking away from the fleet."

"Listen, Korah...give control of the ship back to Captain Hanaz and resume course. You are putting yourself and thousands of passengers at risk. Comply, or you will all die!"

"Get me a visual on the Pearl," Daeson said to Lt. Golan. The left display immediately showed the fleet's formation and one ship splitting away.

Daeson looked toward Ensign Walla.

"The *Pearl* is still separating from formation," Lt. Golan reported.

"Open a channel to Viper One again and make sure the *Pearl* hears this," Daeson ordered.

"Viper One, lock weapons on the engines of the *Pearl*. If it doesn't return to course in one minute, open fire and disable the transport. Acknowledge."

Every head turned to stare at Daeson, but the fierceness of his countenance did not change.

"Viper One, acknowledged," Tig replied.

The bridge of the *Liberty* watched as Viper One immediately executed a barrel roll over the fleet to end up on an intercept course with the *Pearl*. In no time Tig was positioned directly behind her.

"Weapons locked."

"Korah, return control of the ship to Captain Hanaz immediately and your actions will not be held against you. Continue, and I will personally make sure you are executed for mutiny."

The seconds ticked by as the Pearl drifted further and further from formation while the asteroid field came closer and closer. Daeson quit breathing as one minute came and went.

"Weapons locked and ready. Confirm," Tig radioed.

Daeson waited, the bridge heavy with silence.

"*Liberty*, this is Captain Hanaz of the *Pearl*. We are resuming course, vector one, three, mark two."

Daeson started breathing again along with the rest of the bridge.

"Viper One, provide cover until the *Pearl* is back in formation," Daeson ordered.

By now the asteroid field loomed large before them, an impassible ocean of destruction. And the Raylean fleet was flying full speed into its rocky storm.

"Admiral, the ships to the rear are taking fire," Lt. Golan reported.

"Open a channel to *Voyage*."

"Channel open," Ensign Walla reported a second later.

"Captain Mallok, what's your status?" Daeson asked.

"We're taking fire, but our shields are holding. They're still outside lethal range." Mallok's voice was steady, just as Daeson knew it would be.

"Reroute power to rear energy shields," Daeson returned.

"Already done. What's the plan, Admiral?"

"We're working on that. Standby."

Daeson looked at Lt. Golan. "How long before the Jyptonians are within lethal firing range of *Voyage*?" Daeson asked.

"Eighteen point six minutes at current closing velocity, but if they launch concussion missiles even at this distance, with nowhere to go we can't outrun them." Lt. Golan glanced up from his glass console. "We'll be entering the asteroid field in three minutes."

"Whatever you have planned, Admiral, now's the time," Trisk said.

All eyes turned once more toward Daeson...eyes filled with hope and fear, yet full of Raylean courage.

Ell Yon...where are you? Daeson whispered in his heart, for he had nothing he could do. His only option was to order a fleet-wide all stop command.

"Ensign Wall—"

"Sir, there's a massive energy field coming right at us." Lt. Golan exclaimed.

"From the Jyptonians?" Daeson asked.

"No Admiral, through the asteroid field!"

A second later, a brilliant white beam of energy enveloped the entire fleet. It seemed to penetrate clear through their shielding and the very hulls of their ships. Everyone covered their eyes to protect themselves from the blinding light. All Daeson could do was imagine ship after ship exploding as the asteroids careened into the unprotected armada. Slowly, the light faded, dimming from the inside and expanding outward. Daeson blinked, desperately trying to get a visual fix on their position.

"What was that?" he exclaimed.

"According to my sensors, it was an extremely powerful repulsion beam," Lt. Golan reported, his voice surprisingly calm.

"Look, Admiral!" Ensign Kwi exclaimed, pointing to the forward screen.

As the energy beam expanded outward, it pushed a cylindrical wake of asteroids along with it leaving an empty tunnel of space.

"Ell Yon!" Daeson said beneath his breath.

The tunnel expanded until it was wide enough to allow the fleet to enter in its current formation. A wall of impenetrable energy deflected every asteroid from their path.

"This is the stuff legends are made of," Trisk marveled, with a smile as big as Daeson had ever seen on the typically stoic man.

"Your orders, Admiral?" the navigation officer asked.

"Ahead full," Daeson ordered.

Ensign Kwi quickly tapped out an adjustment to their course, and the *Liberty* aligned perfectly with the center of the tunnel. As they entered the energy cocoon within the asteroid field, the entire crew stood entranced by the spectacle.

"How is this possible?" someone asked.

"There is only one answer—Ell Yon," Daeson affirmed.

In spite of this joyful moment of salvation, Daeson knew their peril was far from over. The back of the transport convoy would never make it. Time was not on their side.

Chancellor Linden Lockridge sat at the helm of the Jyptonian flagship, *Invincible.* Leaning forward, his fisted hand epitomized the force with which he was going to crush Daeson and his despicable Drudge. His fleet of fourteen destroyers and four squadrons of Starcrafts were aligned in perfect battle formation, the mightiest starship force in the galaxy. Linden's face glowed in anticipation of the devastation he would wreak upon the fleet of transports.

Every captain in the fleet had strict orders not to destroy but to capture the *Liberty.* He wanted Starlore alive for a public execution back on Jypton. Chancellor Treville had assured him of a galactic audience, justice for the crimes he'd committed against benevolent and legitimate authorities everywhere.

"I have you, Starlore. And now let the icy tomb of space open its mouth and swallow you all!"

Linden sneered. "Open fire!"

"My Lord, none of our weapons are in range to be effective," the weapons officer reported.

"I don't care," Linden barked. "I want them to taste and fear their doom even now. Fire!"

The *Invincible* opened fire on the trailing ships of the transport armada. Moments later Linden's ship was immersed in a brilliant white light that seemed to penetrate every corner of the ship.

"What is this?" Linden demanded as the white energy beam slowly dissipated.

"Some sort of energy weapon," came the reply from their sensors officer.

"They have no weapons!" Linden scowled.

"It's not coming from the transports, Chancellor. Its origin is far beyond the Agulla Asteroid Field. It's coming through the slipstream conduit from the Omega Nebula!"

Linden scowled. "What kind of a weapon?"

There was no response. He turned and looked at his bridge crew.

"What kind of weapon?" Linden repeated louder.

Silence. Linden was feeling his rage build, and the Triad began to glow.

"My Lord, the lead ships of the armada have reached the asteroid field."

Linden's rage slowly transformed to dark delight.

Now is the end of you, Starlore. Linden focused on the magnified view, waiting for the armada to halt or turn, but instead they continued onward. He stood up.

"What am I seeing?"

"They're entering the asteroid field," came the sensor officer's reply.

"Impossible!" Linden exclaimed. He stood up and walked closer to the display. He turned around and looked at his crew. "How is this possible?" he demanded.

The sensors officer turned white as he endured the full glare of the Chancellor.

"From what I can tell, my Lord, the energy beam is clearing a path in the asteroid field large enough for the transports to enter."

With teeth clenched, Linden slowly walked back to the command chair. "How long until weapons range?" he demanded.

"Sixteen minutes," came the reply from weapons.

"Then it matters not, for we will obliterate them inside the asteroid field. I want every destroyer's weapons targeted on those ships. Launch concussion missiles first. Fire on my mark!"

"All destroyers report targeting solution set."

I will have your blood today, Starlore, no matter what comes! Linden allowed the image of the fleeing transports to fuel the deep burning hatred within his chest as the Triad pulsed in anticipation, drawing power from the Deitum Prime coursing through his veins.

"Admiral, we need to adjust course to stay within the energy beam. We're close to penetrating on the starboard side," Ensign Kwi reported.

"How is that possible?" Daeson asked.

"The energy beam is...curved, sir."

Daeson turned and looked in astonishment at Lt. Golan.

"What? That's impossible! There is no technology to allow such a thing."

"Yes, sir, it is impossible, but it curves."

"Admiral, a curved flight path in the asteroid field will keep us out of weapons range of the Jyptonian fleet should they pursue us into the beam," Trisk added.

"Of course," Daeson said. "Remarkable! What of the trailing ships? Will they make it in time?"

"For protection from Jyptonian energy weapons, yes, but if they launch concussion missiles, the last four transports will still be in range before the curving field can hide them. Even then, if they can maintain a lock on us through the asteroid field, the missiles could follow."

Daeson frowned.

"Open a channel to Viper One and Viper Two.

"Channel open," reported Lt. Walla.

Daeson knew what he had to ask of them, but forming the words was difficult.

"Tig…Rav, we're not going to get all ships into the asteroid field in time."

There was a moment of silence as Daeson's unspoken order was received. Everything inside him screamed against the inevitable. He could not ask the two he loved the most, one his bonded soul mate, to risk even more.

"Roger that. We'll buy you the time you need," came Tig's reply.

"Tig—," Daeson began.

"Message received and understood, *Liberty*," Tig interrupted.

Daeson hung his head. He knew Tig would do everything in his power to keep Raviel alive. A lump formed in his throat. Surely there was something that could be done.

"Admiral," Lt. Golan looked up from his console, face grim.

"The Jyptonian fleet just launched one hundred sixty concussion missiles."

Righteous anger filled Daeson's soul.

"How long until impact?"

"Seven minutes," Lt. Golan returned.

The front display zoomed in on the ominous approaching missiles, but the visual was lost a moment later as the *Liberty* curved within the energy tunnel.

"Captain Trisk, you have command of the ship. Take *Liberty* through the asteroid field."

Trisk turned and looked at Daeson.

"What are you doing?" he asked. "All we have is a shuttle, there's nothing else you can do!"

Daeson turned a cold and icy stare toward Trisk. It ended the query.

"Yes, Admiral…Ell Yon be with you!"

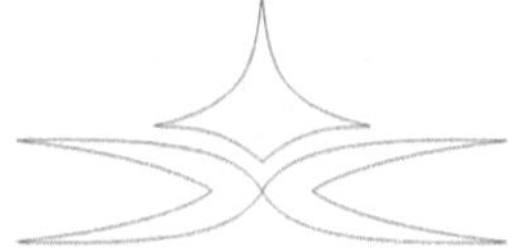

CHAPTER

15

The Greatest Sacrifice

Raviel saw Tig pull his Starcraft up beside hers. The fleet of Raylean transports, three and four across, formed a convoy that stretched ahead of them as far as they could see. All but two transports were now inside the energy tunnel. The sight was magnificent.

Raviel clicked on her private channel with Tig.

"Don't think I don't know what you just told Daeson. Make no mistake, Tig, I'm in this till the end."

She looked over at Tig in his Starcraft and saw him looking her way. In spite of the dire circumstances facing them, Raviel couldn't help feeling proud about where she was and what she was doing. She had spent her whole life dreaming of this very day, and here she was piloting a Starcraft, defending the Raylean people from the evil Jyptonian regime on behalf of Sovereign Ell Yon. She could think of no better way to serve and sacrifice her life than for such a cause as this. Chills flowed up and down her spine as she thought of it.

She saw Tig nod his head.

The com channel clicked open.

"I know it," Tig replied. "But Daeson doesn't need to know it. Follow me, Viper Two!"

Tig's Starcraft broke high and left in a tight Immelmann maneuver. Raviel followed. Now flying in the opposite direction of the transports, they came face-to-face with the most powerful armada in the galaxy.

"You ready for this, Rivet?" Raviel asked as she zoomed in on the Jyptonian fleet with her optical scanner. The image nearly took her breath away as her display filled with considerably more than a hundred concussion missiles coming straight at them, with fourteen destroyers and four squadrons of Starcraft as a backdrop. Her visor began filling with targets until it was impossible to discern one missile from another.

"Let's get busy, shall we?" Rivet replied. The channel with Tig opened and Rivet continued. "The most effective defense is to launch all of our concussion missiles at once and detonate them at the leading edge of the salvo. Then we target individual missiles with our plasma cannons. Because of our enhanced Starcraft, I can simultaneously fire the phaser burst guns while you operate the plasma cannons, my Lady."

"Good plan," Tig replied. "Arm all concussion missiles and fire on my mark."

Raviel touched her display to arm her four concussion missiles. "Missiles armed and ready," she replied.

She heard Tig click on his mic. "Roger that, Viper Two. Three...two...one...fire!"

Eight concussion missiles rocketed off the wingtip rails of both Starcraft. It was a beautiful sight to behold yet seemed paltry considering what was coming at them. Silently, they waited as the distance between the concussion missiles quickly closed. Flying three times faster than a Starcraft, the missiles were screaming towards each other at a closing velocity that was frightening.

"Remote concussion missile detonation in three...two...one...now!" Rivet reported.

The space in front of them lit up like a miniature super nova as their missiles exploded and initiated a chain reaction that took out many more of the Jyptonian missiles. When the explosions faded, their sensors began taking inventory of the remaining missiles.

Raviel checked that her plasma cannons were charged and ready.

"What's the damage, Rivet?" she asked.

"Sensors are detecting one hundred seven missiles still active."

Raviel's heart sank. That was still far too many for them to eliminate. With a little luck, they might be able to take out another twenty or thirty. That still left more than enough to destroy the entire Raylean fleet of transports. Her visor began filling with targets again. She filtered them by distance, keeping only fifteen on display at a time.

"Our plasma cannons will be effective in less than one minute," Tig reported. "We'll only have about three minutes of firing time before they're too close."

Raviel knew full well that detonating a missile inside its lethal radius would also take out their Starcrafts.

"If we set a flight vector toward our transports and continue firing while retreating, we can buy a little more time," Raviel replied.

"Good thinking, Viper Two," Tig responded.

"I like the way you think, my Lady." Rivet's voice came through Raviel's headset. She smiled.

"Cannon's armed and ready," Raviel reported. Her sensors were locked on the first fifteen targets. As the missiles came closer, she would have to reposition slightly to accommodate the widening range of targets.

"Commence firing!" Tig ordered.

Side by side the two valiant Starcrafts blasted away at the coming salvo of death. One by one the missiles were taken out. For every target that disappeared on Raviel's visor display, another was added. As quickly as her hands could fly, her cannons echoed burst after burst of plasma energy. Additionally, Rivet was now able to target missiles with the phaser burst guns. The firing power of the enhanced Starcraft was a sight to behold. But the endless sea of missiles kept coming— the explosions growing closer and closer with each passing second. Their fevered defense was relentless, but it would not be enough.

"Reposition!" Tig ordered.

Raviel flipped her Starcraft one hundred eighty degrees, slammed her throttles to full speed for five seconds, then flipped her Starcraft back around to face the advancing missiles. Tig had done the same, and now they were flying backwards while firing their cannons on the remaining seventy-three missiles. The maneuver would buy them another sixty seconds, but that was all.

While frantically targeting and firing each successive missile, Raviel's mind began to consider the tragic consequences of ducking out once the missiles were within lethal range. She imagined watching the missiles fly past and sequentially destroy the entire fleet of transports. A thousand faces flashed across her mind at the thought of the terror of complete destruction that would wipe them from existence.

"Time to bug out, Viper Two!" Tig ordered, but Raviel did not move, and neither did Tig.

Three more missiles were destroyed right in front of her. They were close.

"I'm with you, fellow warrior of Ell Yon." Lt. Ki's voice spoke calmly into her com link.

"Raviel, you must go!" Tig pleaded.

"You know I can't, Tig."

Silence.

Only seconds remained. Two more missiles exploded. Life was coming to a fiery end.

I love you, Daeson! It was the only thought that mattered to her in these final seconds. Perhaps Daeson would survive and lead some of her people to a new place...a new beginning. It was hope enough.

Then something caught the corner of her eye...a small ship...*NO!*

Daeson pulled the ejection handle in the shuttle. The top of the cockpit split open, and he was thrust up and away from the shuttle. For one brief second, the silence and vastness of space held him captive. His suit and helmet were all that protected him from the cold and instant death just beyond. On each side of him were his two valiant Starcraft warriors, as well as Lt. Ki operating Rivet. Their thrust vector, however, was behind him in the direction of the transports, so they quickly disappeared from his view. In front of him was a wall of over sixty concussion missiles screaming at him. And behind that, a fleet of Jyptonian warships were seconds from being within firing range with their massive plasma cannons.

"Daeson!"

He heard the pained plea from his love through his com link, but there was no time to respond. The next missile to explode would take them all out.

Fear not, for I am here! The Protector whispered through his mind.

Even through his suit Daeson could see the pulsing blue energy of the Sovereign's power. He held up his hand toward the impossible salvo of Jyptonian concussion missiles. They were upon them. From deep within his soul the power of Ell Yon exploded from the Protector in a wall of arcing flame spanning outward.

It was as if every cell in his body was being drained of life itself. The first missile hit the Protector's shield and exploded in front of them. Daeson covered his eyes with his left hand as the space in front of him turned white hot with an endless concussion of explosions. Seconds later, the Protector's shield collapsed. All that remained was the gaseous residue of exploded missiles.

But Daeson couldn't see the carnage. His eyes were shut because opening them would require strength he no longer had. It was as if his body had been utterly drained of energy, almost to the point of death. Knowing such power could not have come from him, he realized that the Protector was channeling its power via the Omeganite through his purged cells. Though Daeson's power was limited, Ell Yon's power was not.

Slowly Daeson came back to life. He vaguely heard the com link chanting a message in his head.

Slowly he turned and opened his eyes to see if Raviel's Starcraft was intact. Though far behind him, both Starcrafts appeared undamaged. He saw both Starcraft engage their thrusters.

"Daeson, are you alright?" Raviel's voice pleaded over the com channel.

"I...am," he mumbled.

"We're on our way!" Tig replied.

Daeson could see the Jyptonian fleet coming fast. Surely, they would be within weapons range in seconds. A moment later, Tig's cockpit was open. It took strength Daeson didn't have to climb into the second seat. With movements that were agonizingly slow, Daeson strapped himself in. Then both Starcrafts punched thrusters to rejoin the transports.

All transports were now well inside the energy tunnel within the Agulla Asteroid Field. Soon they would be out of visual range, but that wouldn't last long. As they entered the tunnel, Daeson detected the first burst of plasma cannon fire coming at them. It was massive and had to have come from one of the destroyers. Daeson's fleet of transports would still be out of range of the smaller plasma cannons the Jyptonian Starcraft were carrying.

"It's coming!" Tig exclaimed. "Do your shield thingy!"

Daeson realized he had nothing left to give. He listened, but the Sovereign was silent. He looked down at the Protector—it was still.

"Sorry, Tig...I've got nothing left."

Daeson stared at the oncoming wave once more. Surely, they hadn't been saved only to be destroyed now? The curve of the energy tunnel might save them from the first salvo of plasma cannon fire, but it would not last long.

The first round of plasma fire exploded behind them against the far wall of the tunnel, seemingly having no effect on the tunnel's ability to shield them from the asteroids. Both Starcrafts were now flying escort to the trailing transport, *Voyage*. When Daeson's mind fully cleared, he was able to re-engage in the fray.

"Hurry up, *Voyage!*" he whispered.

"Viper Two, fly to the front of the fleet and provide cover," Daeson ordered.

"Negative, Viper One," Raviel replied. "I'm staying with you."

Daeson huffed. He clicked the com link. "Raviel, we need protection at the front. I don't know where the Galactic Alliance ships are, but I'm quite certain they haven't left. Get your Starcraft back up to the *Liberty* now!"

The hesitation in response was enough for him to note Raviel's objection.

"Roger, Viper One."

Daeson saw Raviel's Starcraft leap forward along the fleet, speedily catching up with the *Liberty*.

If the Jyptonian fleet followed them into the asteroid field, there would be nothing to stop them. What could save them now?

Daeson brought up a rear view on his display, waiting to see the pursuit of the Jyptonians around the curve of the energy tunnel. How could the Rayleans possibly survive this?

The image of Admiral Gorzak appeared before Linden, his face cold stone.

"How many did we destroy?" Linden asked.

Admiral Gorzak hesitated. "Our sensors aren't detecting any transport debris."

"What? Our concussion missiles did nothing?" Linden fumed with anger. "How is this possible?" he demanded.

Admiral Gorzak's eyes narrowed. "I'm not sure. There was an energy wave that hit the missiles and detonated them before they could reach the transports."

Linden fought to control his anger as he eyed the admiral. He was half the man's age, but Linden was the supreme authority here.

"Chancellor Lockridge," the admiral continued. "The transports have almost all entered the asteroid field. What are your orders?"

"Those fools!" Linden exclaimed. "Now they have nowhere to go. And what of the Galactic Alliance fleet?"

"We will be in firing range before they will," Gorzak answered.

"Good," Linden retorted. "I'll not let them steal the victory from us this day. Order them to stand down."

The admiral raised an eyebrow. Linden huffed.

"*Request* them to stand down. As soon as we are in range of those transports, I want every ship to open fire!"

The admiral turned away to receive new information from his bridge crew. When he turned back, he was scowling. "It seems we are facing an unexpected challenge. The energy tunnel they are travelling through...curves," the admiral stated flatly. "Our plasma cannons will not track them. Even our concussion missiles will have a difficult time tracking them through the asteroids."

Linden stood up and walked closer to the admiral's image. "What do you mean curves? That's impossible."

He turned and looked at his sensors officer.

"Confirmed sir. It curves. Nearly all of the transports are already out of visual range. Our weapons will not reach them."

Linden felt the blood coursing through his veins as his anger rose. What trickery was Daeson using?

"I recommend flight vectors that will navigate our fleet around the asteroid field and intercept them on the far side." The admiral nodded as if there were no other options.

"What?!" exclaimed Linden. "And risk losing them at the nearest slipstream conduit? No, Admiral. We will pursue and destroy them!

"But Chancellor, we have no way of knowing how long the energy beam will remain. I—"

"I don't care!" Linden exclaimed. "We will destroy them here and now! Get me the Starcraft squadron commander!"

Linden's rage was building, and the Triad responded accordingly.

The image of a steely-eyed major appeared next to Admiral Gorzak. He lifted his visor so Linden could see him eye to eye.

"Yes, Chancellor," Brehan responded. Once Linden became Chancellor of Jypton, he quickly began surrounding himself with people he knew he could trust. This included his long-time friend, Brehan.

"Major Wasak, lead us into that asteroid field and decimate those transports!"

"Yes, sir!" the major snapped.

"Chancellor," the admiral's face was firm. "If that field collapses, we will lose every ship!"

Linden took a step toward the admiral. "Am I to question your resolve to crush these rebellious traitors when they are within our reach?"

The admiral lifted his head slightly. "Of course not, Chancellor. I am merely suggesting that it would be foolish to jeopardize the life of the Chancellor unnecessarily when our fleet can easily accomplish the task without you. Your safety is paramount for the planet of Jypton."

Linden froze as he considered the admiral's counsel. He glared at the admiral, then returned to his chair. "Bring me the charred corpse of Daeson Starlore," he ordered.

"Yes, Chancellor Lockridge."

Linden sulked, frustrated that Starlore would not die by his own hand or be publicly executed, but was comforted with the thought of the decimation of the entire Drudge people.

"I want a visual on the entire attack," he ordered.

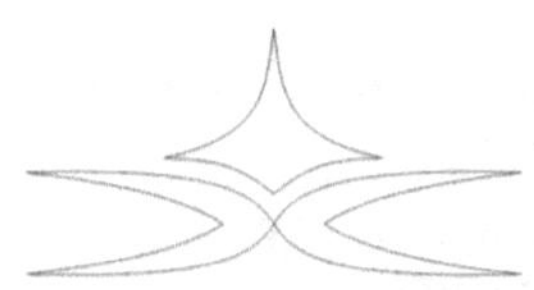

CHAPTER

15

The Tears of Battle

Daeson ordered every transport captain to push the engines as hard as they could go. Keeping out of visual range of the Jyptonian fleet was their only hope now. He imagined that the squadrons of Starcraft would come first, since they were nimble and quicker than the destroyers. With little room to maneuver, he and Tig wouldn't last long against them.

"*Liberty,* this is Viper One, what's your status?" Daeson radioed.

"Still clear ahead. We should exit the asteroid field in thirty-two minutes."

"Roger that. As soon as you exit, make straight away for the Omega slipstream conduit. It's the closest one and our only chance of escape."

"Roger, Viper One," came Trisk's reply.

The minutes lingered, and it was agonizing seeing the throttles of their Starcraft at only forty percent.

Daeson felt like they were trying to escape a charging Kolazo Beast by walking away. Getting a lock on anything inside the asteroid field was impossible, and they had no idea when the carnage from behind would begin. Daeson's eyes were glued to the rearward image on his panel.

"Are we going to make it, Daeson?" Tig asked.

"If they don't follow us through the energy tunnel, we may have a chance. If they maneuver around the asteroid belt, there's no way they could reach us before we make the slipstream conduit," Daeson said hopefully.

"And if they follow?" Tig asked.

"If they follow, there's not much we can do, old friend. Not unless you've got some super Starcraft tactic for taking out four squadrons in a confined space."

"Yeah...I guess I missed that class at the academy," Tig quipped.

All of a sudden, the space around them lit up in multiple fiery bursts of plasma energy. Their Starcraft ratcheted from the impact, but the shields held.

"We can't even return fire in here," Tig said.

"We have to protect that transport," Daeson replied as he quickly worked to reroute some power to their energy shield. "Their shields wouldn't last two hits."

The concussions from the Jyptonian Starcrafts were now continuous, and their energy shield was dropping fast. Eighty percent...sixty...forty...twenty-five. Four more hits and it would be over. Daeson looked down at the Protector.

Where are you now, my Sovereign?

Two more cannon blasts ripped across the stern of their Starcraft, and Daeson could tell by the violence of the last hit that there was nothing left to protect them.

"E-shield is down to five percent."

Daeson could hear defeat in Tig's voice. He braced for impact and wondered how painful an icy cold death in space would be.

"The next one—" Tig began, but all at once the plasma cannons stopped—the silence was surreal. Daeson glanced at his display and witnessed the unimaginable.

From the captain's seat aboard the *Invincible*, Linden watched with gleeful anticipation as the visual feed from Major Wasak's Starcraft fed the display in front of him. Racing toward final victory, he watched as Wasak and his squadron pounded Starlore's Starcraft with plasma cannon fire.

"And now you die, Daeson Starlore. My revenge is complete!" Linden lifted himself out of his seat absorbing every delightful moment of his victory. Then, at the pinnacle of his ultimate triumph, the plasma cannon fire stopped. From the left side of the screen, a Jyptonian Starcraft exploded in a fireball that nearly took Wasak's Starcraft out.

"No!" Linden yelled. "Finish him!" he yelled.

But Wasak did not hear the order. A massive asteroid filled the display and then the screen went blank. Linden turned to his sensors officer.

"What happened?" he demanded. "Get me that visual back!"

"I've lost the signal, Chancellor."

The display automatically transitioned back to a magnified view of the energy tunnel from the perspective of the *Invincible*. Deep within the asteroid field, dozens of explosions could be seen. Like a chain reaction, the explosions followed the energy tunnel outward toward Linden.

"Chancellor, the energy field is...collapsing!"

Linden looked on in horror as the wake of explosions followed the curved tunnel, decimating every warship he had. Daeson Starlore's final act of betrayal was more than he could bear. It was impossible! Linden wasn't supposed to be the one to lose. He never lost. The rage mounted inside him until he could not maintain control. His eyes glowed red as the Triad pulsed with unimaginable power. His muscles swelled and his body became an unstoppable vessel of destruction.

The entire crew of the bridge cowered against the outer walls as Linden smashed his fists into consoles and displays. Then the Triad erupted in a massive beam of red energy that scorched the front display, ultimately breaching the hull of the ship. The scream of the Jyptonian Chancellor echoed as the Triad sliced the forward third of the *Invincible*. As the air spilled out into the icy tomb of space, Linden's scream faded to death.

Just behind Daeson and Tig, the energy tunnel was collapsing. Massive asteroids were spilling into the space cocoon. A few of the pursuing Starcraft attempted to dodge them at first, but the speed at which they were flying made it impossible. Within seconds, all Daeson could see behind him were multiple explosions and fragments of Jyptonian ships being ground to nothing by the millions of asteroids that now crushed in on all sides.

"What's happening, Daeson?" Tig asked.

"The energy tunnel is collapsing, Tig. Don't stop. Whatever you do, don't stop!"

Following just behind them, the collapse of the energy tunnel continued.

"Ell Yon has saved us once again!" Daeson exclaimed.

Daeson reported what was happening to Raviel, Trisk, and all of the ship captains and their crews. He could almost hear the jubilant cheers of three hundred thousand Rayleans from the transports.

Twenty minutes later Trisk let Daeson know that the fleet was exiting the Agulla Asteroid Field. Daeson took a deep breath, anxious to be clear of it himself. But in the back of Daeson's mind, there was a splinter of uneasiness that would not allow complete rest...not yet.

"*Liberty*, this is Viper One. What are your long-range scanners showing?" Daeson asked. Inside the asteroid field, scanners proved unusable. They were flying blind.

"Standby. Checking now, Viper One," Trisk replied. "All clear, Viper One."

Daeson closed his eyes and rested his head against the headrest of his seat. Could it be over?

"Viper One, this is Viper Two. Negative on the all clear. My long-range scanner is picking up multiple ships bearing one, five, three, mark eight."

Raviel's voice was calm and steady, but Daeson felt the tension in her voice. Her enhanced Starcraft would have the ability to see further, as Lt. Ki had told him.

"The Galactic Alliance," Daeson said aloud without transmitting back to the *Liberty*. Zari Treville's ships were fast...the fastest in the galaxy, and he was not done with them. By now the Galactic Chancellor would have discovered the destruction of his greatest ally, and his fury would be greater than that of Linden himself.

"Viper One, did you copy? Signatures indicate the ships are Galactic Alliance," Raviel queried.

Daeson clicked on his mic. "Copy, Viper Two. *Liberty,* can you make the Omega conduit before interception?"

A few seconds passed.

"Roger that, Viper One, but it looks like the back of the fleet is going to be a bit short on time. We estimate they'll be in weapons range in approximately forty-three minutes."

"Copy, *Liberty,*" was all that Daeson could say.

The next few moments were lived out in silent contemplation as they continued their miraculous journey through the asteroid field, only to be faced with a more powerful enemy than the starships of Jypton. Daeson recalled the darkened eyes of Chancellor Treville from months earlier and shuddered.

Even then Daeson had known there was something more than the desires of a power-hungry chancellor at work in Treville—something ancient and dark. From the first time Daeson met Treville, Daeson could sense the imbalance of power between Linden's father and Treville. Linden was only just beginning to understand, but his father had known differently, having experienced years of influence alongside the Chancellor of the Galactic Alliance.

Ell Yon, what else must your people endure? Is there a limit to what you will or can do to save us? Daeson wondered. The Rayleans certainly had no power to wield of their own against such a force.

Daeson's cockpit display flickered, and he attempted to readjust, hoping to have his scanners come on line once they exited the asteroid field. The display flickered again, and this time an image appeared, one that caused the hair to stand up on the back of his neck. The cold, dark eyes of Zari Treville were staring back at him. Daeson tried to adjust the display, but it didn't yield.

"Hello, Daeson Starlore," Treville said calmly.

"Tig, are you getting this?" Daeson asked over his cockpit mic.

"Getting what?"

"Don't deceive yourself, Daeson," Treville continued. "Getting through one slipstream conduit isn't going to save you. I'm coming, and there's no stopping me."

Daeson tried again to block the image and figure out how Treville was doing this.

"I knew when I met you back on Jypton many months ago that you were special. Now that Lockridge is gone, I can speak candidly with you."

Daeson stopped and looked closely at the image. "What do you mean, gone?" Daeson asked. He wasn't sure Treville's com trickery was actually two way.

"Ah...of course...you have no way of knowing." A wry smile crossed Treville's lips. "Linden has destroyed himself...unable to control the power I gave him—power you could have."

Daeson closed his eyes. Was Treville lying? Was Linden really dead? Daeson looked on the image once more and tried to interrupt the signal.

"You and I both know that Lockridge was weak." Treville's eyes lured and enticed. "His emotions owned him. I need someone strong to help rule the galaxy. Someone like you."

Daeson froze. *Rule the galaxy?* The offer jolted him. Daeson dared to look directly into Treville's eyes and saw Lord Dracus staring back. Chills flitted up and down his spine. He felt a warm glow on his forearm. Daeson broke the dragon's gaze and looked down—the Protector was pulsing deep angry colors.

"This is an offer that I will only make once, Daeson, and your time is short. Death...or power?" Treville lowered his head—the gaze of complete Immortal power overshadowed him.

Daeson gazed back into the eyes of darkness. He did not hold back as his passion to serve the one Immortal who knew no evil filled his soul.

"Not now, not ever, not in a thousand years would I consider such a thing. The Sovereign Ell Yon is the one I serve, and by his power you will be overcome!"

Treville's countenance turned darker still. His eyes filled with a portion of hate and loathing that a thousand nightmares could not contain.

"I will destroy you and your wretched people, Starlore. Today you shall all die. And should one single Raylean escape my judgment, I will hunt him from the moons of Kalari to the suns of Antibulla...I will destroy you all and will purge every corner of the galaxy of this despicable race of people you call your own. This I vow!"

Daeson felt the Protector searing his arm. He held it up.

"We're getting a resonant feedback loop on the interphase channel," a voice behind Treville quavered within Daeson's earshot. The chancellor of the Galactic

Alliance scowled just as a burst of energy exploded from the Protector. A fraction of a second later, scorching blue flames erupted across Treville's face. It only lasted a second, but Daeson saw the scorched gash across Treville's right eye and cheek. He screamed, and the image went blank.

Daeson sat stunned for a moment, gazing down at the Protector, fearful of its power once more.

"What's your plan, Daeson?" Raviel asked on a private channel.

"Ah…say again?" Daeson replied.

"What's your plan? You and I both know we can't take three hundred thousand Rayleans through that conduit near the Omega Nebula. We barely survived the Omegeon particles and had weeks to recover."

Daeson took a deep breath and tried to regain his thoughts.

"Give me a minute, Rav."

"You okay?" she replied.

Daeson took a couple of deep breaths as he pushed the encounter with Treville out of his mind so he could consider their options. He clicked his mic.

"You're right, Rav. But when the Malakians upgraded my Starcraft, they also installed a complete map of every conduit in the galaxy. There's a conduit we didn't know about. Have Rivet show you the map near the Nebula."

A moment later Raviel's voice came through. "Incredible! We need to get this map to the rest of the fleet."

"Roger that," Daeson replied. "Set up a data link to the *Liberty* and begin transmitting. Give Trisk the coordinates of the next closest conduit. We just have to hope that the Galactic Alliance doesn't know about it, or our escape will be short-lived."

A few minutes later *Voyage* and Viper One exited the asteroid field just as the last of the tunnel collapsed. The energy beam had now completely disappeared. Daeson immediately scanned and located the Galactic Alliance fleet. Their direct journey through the Agulla Asteroid Field had bought them time but not enough.

Treville's fleet was closing in fast from a position right and aft of the Rayleans. Tig flew their Starcraft up along the Raylean formation of transports to inspect for any damage. Raviel met them half way and dropped into a fingertip formation with Tig and Daeson.

"Viper Two, I want you to stay with the *Liberty*," Daeson said, looking over at her.

Raviel lifted her visor and looked at him in unbelief. "I have the most powerful Starcraft in the galaxy and a copilot that can fly this thing better than I can. You know that makes no sense, Daeson. You need us back here, and that's where I'm going to be."

Daeson remembered the first time he noticed Raviel. As a lowly Drudge she had squared off with Xandra, a Jyptonian Elite. The courage in her heart was unique. He couldn't help but love her all the more for it. Besides this, her logic was flawless. He saw Rivet look his way and nod.

"Very well, Rav. You be careful. That Starcraft is the best defense we've got for the entire fleet. You need to keep that in mind when it comes to taking risks."

He hoped that appealing to her sense of logic would somehow minimize her willingness to sacrifice herself, but he doubted that it would have any affect.

Thirty minutes later the *Liberty* was nearing the Omega slipstream conduit. The two Starcrafts positioned themselves near the entrance to guard their precious cargo.

"Viper One to *Liberty*, confirm receipt of the updated conduit map and the follow-on coordinates for the next jump," Daeson inquired.

"Copy, Viper One," Trisk replied. "Data received and coordinates set. The map has been transmitted to the rest of the fleet as well. We will be entering the conduit in two minutes."

"Ell Yon be with you, *Liberty*," Daeson said.

"And with you both, Viper One and Viper Two. Fly well!"

A moment later the conduit jump drives of the transport energized. In the blink of an eye, the ship disappeared. Two minutes from that moment, they would arrive over one hundred twenty light years away...the distant glow of the Omega Nebula waited for them. One by one the transports entered the conduit and disappeared. The two Starcraft flew in nervous cover patterns over the remaining seventeen ships, but the Galactic Alliance ships were almost on top of them. Daeson estimated that at least ten transports wouldn't make it to the entrance of the conduit in time. Their E-shield had recovered to fifty percent, but against such power, it didn't matter much. A Galactic Alliance destroyer could obliterate them with one cannon shot.

"Viper Two, engage your cloak."

"I can't fire my cannons when I'm cloaked," Raviel replied.

Daeson didn't try to argue. Raviel was going to fight no matter what he did. Now that the threat was so real and so close, it angered him.

"They've launched twenty concussion missiles," Rivet reported. "Plasma weapons range in ten seconds."

"Here it comes," Tig said, charging up their cannons. "It's been an honor serving you, Admiral Starlore."

"And you as well, my friend. Target as many of the missiles as possible. Because of the range, we can avoid the plasma cannon fire. They are firing their plasma cannons as a cover for the missiles coming behind."

"Roger that," Tig replied. Both he and Daeson knew that their efforts would be futile.

Daeson looked down at the Protector—silent and still. He didn't understand the ways of Ell Yon. He faced the notion that if Ell Yon used the Protector through Daeson once more, he wouldn't survive. But if it meant saving the rest of the transports, Daeson was willing. He lifted his hand up toward the coming destruction, but the Protector remained still.

"Daeson, sixteen starships have appeared out of nowhere!" Raviel radioed.

He zoomed in on the ships as the first wave of plasma cannon fire hit. The shields of the massive ships easily absorbed the energy of the cannon fire. A barrage of powerful phaser and plasma cannon fire erupted on the approaching concussion missiles and destroyed them all. Seconds later an orchestra of phaser and plasma cannon fire lit up the space between the newly arrived starships and the Alliance fleet. The display of energy bursts was so bright that it watered the eyes. Smaller star fighters launched from the ships to engage the Galactic Alliance fighters. The battle escalated to an intensity Daeson found fearsome and frightening to watch.

"I've seen those ships before!" Daeson replied. He recalled the visions the Protector had given him and the scene inside Ell Yon's battle room, with displays capturing such engagements throughout the galaxy as the Commander directed it all.

"They're the ships of the Immortals!"

"We're going to make it!" Raviel returned.

The next few minutes were anxious ones as they flew cover for the remaining transports...waiting... hoping the Malakian force would be successful in keeping the Galactic Alliance fleet at bay.

"Just two more," Daeson whispered to himself.

"Daeson, two Galactic Alliance fighters have broken free from the battle and are heading our way!" Tig exclaimed.

Daeson watched as a Malakian fighter pursued, but the Galactic Alliance fighters were already firing. Now only the *Voyage* remained. Viper One and Two returned fire, aligning themselves to take the impact of the cannon fire. Daeson saw the slipstream jump drives of the *Voyage* engage as the first volley of cannon fire hit them. Their E-shield immediately dropped to zero percent. These fighters were much more powerful than the Starcrafts of the Jyptonians.

"Viper Two, what's your status?"

"E-Shield at ten percent!" Raviel replied.

"The *Voyage* is away," Daeson returned. "Enter the conduit now!"

Both Starcraft maneuvered aggressively to dodge the next burst of cannon fire. Daeson saw one of the two Galactic Alliance fighters explode in a fire ball from the trailing Malakian fighter. The other Alliance fighter was hot on their tail, and the Malakian on his, but the slipstream conduit entrance seemed too far. Tig purposely slowed to allow Raviel to enter first. Seconds ticked. Raviel rolled left to avoid one shot. Tig rolled right to avoid another.

"Engage slipstream jump drives now!" Daeson ordered.

"Missiles fired!" Rivet's voice erupted over the com channel just as they entered the conduit.

The world of battle melted away as the slipstream jump drives of Viper One and Viper Two engaged. At that moment, the missiles the Alliance fighter had fired entered the conduit with them. Daeson looked over at Raviel as one missile approached her right wing. Its proximity detector detonated and the resulting blast ripped through her remaining E-shield, tearing into her ship.

The concussion from the first missile sent a shock wave that diverted the second missile toward the slipstream conduit wall. The successive concussions were just fractions of a second apart, but the resultant quantum anomaly changed Daeson's life forever. Raviel's Starcraft tumbled uncontrollably left toward the conduit wall where the second missile had exploded and torn open a rip in the fabric of the keeper of space and time.

"Daeson—"

One word...one word was all he heard. A plea...a call for help. Before Daeson could utter a response, Raviel, Rivet, and their Starcraft were sucked out of the conduit and instantly disappeared.

"No!" Daeson screamed. "We have to go back, Tig!"

"How, Daeson? How?"

Daeson held his hands up to the canopy. He knew there was no going back. Slipstream conduits were a one-way nonstop journey. Nothing like this had ever been recorded in slipstream history. It was very likely that the instant Raviel's ship exited the conduit, it disintegrated to nothing. Daeson's heart stopped, and the tears hurt as they fell from his eyes. He was numb, wishing somehow he could turn back time for those few seconds and make it right. He had lost her, and his soul tore in two.

Two minutes later their Starcraft appeared behind thirty-seven intact transports aligned in perfect formation. They had all made it...all except one. Already they were on course for the next conduit. The effects of the Omegeon radiation would be severe and quick. There was no time to delay.

Daeson became desperate to find a way back, but none of his thoughts even remotely made sense. The Galactic Alliance was waiting at the entrance of the conduit they had just exited and might be coming through this side of the conduit at any moment. Here the Omegeon particles threatened to incapacitate the entire Raylean fleet unless they made the nearest conduit entrance in the next few minutes. There wasn't even enough time to explain or petition for some alternative action. Daeson felt propelled onward by uncontrollable circumstances that demanded he abandon his love, regardless of whether she was dead or alive. The horror of these few minutes tortured him.

The *Liberty* was hailing them, but Daeson heard nothing. Tig responded—Daeson didn't hear what he said. He couldn't muster the mental courage to live beyond the last two minutes of his life. Over and over again he heard Raviel's voice reaching for him...pleading with him. Images of Raviel floating aimlessly in the void of space far from any planet or station tormented him, as the forces of duty, threat, and physics thrust him further and further away with each passing second.

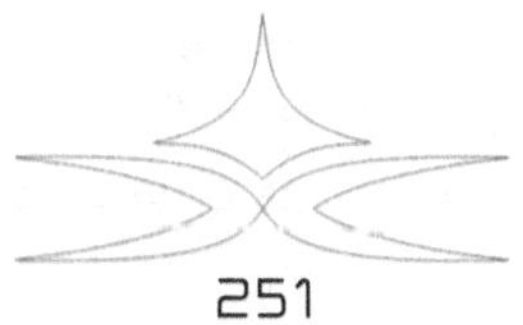

CHAPTER

17

The End of Time

"I will give unto the Rayleans a world abundant in resource and life. They will possess a new world in the midst of many, and they will be a people once more. I will visit my promise upon them and will lift their darkness and free them from their bondage."
- Sabella, Oracle of Ell Yon

The Raylean fleet of transports made it through the Omega Nebula slipstream conduit and made two more jumps to ensure they were indeed free from possible pursuit by the Galactic Alliance and clear of Omegeon particles. With each successive jump, the possibility of determining Raviel's fate became nearly nonexistent. Every light year they travelled away, Daeson's pain magnified. The survival of three hundred thousand Rayleans cast out into space superseded all else. It was simply the momentum of causality. There was much to consider...to plan...to do to ensure the survival of this new space-faring people. Yet Daeson could hardly force himself to rise to the task. His anguish over Raviel paralyzed him.

Daeson barely heard the quiet conversation between Tig and Trisk in the hours that followed. As soon as the threat to the transports was completely eliminated, Tig maneuvered their Starcraft into the shuttle bay of the *Liberty*. Once on board, Daeson revived. As the bay pressurized, he unstrapped and anxiously waited for the canopy to open.

"Open this thing, Tig!"

"It's not safe yet," Tig replied, pointing to the red light on the bay wall that indicated an insufficient atmosphere.

Daeson considered overriding the canopy-open action from the rear seat, but just then the bay's green light illuminated. He heard the whoosh of air escape the cockpit as the canopy seal broke. The canopy rose away from them much too slowly, and within seconds Daeson was out of the seat and climbing down the ladder as it extended from the underside of the Starcraft.

The bay doors opened as Daeson approached.

Trisk greeted him. "Daeson, I'm sorry," Trisk began, but Daeson interrupted.

"Are the transports secure?" Daeson asked.

"They are."

Daeson nodded, then pushed past him. Trisk turned to Tig, a look of confusion on his face.

Hearing shouts of jubilee throughout the ship angered Daeson. It shouldn't have, but it did. He made haste, straight to the one man that could offer him hope if there was any hope to be had...Sci-tech Master Boytt. He hurried to the starboard bow where a conference room had been converted to one of the sci-tech labs for the fleet. Once there, he pushed past sci-techs anxious to congratulate him and found Master Boytt. Boytt was not smiling like the others. The man had discernment uncharacteristic of a sci-tech. With one look at Daeson he dismissed his associates.

"Come," Boytt said, pulling Daeson by his arm into a small chamber reserved for storing the tech secrets of the Rayleans.

Once the door slid closed behind them, Daeson felt his emotions rising dangerously to the surface, threatening to utterly conquer his composure as fleet admiral. He looked at Boytt, eyes reddening. "I lost her." The sound of his own voice proclaiming the fate of his love was too much. Tears spilled from his eyes.

Boytt's face reflected the painful reality of Daeson's words.

"I lost her, and I need you to help me find her."

Boytt squinted. "What happened?"

Daeson took the next few minutes to describe in detail the horror of those fateful few seconds inside the slipstream conduit. He knew the details well for he had lived them over and over hundreds of times already. When he was done, he looked at Boytt with hopeful eyes.

"Master Boytt, is it theoretically possible that she could have survived?"

Boytt tried to hide it, but his countenance only added to Daeson's sorrow.

"Possible at all?" Daeson pleaded.

Boytt looked at Daeson and frowned. "Anything is theoretically possible, Daeson, but likely?" Boytt hesitated. "I'm sorry...the odds are nearly zero."

"Why?" Daeson demanded.

"Because transitioning from slipstream velocity to sub-light speed is something we don't even fully understand yet. The conduits were created by the Immortals and are far beyond our ability to comprehend. Raviel may even have experienced some type of space-time quantum effect that we haven't ever observed before. We simply don't have the math and physics to evaluate such an event."

Boytt paused, appearing to struggle with how to console Daeson. "Come with me," he said. Outside the storage chamber, Boytt took Daeson to a large display. He brought up a map of the stars, showing the space near the Omega slipstream conduit.

"Even if her ship did remain intact and she did survive, it means she is probably traveling at or near light speed somewhere between the Omega slipstream conduit entrance and exit, which is over one hundred twenty light years apart. Just finding her would take a miracle, not to mention the time dilation she would be experiencing."

Boytt put a gentle hand on Daeson's shoulder. "I'm sorry, Daeson. I know that's not what you wanted to hear. Raviel was one of the most amazing young women I've ever known. I wish with all my heart that I could do something to make this turn out right."

Daeson stared blankly at the display of space where the Omega conduit was. Raviel was truly gone. That fact tore away nearly every shred of his desire to carry on. Without her, he felt utterly lost. There was a hole in his soul that was impossible to describe or to fill.

It took everything within him to make a brief appearance on the bridge to ensure that Trisk had what he needed, but then he found his quarters and buried himself in sorrow.

Daeson retreated for a time, and no one faulted him. They had all suffered loss and knew the pain that accompanied such a thing. In Daeson's despondency,

Trisk and Tig rose to the occasion, but as the days passed by and the needs of the people pressed hard upon him, he slowly reengaged and began to lead the Rayleans once more.

The Protector was their lifeline to survival, and Daeson relied upon it exclusively in the harshness of space, with so many people and so many needs. As their limited supplies were quickly exhausted, murmurings began. After all, how could they possibly survive long without a continual supply of water and food? Daeson felt every comment and every uttered doubt, denying him the motivation to rise up from his personal despondency.

On a day shortly after their deliverance from Jypton, Daeson stood on the bridge of *Liberty*, waiting to address the people. He could hardly keep from looking for Raviel, hungry for the encouragement he needed, but she was not there. He glanced toward Ensign Walla.

"Com link established, Admiral," reported Walla. "The entire fleet will see and hear you."

Daeson stared at the display in front of him. Multiple inset views showed thousands upon thousands of Rayleans gathered together on the thirty-seven transports to hear the words of the man who had done the impossible.

Speak words of hope...my words!

"Fellow Rayleans, we find ourselves as sojourners in the vastness of space with no place to call our home, yet by the hand of Ell Yon, we have been made free for the first time in over twelve hundred years. *You*...you are the ones that have lived this miracle of liberty. You are the ones that must remember this day forever and tell it to the generations to come, for mighty was the hand of the Sovereign Ell Yon against the forces of Jypton and against the forces of the Galactic Alliance.

"Never before in the history of the galaxy has such a thing been accomplished. Through the Protector, Ell Yon has promised to never leave us or abandon us. The wisdom and power of the same Immortal that delivered us from Lockridge is with us now and will be with us forever. Our journey ahead will be long and difficult…I will not lie. But out here among the stars is a place for us…a home world that we will call our own…a planet Sovereign Ell Yon has promised to us."

An audible response rose up from the displays. Daeson could feel the heart of his people swelling with hope.

"The Protector is Ell Yon's evidence of this promise. This day Ell Yon delivered us from the bondage of Jypton. There is coming a day when he will deliver us from the bondage of Dietum Prime and grant us the gift of immortality. One day a deliverer much greater than any mere mortal will come and lead you, purging that which has diseased our genetic code. It is our remembrance of this day that will prepare us for such a time. Through the years to come, we must have solidarity…we must unite in heart and deed!"

Daeson's impassioned words stirred the hearts of nearly every Raylean. He lifted his hand high in the air, the Protector arcing its beautiful power.

"We are one under the Sovereign!"

"One under the Sovereign!" echoed the people with hands lifted high. The chant rose in volume until with one voice they all proclaimed their allegiance to the one who had delivered them.

Daeson's words gave the people exactly what they needed as they looked ahead to the impossible task of survival in space, but in the quiet silence of his quarters, Daeson wept. Both joy and immense sorrow filled his heart, for he could not yet fully give Raviel over to death. In spite of multiple requests for answers and guidance regarding Raviel, the Protector was silent. It was a silence that thoroughly tested his trust in Sovereign Ell Yon. Not truly knowing the fate of his love threatened to haunt him to the very end of time.

EPILOGUE

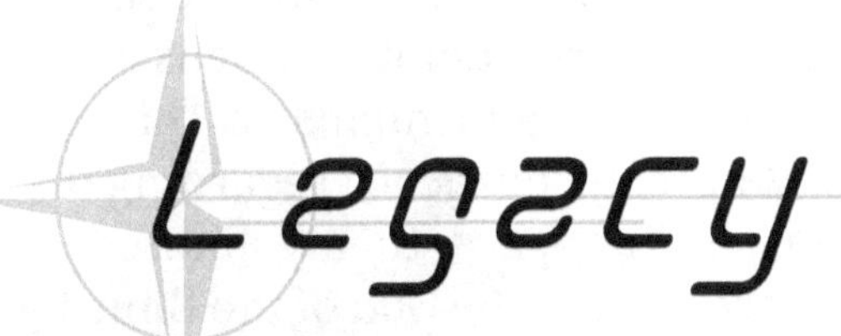

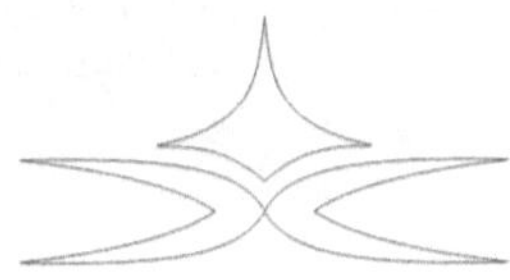

Brae's eyes slowly closed as Elias finished the last words of his story. He brushed a few strands of hair from her face, gazing down at the beautiful, sweet features of his daughter. She looked so much like her mother that Elias fought back painful emotions.

"Oh, Brae. If only I could prepare you for what is to come!"

Elias stood up and pulled the blankets to just under Brae's chin. The stories of the great and mighty Ell Yon always stirred his soul, even if it was he who told them. He bent down and kissed her forehead.

"I love you, little lady. Dream of grand adventures, for one day you shall surely live one."

AUTHOR'S COMMENTARY

The canvas of life upon which God has given us the ability to create story is truly remarkable—an undiscoverable universe, emotions, senses, a world of unrepeatable humans, and minds to think of untold adventures. My greatest concern regarding the writing of this series is in regard to my limited ability to appropriately represent the God of the Bible by the use of metaphors. Please do not make the mistake of assuming that science and technology can in some way explain away the supernatural marvels of God, His holiness, power, wisdom, and love. The full character of God is unknowable, and thus attempting to depict Him in all of His glory is a frightful endeavor. I pray that you return to His Word and fully embrace the profound descriptions of truth without fiction found there. It is my purpose in writing these words to point you once more to the glorious God of heaven and earth, His Son Jesus Christ, the Holy Spirit, and the radical intersection of supernatural love through the redemptive power of the gospel.

~Chuck Black